First Command

Alliance Cadets, Volume 1

Charles K James

Published by Megavoltage Publishing, 2021.

Copyright © 2021 by Megavoltage Publishing

All rights reserved.

No part of this book may be reproduced or used in any manner without written permission of the copyright owner except for the use of quotations in a book review.

This novel is a work of fiction. Characters, names, and places appearing in this work are fictitious or are used fictitiously. Any resemblance to actual events, locales, or persons—living or dead—is purely coincidental.

FIRST COMMAND

FIRST EDITION, June 2021

ISBN 978-1-7777109-1-0

Author: Charles K James www.charlesjamessfauthor.com

Editor: Adria Laycraft www.adrialaycraft.com

Cover Art: www.miblart.com

To Big Al and Josie Niskanen.

Thanks for always believing in me.

CHAPTER ONE

An old space corvette appeared in the Dienne star system with a thud that sent gravitational ripples through space. Cassiopeia Requin slammed against her restraints. Her gut squeezed bile up the back of her throat.

Cassi tried to hold her chin up, to breathe in the cool recycled air. She tried to project confidence from within her bright orange pressure suit. The flight instructors were watching her, evaluating her, assessing her character as much as her technical competence. For the duration of the mission, Cassi was the acting commander of the Alliance Expeditionary Fleet Spacecraft *Triumph*.

And mission commanders did not barf.

With the transit sequence complete, the other cadets ran through their post-transit checklists, verifying that the *Triumph's* critical systems were operational.

"Life support—go."

"AXON—go."

"Signals—go."

The seven cadets on board were strapped into control stations, safe inside self-contained pressure suits, and double bubbled within the spacecraft's pressurized command module.

A glowing blue and white planet bathed the cadets with serene light through the spacecraft's windows. They had come out of the transit close enough to see the mix of oceans, clouds and vast patches of land on Dienne.

As much as Cassi wanted to admire the beauty of the alien world, she had to focus on the challenges in front of her: get the *Triumph* into orbit and execute the drop.

The transit process was subject to uncertainty. For an instant they had been encased in a superluminal warp field—an isolated bubble that crossed light years in a matter of seconds. Then the warp field collapsed, and they appeared more-or-less where they intended to arrive, but they didn't know their precise location in relation to the planet. Without guidance buoys, they needed a series of radar measurements to establish their position.

And Cassi had to keep her breakfast at the bottom of her esophagus.

"All systems operational—" Bauer, the cadet acting as the mission's executive officer, stopped in the middle of his report. "What is it Pelly?"

"We're too close for the velocity we're at, sir."

Cassi's gut gurgled. She tried to concentrate on the orbital mechanics.

Wrong velocity. If they were traveling too fast, they wouldn't fall into orbit. They could shoot right past Dienne. They had to execute a braking burn.

Humid air fogged the inside of her helmet.

Two flight instructors at the back of the module watched the cadets—watched and judged.

Every cadet had to qualify as an astronaut—earn their stars. To do that they had to fly a decommissioned corvette out to an arbitrary planet, establish a stable orbit, drop a landing shuttle on it and return with a viable soil sample. Then they had to transit back home, all without assistance from the flight instructors.

If you failed, you washed out of the program.

So far they were doing alright. Having simulated the mission dozens of times, prepared for countless problems, the cadets knew what they were doing. All they had to do was get their spacecraft on course for a stable orbit.

Commander Dodd, the senior instructor glared directly at Cassi from inside his helmet, his woolly eyebrows low over his eyes. He tapped the tablet cradled in his arm with a stylus.

Tap. Tap. Tap.

It wasn't just Cassi's astronaut qualification on the line. If one cadet failed the exercise, they all failed.

"Navigation—" Her stomach did a somersault. "Calculate the correction."

"Aye, ma'am."

Bile crept up Cassi's throat. She couldn't keep it down.

"Bauer, you have the conn."

Her second in command glanced at her, eyes wide, as if to ask what she was doing. A mission commander didn't just hand over control of the mission, not like this. "Um... aye, ma'am. I have the conn."

Cassi unbuckled from her control station and launched herself through the microgravity environment to the little sanitation cabin at the back of the command module. She flung open the door, grabbed the vacuum cleaner toilet hose with one hand and pulled at her fishbowl helmet with the other.

Her stomach heaved. The muscles in her gut constricted without permission. Her gloved fingers fumbled at the latch.

It wouldn't come off!

She tried to hold it down, but the rocket had launched. A burning mix of stomach acid and liquefied omelet breakfast erupted through her mouth and nose, splattered against her helmet's face shield, and bounced back into her face.

Cassi clawed at the latch.

The warm vomit blurred the transparent visor and crept down her neck and into the rest of her pressure suit.

Someone grabbed her and pulled her back, out of the stall. They popped off her helmet. Mucus globules of stomach flotsam burst from her helmet into the command module. They coalesced in the absence of gravity, floating, sticking to Cassi's hair and skin and scattered through the enclosed cabin space.

The other cadets tried to contain their reactions. Grunts and "ughs" were stifled, but not completely suppressed.

Emica Junko grabbed the toilet hose and pushed the funnel up to Cassi's mouth. The machine latched onto her face and sucked away everything else that came up with an awful slurping that resonated through the otherwise quiet command module.

The junior flight instructor, Lieutenant Singh, drew his hands up and pressed fingers against the transparent polymer of his face shield, as if to cover his mouth.

Emica patted Cassi's back as globs of puke latched on to her own pressure suit. "Easy," she said, her voice calm, as if this happened everyday. "Take some deep breaths. You okay, Cassi?"

With her stomach empty, the wave of abdominal convulsions passed. Cassi took a deep breath of the cabin air, trying not to inhale anything solid or liquid floating around in front of her.

Emica used the hose to suck at the jelly-like floaters, catching the lion's share of them, the system making a wet gurgle each time it sucked one up.

Lieutenant Singh, Commander Dodd, Pelly, Kroyle, Quinton, Sijani, Bauer... they all stared at Cassi.

She wanted to push Emica out of the way and lock herself in the washroom. She wanted to cry. Even beyond failing as a leader, there were consequences to these kinds of accidents. Assuming she hadn't just washed out of the entire program, for the rest of her career she would be known as the cadet who barfed all over herself in a pressure suit and caused her crew to fail their astronaut quals.

Dodd scribbled on his tablet.

The *Triumph* rumbled.

Social catastrophe aside, they were still going too fast.

Commander Dodd hadn't actually said the word *fail* yet. In fact, he hadn't said anything at all. Neither had Lieutenant Singh. Dodd just kept tapping his stylus against his tablet.

Tap. Tap. Tap.

Emica wiped some splatter off her own face shield. "Are you alright, Cassi?"

Cassi's stomach felt better now that it was empty. The inside of her mouth and her nasal cavity burned, and the awful smell certainly would keep her from eating eggs anytime soon, but she could function.

Emica ran the vacuum down Cassi's neck, reached down her suit and cleaned up the worst of the wet mess that was now stuck between her skin and the fabric of her undersuit.

Tap. Tap. Tap.

They were still traveling too fast.

Cassi took a couple deep breaths and placed a hand on her friend's shoulder. "Em, you need to get back to your station." Emica was the navigator. To correct their velocity, she would need to calculate the burn.

Emica offered a timid smile through her face shield, the kind of smile you give someone to tell them that everything is going to be okay, even when you're fairly sure it won't be. "Aye, ma'am."

With as much grace and dignity as she could muster, Cassi wiped out the inside of her fishbowl helmet, secured it in place and returned to her console to resume command. At least for the moment, she had to pretend as if nothing had happened.

The blatant mix of disappointment and frustration on Bauer's face did not escape her. He didn't say anything, but he'd come into the mission already upset that she had been selected to command over him. His test scores were higher on almost every metric the program used. Bauer deserved to be the mission commander.

Yet he was in the number two seat, and she had just blown the mission.

Bauer and everyone else had been so fixated on her, they hadn't done anything about the fact that the *Triumph* was about to shoot past the planet it was supposed to swing around.

Cassi buckled herself back in at her station and cleared her throat. "Bauer, double check our orbital position and velocity."

She didn't see him roll his eyes, but something in the way he delayed his movement and turned away from her suggested he didn't feel the task was a high priority.

Pelly showed Bauer the radar numbers. Pelly was only fourteen years old and the youngest kid who'd ever earned his way into the Cadet Corps' astronaut officer program.

"See?"

Bauer furrowed his brow, then shook his head. "Relax Pelly. We're fine."

"No, sir. We're not. We're too close to the planet."

Bauer tapped his display. "This is our position right here. AXON is updating the recommended velocity as we go. We're in the recommended tolerance."

AXON was the *Triumph's* artificial intelligence supercomputer.

"AXON's reporting wrong. The radar reading is off."

"How could the radar reading be off? It's radar."

Even though Pelly was a prodigy of sorts, he often got overzealous.

"I'm not sure, sir. Maybe it's bouncing off the atmosphere or something, but it's incorrect... by a few hundred kilometers. We're travelling too fast. We need to brake. Now!"

Bauer reached over and tapped Pelly's terminal. "You focus here... on control systems, life support... engineering stuff. Navigation is Junko's job. Making sure she's doing it right is my job. And AXON's job. And AXON says it's fine."

Pelly looked like a kid trying to explain something to a parent who'd already stopped caring. "What does it matter who figures it out?"

Quantum-scale errors in the transit process amplified over light-year distances. A spacecraft could only transit so far before it had to stop and assess its position. When the *Triumph* appeared in orbit it had to measure its position relative to the planet and adjust its velocity, which it had done.

Emica checked that the instant they arrived.

Bauer double-checked it.

Pelly said it was wrong.

"How do you know AXON is off?" Cassi asked.

"I have an astronomy app on my tracker. If you know how large something is and you take a picture of it, you can calculate how far away you are."

"You want us to trust a freeware app on your tracker over an Alliance artificial intelligence supercomputer?"

Pelly didn't waver. "I want you to trust basic geometry."

"How could the radar reading be off though?" Emica asked.

"I don't know," Pelly admitted. "Maybe the radio waves are bouncing off the ionosphere. Maybe it's a software glitch. But if we don't do something fast, we're going to blow right past this planet. And we won't complete the mission."

Kroyle, the cadet at the spacecraft's helm, looked back and forth between Pelly and Bauer, then over to Cassi. "What should I do?"

Cassi swallowed. Not only had she just been utterly humiliated, but now she had to choose between Bauer and Pelly. That shouldn't have mattered. It was a physics question. But she couldn't just pretend that Bauer wouldn't find a way to retaliate if she sided with Pelly. And if she sided with Bauer, Pelly would shut down, like a turtle pulling into a shell.

She glanced at Lieutenant Singh as if he might offer a hint.

"You're the mission commander, Cadet Requin," Singh said. "Don't look at me."

Maybe this was part of the test. The flight instructors always threw something unexpected at them in the simulations. Normally it was something like a fire drill, though. This was a sinister trick if that's what it was.

The putrid aftertaste of vomit and the burning sensation in the back of her nasal cavity weren't doing much to help her focus. But the fact that the lieutenant said anything at all was promising. If they had already failed, it wouldn't matter what she did.

Cassi took a deep breath. She'd always thought it would be so much fun to sit at the command station, so important, so powerful. She'd been ecstatic when she realized she'd drawn command for the live mission. But then the pressure to shine bore down on her and kept her up for nights on end, running through the math, the drills, the potential errors.

At least now that she'd barfed, any pressure to shine was off.

Mathematically, Pelly was right. It was better to go with the math and sort out the social consequences than the other way around.

"Cadet Junko," Cassi said. "Calculate a braking burn to correct our velocity using Cadet Pelly's revised position coordinates."

Bauer rolled his eyes.

Both Singh and Dodd started writing.

"Aye, ma'am."

Bauer adjusted the restraints on his chair, shaking his head. "Crew prepare for retro burn maneuver."

"I've got the correction," Emica announced.

Bauer confirmed the calculation.

Kroyle sat right in front of and below Cassi. He arced his back and glanced up at her, waiting.

"Execute braking burn, on your own time, helm."

The corvette shuddered as the thrusters flared. The crew were thrown forward as if someone had just flipped a gravity switch at the front of the room and dialed it up to high. Cassi's pressure suit constricted around her to keep her from passing out. She closed her eyes and concentrated on keeping her stomach steady.

When the rumbling stopped, she checked the *Triumph's* trajectory. Everything looked good.

"Pelly?"

The cadet checked the tracker computer on his left forearm. "We're good ma'am. The radar is still off though."

Cassi looked at Dodd. Same cold grimace.

Bauer didn't say anything.

Emica put the outside view back on the main window, flooding the bridge with so much white light that Cassi had to squint.

Just like that, they were back on track.

Now they just had to prep the dropship, drop it, pick up some dirt, and repeat the transit back to Avalon. Easy.

In her peripheral vision, she caught Dodd and Singh glancing at each other. The cadets hadn't failed yet. They could still pull this off.

But then Bauer cocked his head and furrowed his brow at his terminal.

"What's wrong?" Cassi asked.

"Well, I don't know if this is what was throwing our radar off, but there's another spacecraft in orbit."

Dodd leaned over and checked Bauer's terminal. His eyebrows lowered. "That's not supposed to be there."

CHAPTER TWO

"I'm getting a signal from them," the acting communications officer, Taura Sijani reported. "It's an emergency beacon."

Commander Dodd shifted uneasily in his seat. "Cadets, this is not part of the exercise."

Emica adjusted the optics to zoom in on the source of the signal. The other craft tumbled through space on the edge of Dienne's upper atmosphere, stuck in an endless series of somersaults.

Pelly's eyes widened. "That's a Phoenix Mark Three."

Just about everyone in the *Triumph's* command module turned to look at the acting flight engineer. "Haven't you guys ever seen Devils of Dalton? Space Patrol Five? Starship Dogs?"

Cassi wasn't sure what the fourteen-year-old cadet was getting at. Neither, it seemed, was anyone else.

"The Phoenix Mark Three is like the standard pirate spacecraft in every action movie and video game made since like... humans colonized space."

"They're not pirates," Bauer said. "They're in trouble."

Sijani put the emergency broadcast on audio.

The audio squelched and clicked and a computer-generated voice spoke. "Automated transmission: *Lucky Bee*. Emergency protocol: loss of life support systems. Crew status: three members alive, three deceased. Crew in stasis pods. Emergency protocol: approaching atmosphere at high velocity. Warning: hull integrity failure in thirty-three minutes, seven seconds..."

The audio went on, a haunting mechanical scroll through a list of critical information. The main screen showed the beacon file—an electronic header containing minimum essential data—downloading into AXON.

At Dodd's signal, Sijani turned off the audio with a heavy click. The beacon's periodic ping continued to sound. Their own spacecraft's environmental conditioning systems hummed quietly in the background.

Singh turned to Dodd and mouthed something. Cassi couldn't quite make out what it was, but from the way his head moved inside his helmet, she knew he was balking.

"Sir, we have to respond," Cassi said.

Dodd hesitated, then shook his head subtly.

Cassi checked her display. "We have enough fuel. More than enough. It's just a minor course deviation."

"It's not that," Lieutenant Singh said. "I think we all want to help them. But an approach on a ship that's rolling like that is dangerous. This is a basic flight test. None of you are qualified astronauts yet."

The *Bee*'s beacon pinged again. The sound resonated inside Cassi's helmet, an electromechanical call for help.

The crew could survive in stasis-pods, flash-frozen and orbiting through space indefinitely like asteroids. Someone could come back for them... a proper rescue mission. But the spacecraft had thirty minutes before its hull integrity failed.

It was about to fall into Dienne's atmosphere and burn up.

Sijani looked back at Cassi and then the flight instructors. "Can we at least send them a message? Let them know that we've seen them and we're going to send help?"

"The crew are in stasis pods," Singh said. "They won't hear anything."

"We could still send something, couldn't we, sir?"

"Ask your mission commander," Dodd said.

"Send the message," Cassi ordered.

As Sijani radioed the *Bee*, Cassi studied its flight path. Something about it made her uneasy. She wondered if the reason their position reading had been off was because somehow, they were picking up a signal from the *Bee*. That didn't make any sense either though.

She turned to Pelly. "Can you establish a remote connection to their flight systems? Hack into it? Maybe we can fire their thrusters remotely, at least enough to stabilize their orbit."

"I can try." Pelly began working on it.

"Junko, start—"

"Orbital correction," Emica finished Cassi's order for her. "I'm on it."

An annoying kludge tone came from Pelly's terminal, an audible kick in the face. He tried a few more things, but the kludge kept repeating. "I can't get in. It's like something is actively keeping me out, ma'am."

"Cadet Requin," Singh's voice cracked. "We haven't given you any orders to engage with that spacecraft. Carry on with the planned mission."

The air inside Cassi's helmet still smelled of vomit. It was growing more humid, a thin cloud of vapor collecting on the inside of the transparent polymer, obscuring her vision. The other cadets looked at her: Kroyle, Emica, Sijani...

The *Bee* didn't have much time left.

"Sirs, we have to help them."

"We can't, Cadet Requin," Dodd said.

"It's intergalactic treaty law—"

"That's enough, Cadet." Singh's voice sounded calm. His anger came through in a sub-tone that wouldn't be present on any recording. "Carry on with the registered flight plan, or you'll all fail this exercise."

Aye, sir. Cassi's mouth formed the words, but she couldn't bring herself to give them any voice. Instead, she doubled down. "Lieutenant, with all due respect, I am the mission commander. Under intergalactic law, all spacecraft are obliged to render assistance to any other spacecraft in peril if they are able to do so. Standing orders in the Alliance Cadet Corps dictate that cadets must conduct all operations in accordance with intergalactic law. It would be a dereliction of duty for us not to respond."

"You're the *acting* mission commander, Cadet Requin. You don't have any actual authority here."

Emica twisted right around in her restraints. The visual of the dark tumbling saucer-like spacecraft against the bright blue backdrop of Dienne was right behind her head. "I have a flight solution. But we have to execute now, or we'll lose them."

"Commander Dodd," Cassi tried focusing on the senior officer. "Are you ordering this crew to ignore a life-threatening distress call?"

Dodd swallowed and looked at Singh who shook his head.

Sijani stared at Cassi, her glare so intense it felt on the verge of cutting through Cassi's pressure suit.

The odds were that there wasn't much they could do to save the crew of the *Bee* in the first place.

Dodd cleared his throat. "Cadet Requin, you are ordered to carry on with your mission as planned."

Cassi swore under her breath. "Aye sir, mission as planned. The plan is to act in accordance with intergalactic law. Helm, execute burn."

Kroyle nodded and swallowed. "Adjustment burn in three... two... one..."

The *Triumph* rumbled as it bled off kinetic energy and dropped in orbit to match the *Lucky Bee*.

Feigning a misinterpretation of the flight instructor's orders wouldn't stand up once they got back to Avalon, but it was something.

"Cadet, stand down!" Singh ordered.

Dodd lifted a hand. "Belay that. If we're going in, we have to commit."

They came up on the little saucer faster than Cassi expected.

Interfacing with AXON, Emica figured out the complex and subtle pattern of adjustments they needed to match the *Lucky Bee*'s roll pattern. Kroyle executed, manually adding in small adjustments for where AXON didn't get the roll perfect.

Cassi's uniform felt uncomfortably tight. Her skin was wet with sweat and still sticky from the bile that had worked its way into her undersuit.

Singh glared at her now. Cassi was pretty sure any future of her ever being a spacecraft captain was doomed.

Emica and Kroyle were doing a good job lining up with the *Bee*. Now, if Cassi ignored the spinning planet in the background, the two spacecraft were almost stationary relative to each other, with the *Triumph* slowly closing the gap between them.

Both spacecraft were already starting to heat up as the atmosphere around them grew dense. Pelly adjusted the climate control systems inside their own spacecraft to compensate.

"We have about fifteen minutes," Bauer said. He looked at Cassi. "That's not going to be enough time to extract anyone from inside."

Cassi's mind raced. "We don't have to extract anyone. If we can dock with them, we can execute a slow burn and lift them into a higher orbit. Once they're stable, we can go in and pull them out, or even leave them and send a proper rescue mission back."

Dodd cleared his throat. "Where we're at, that's the best course of action."

"Three hundred meters..." Emica reported.

"Slow it down, Kroyle," Bauer ordered.

"Two fifty…"

"I got it, sir," Kroyle said. He fired the retro thrusters in little bursts to slow their approach.

"Two hundred…"

The *Triumph* bucked like a car hitting a speed bump on a highway, the kind of jolt that Cassi felt straight through her spinal column.

"What was that?"

An alarm chimed. "We're venting—"

Singh swore.

"Seal the module," Cassi ordered.

Pelly: "Ma'am… I think… we're under attack."

The ship bucked again. This time not a single bump, but a series of heavy thuds, like a speedboat smacking against rough swells. Cassi slammed against her restraints.

Attack? That didn't make any sense.

The *Triumph* made painful, screeching, ominous sounds that reverberated inside Cassi's helmet. A loud whoosh like an air tool with its valve open made it almost impossible to hear anything else.

AXON scrambled to address the litany of technical problems popping up all through the spacecraft. Warning beacons flashed across Cassi's display. In training, the flight instructors almost always threw some kind of glitch at them. They were all trained to handle problems, even big ones. Sometimes, when they were feeling particularly nasty the instructors would throw 'compound glitches'—two or three problems that interacted with each other, each making the others more challenging to solve.

But now everything had gone wrong at once.

A part of her expected Dodd to take over, but if he or Singh were issuing orders, Cassi couldn't hear a thing they were saying.

"Kroyle!" Cassi called. She tried to keep her voice steady, but loud. She leaned in as close to the microphone as she could. "Stabilize the flight path."

"But I'm not..."

"Do it!"

He jostled the spacecraft around, hitting them all with heavy centripetal deceleration and the dizzying tumble slowed.

Little globules of quivering blood floated across Cassi's field of view. A couple touched and stuck to her helmet, running across the face shield.

Behind her, Commander Singh lay back in his restraints. The face plate on his own helmet had been shattered. Little globs of blood and shards of broken polymer floated all around his head like a deadly raincloud frozen in time. Pieces of console paneling, coolant hose junctions, valves, gaskets and bolts... had all broken loose and spun free in the command module, like shrapnel.

Blood spewed from a slice in Singh's face. He was still conscious, but barely, writhing in pain. He tried to work a hand in through his broken face mask, probably to put pressure on the wound, but the broken polymer sawed at his hand like shark teeth.

Dodd clutched his right arm against his chest. The fabric across the shoulder of his pressure suit was torn.

The sound from air blasting through the hole in the module bulkhead subsided as AXON heated specific grids on the mesh embedded in the module's torronite shell, melting it and electromagnetically pushing it toward the rupture.

Bauer stared at his terminal. "The *Lucky Bee* fired on us... ion cannon."

On the main screen the *Lucky Bee* was stable now too and closing in, a set of four docking talons outstretched.

CHAPTER THREE

"I told you they were pirates," Pelly said. "But does anyone listen to me? Ever?"

"They hit the *Triumph's* plasma cannon," Bauer reported. That was the only offensive weapon the decommissioned corvette had.

Kroyle shouted. "Lieutenant Singh needs first aid!"

Bauer ordered Quinton to help. As Quinton unbuckled himself, Dodd grunted. "Belay that, cadet."

Quinton stopped. "I... the lieutenant needs first aid, sir."

"If they hit us again while you're unrestrained, you'll get slammed against the bulkheads," Cassi said. "Hard."

"Signals," Dodd spoke through gritted teeth. "Ask them what they want."

Sijani sent the message by text.

No message came back as the *Lucky Bee* closed the remaining gap between the two ships.

"They're after our tech," Pelly said. "That's what pirates do. The *Triumph* has Casimir ramjets, a FLASH inverter, a VECTOR core... they're all worth a fortune on the black market."

Pelly hesitated once he realized everyone was listening to him. His voice got lower. "They probably want to kill us and dump our bodies. We'd just burn up in Dienne's atmosphere. Then they wipe the memory on the computers. If anyone asks, they came across an empty spacecraft. Most people involved in black markets don't ask too many questions."

"Get us out of here," Cassi said. "Cadet Junko—"

"Already on it. Calculating…"

The *Lucky Bee* closed in. The main view screen showed the pirate vessel looming ever closer, closing a gap that was now only thirty meters… twenty-five… twenty…

"Come on…"

Ten… five…

Kroyle fumbled with the controls. The *Triumph* rolled as he tried to create just a little extra space with the maneuvering thrusters.

A pang came up through the floor as the *Lucky Bee's* docking prongs latched onto the *Triumph's* hull.

"Got a solution!"

Kroyle hit the execution command. The Casimir ramjets grabbed onto the quantum foam of the space vacuum and drove forward, like a hot rod squealing its tires on hot asphalt.

But their trajectory calculation hadn't accounted for the added mass of the *Lucky Bee,* now tethered to their hull. As the ramjets fired, both ships swung in a massive arc and dropped into the blue glow of Dienne's atmosphere.

Klaxons rang out, warning chimes blended in, and bright red text scrolled across Cassi's command terminal and the bridge's central screen.

The *Triumph* shook.

Cassi slammed around in her harness with a centripetal force so strong it was hard to breathe. Her pressure suit constricted, squeezing her body tight to keep the blood in her head, to keep her from losing consciousness.

Another deafening rush of air dominated her audio.

"We're venting!" Pelly called out. The command module was losing air pressure, blowing gas out into space. And that was working like a manoeuvring rocket, throwing them further off course. AXON was incredibly good at calculating velocity and acceleration from its engines, but a push from a random vent had to be adapted to. The computer couldn't keep up to the rapid changes.

"Kroyle, get control of the roll!" Cassi ordered, as if the force of her voice might somehow make a difference.

The pilot fought with his controls and swore. The spacecraft bucked and strained, like a bull let out a rodeo gate with a rider who wouldn't let go.

Cassi turned to Pelly. "Where? Which module is breached?" The *Triumph* was designed as a series of nearly independent modules or cells, each with their own controlled environments. Like a cluster of balloons, if one popped they could seal off the rest and be just fine.

"Um... all of them..."

AXON issued another verbal warning. "Decomp. Decomp. Decomp."

The cabin pressure in the command module was almost gone. Dodd tried to pin the tear in his suit together with his good hand, but it was leaking. And Singh gulped for what remained of the cabin air like a landed fish.

"Get into the stasis pod, sir!" Cassi shouted.

Dodd looked up, his eyes wide, vacant, like he hadn't heard.

Bauer unbuckled himself.

"Bauer!"

But Cassi didn't have the power to stop him. Anson Bauer peeled out of his restraints and crawled to the senior flight instructor. He held tight to the restraints and command station scaffolding to keep from getting flung against the bulkheads. The g-forces were like those of an amusement park ride, gentle, weightless, and then crushingly powerful.

Bauer pulled Dodd out of his restraints. The commander screamed as the g-forces pulled at his injured arm. Mashing his palm against the stasis pod emergency button, Bauer opened a small red panel at the back of the command module. Dodd shouted something, but Cassi couldn't hear him.

Bauer pushed him down and in then closed the door.

AXON issued another alert. "Stasis capsule CM02—activated."

With a heavy power surge, the *Triumph* flash froze the senior flight instructor.

"Stasis process completed," AXON reported. "Change of command protocol... commanding officer: Lieutenant Arjun Singh AVLN D34 617 983. Updating user security rights."

The strain on Bauer's face was obvious. The window on his helmet fogged and sweat beaded on his temples. He clenched his teeth as he crawled back for Singh.

"Air pressure critically low," AXON stated.

Singh blew whatever air he had out of his lungs to prevent any rapid decompression injury. He clawed at his restraints, but the blood all around his face blinded him. It stuck to his gloves and his fingers slid helpless off the buckles. Without any pressure Singh's blood would start to boil, giving rise to thousands of tiny air embolisms, any one of which might kill him.

Bauer snapped Singh free of his restraints, grabbed him by the shoulders and hauled the flight instructor out of his command station. They shot down to the other stasis pod, where Bauer kicked it open and slam dunked the lieutenant in.

"Stasis capsule CM01—activated."

In a half second, it turned the flight instructor into Arjun Singh flavored ice cream.

AXON reported again. "Stasis process completed. Change of command protocol... processing... Change of command protocol... processing... emergency field promotion protocol. Cadet Cassiopeia Requin AVLN T72 715 524 promoted to minimum rank for vessel command: ensign. Change of command protocol... commanding officer: Ensign Cassiopeia Requin AVLN T72 715 524. Updating user security rights."

With the two actual qualified astronauts flash frozen in stasis pods, Cassi was no longer just the acting mission commander. She suddenly had full command of the *Triumph* and her crew, with all rights and privileges afforded to the post.

The spacecraft bucked again, slamming Bauer against the ceiling. For a brief moment his body seemed as helpless as that of a crash test dummy. But he shook his head and climbed back to his command station. Cassi reached over and helped him with his restraints.

As stupid as it had been, Bauer had just saved the lives of both flight instructors. Cassi wasn't sure whether she should admonish him or commend him, though for the moment it didn't really matter.

Everyone was alive, but they were still in deep trouble.

Together, the *Triumph* and the *Lucky Bee* spiraled into Dienne's atmosphere. Their hull temperatures rose. Pressure in the cabin had dropped to something unreadable. For the moment all that kept each cadet alive was the thin nano-mesh fabric that made up their pressure suits. Dienne kept rolling past the view screen, entering and leaving from different positions.

Cassi felt dizzy, disoriented.

Then, a ball of white-hot fire engulfed both spacecraft.

CHAPTER FOUR

The *Triumph* shook and spun.

The *Lucky Bee's* docking talons snapped, sending the *Triumph* into a completely new death spiral. The atmosphere was thick enough now that the drag on the spacecraft drove its trajectory.

"Kroyle!" Cassi called out. "Steer into the spin!"

But when she looked over at the pilot, his terminal was black. Tendrils of dark vapor rose from the console into the vacuum of the command module and drifted toward the rupture in the hull, and across his face. Kroyle fought to reinitialize the panel, but he was blind.

AXON should have taken over control of the ship as soon as they broke from the planned trajectory. The spacecraft's artificial intelligence was supposed to be a safety net, an autopilot. But the computer was locked up, frozen in some kind of cyber-paralysis from a million different circuits flooding it with emergency signals. At the *Triumph's* current rate of descent, the ceramic panels on its surface were going to fry and AXON seemed content to allow that to happen.

"Bauer," Cassi said. "I'm transferring piloting control to your station."

"Got it."

Bauer systematically fired the thrusters. A kick hammered the fuselage followed by a thrum that rumbled Cassi's bones. Bauer rocked the *Triumph* back and forth as he fought to compensate for the angular momentum they'd gained. He forced them into a stable-ish trajectory, at least eliminating the tumbling.

"We're still falling," he shouted. "Where's AXON? If I punch this thing too hard it'll rip the wings off."

What they needed was a burn solution. But with AXON locked up Cassi had to do the math manually. She scratched it out on a virtual screen and came up with a force that wouldn't turn them all into pancakes. Hopefully.

Bauer entered it. "Three... two... one..."

The restraints crushed her ribs and chest with such mammoth weight, she couldn't inhale. Her blood pooled in her face. Her lips swelled. Little pinpricks of starlight flashed in her peripheral vision. She was going to pass out.

A moment later, or maybe longer, Cassi returned to a murky consciousness. Her head spun. Sound came through her helmet warped, muffled and distorted. New warning klaxons screamed. Bauer was saying something to her.

"I can't hold it..."

Cassi shook her head. The force from the braking maneuver had dissipated, but the *Triumph* was bouncing through its flight path. The spacecraft was damaged. It was designed to act as an atmospheric entry vehicle in an emergency, and they had all piloted it through planetary landings in simulations, but Bauer's terminal was covered with red warnings—messages from unresponsive hydraulics, nonsense gauge readings, and damage reports.

Bauer shouted. "I can't control it, Cassi. We have to ditch."

The *Triumph* soared over Dienne like a wounded bird. Beneath them alien trees that pushed up through rocky terrain sped past in a blur of green, blue and violet. Jagged sedimentary slate-rock broke through the flora, like cheese-grater teeth waiting to grind up the *Triumph's* torronite hull.

Though she could barely hold her head stable enough to focus on her terminal, Cassi desperately searched for a patch of land smooth enough for an emergency landing. Dienne's wilderness lay untouched—growth on growth, trees that reached like skyscraper spikes high into the air, and older decaying trunks bleached by the alien sun, lay like bones within the growth, patches of swampy sludge and tar, and ominous lakes that seemed to suck in light.

The ground came up fast. Bauer managed some control over their flight path. With one hand he reached over to Pelly's terminal and shouted to the kid to lock something down. The thrusters were overheating. Any moment they were going to lose what little control they had.

"Where should I put it down?"

"There." Cassi pointed to a lake. The water would cushion their landing and put out any residual fires. There was a risk the *Triumph* might sink, but their pressure suits were completely self-contained, designed to protect them from the cold vacuum of space. They could survive submersion.

Bauer grunted acknowledgment and lowered the *Triumph's* nose. The ground whipped by faster as they approached. The ship was technically slowing, but the decreased proximity made it harder to track anything. All the trees blurred into one another.

Then water.

Bauer raised the nose.

One of the thrusters sputtered and died.

The *Triumph* rolled and pitched and hit the surface with a bone-rattling smack. The fuselage rumbled and vibrated as its lower half skidded over the lake.

The nose caught. The spacecraft cartwheeled and twisted in aerobatic turmoil. The wings ripped off. Hot ceramic panels flash-heated water into geysers of steam.

Cassi's restraints slammed into her from multiple directions, as if the spacecraft was trying to rip her body apart and preserve her life all at the same time. G-force alerts flashed.

The other cadets cried out, swore, and tried to hold on.

The spacecraft landed upside down, skidded through a bay and thundered to a stop, washing up on a beach of pebbles and whitewashed driftwood.

Everything got a lot quieter.

AXON's warnings spewed new walls of text across Cassi's command screen. The artificial intelligence reported that everything from the nuclear generator to the radar was offline. The hull's structural integrity was compromised. Four of six thrusters were no longer functional. The other two were completely missing. Life support was down.

Holes in the hull meant Dienne's atmosphere was leaking into the command module.

Cassi took a deep breath. The recycled air inside her pressure suit still had that putrid smell from her own barf. Because they'd landed upside down, she hung, suspended in her restraints. Blood pooled in her skull. Dienne's gravity pulled something wet up past the neckline of her undersuit.

Ignoring AXON's warnings for a moment, Cassi swiped over to her personnel screen and checked everyone's vital signs, running down the list of cadets. Everyone still had a heartbeat at least.

She checked the stasis pods. Both were functioning.

They were banged up. Cadets moaned and complained. Cassi heard someone sobbing. But they were all alive.

She took a few more breaths. Her fingers were trembling. Her heart galloped. She was in shock. They were all in shock.

For a long time no one said anything. They just hung there, upside down, as if they were waiting for a failed simulation to end. Or for someone to tell them what to do. Or a rescue team to kick in the hatches and medics with fluorescent orange vests to unbuckled them one by one, lay them on backboards and shine intense little pen lights into their eyes.

But no one was coming.

The *Triumph* creaked. Gas lines hissed. Fluids dripped.

Bauer rocked gently back and forth in his restraints. "I think I can safely say that we've failed our astronaut qualification."

Cassi wondered if she should say something to him, tell him he did a good job landing the spacecraft in one piece. But it was Bauer. He'd just grunt, as if he had it under control the whole time.

He was older than her and she knew he resented the fact that she'd been chosen as the mission commander over him. If she said anything that sounded too much like a canned attaboy, he'd take it for condescension.

He looked like he might say something to her too, but he didn't.

They were alive. The spacecraft wasn't about to explode. Everyone's pressure suit seemed intact, so they didn't have to worry about pathogen contamination, at least, until Pelly pulled off his helmet.

CHAPTER FIVE

"Wait!" Cassi shouted. But it was too late. Pelly popped open the double latch, twisted the lock and pulled the helmet off his head, breaking the gummy green seal between it and the metal collar on his pressure suit.

The cadet took a deep breath. He filled his lungs with the alien air and pushed it out, eyes closed. When he opened them, he looked around at the other cadets all staring at him.

"What?"

Sijani coughed inside her helmet. "We don't know the air's okay to breathe."

Pelly smirked. "Didn't you guys read the mission background appendixes?"

The cadets had known the general aspects of the mission for months. But every cadet crew was sent to a different planet so the details of the mission would be different for each test. Most of the target planets were either colonized worlds or planets with major Alliance operations. Dienne was an unknown, and they'd only learned it was their objective twelve hours before the launch. That was part of the test.

No one had time to read the mission background appendixes—unless they had a brain that could process text like a supercomputer.

Pelly went on. "Dienne is a Goldilocks planet—totally habitable. Gravity within ten percent of Earth's... its atmosphere is breathable. They've had survey teams on the surface for like eight years now. The first fully independent colony is due to be established in the next two years."

Sijani crossed her arms. "Yeah, but what about alien pathogens? We don't have the advantage of billions of years of evolutionary trial and error to protect us here."

Pelly shrugged. "Dienne pathogens don't have billions of years of evolution honing their ability to attack us either."

Xenoimmunoconditioning—inoculating human colonists against alien pathogens— was an arduous field. Surveyors would typically collect as much information about xenopathogens as they could over the span of a decade. Those got run through simulations and systematically applied to experimental models allowing effective vaccines to be developed. But that all took time and although there were a set of standard xenovaccines that all Alliance Cadets were required to get, they weren't designed specifically for the microbes on this planet.

Emica looked at Cassi. "Well, it's Cassi's decision."

"The mission's over, Junko," Bauer said, unbuckling himself and climbing down onto the ceiling that was now a floor. The implication was that with the mission over, Cassi was no longer the mission commander and therefore no longer in charge.

Emica shook her head. "When Commander Dodd and Lieutenant Singh were put in stasis, AXON issued a field promotion. Cassi is now officially *Ensign* Requin."

A micro expression of anger twitched through Bauer's face, almost too quick to notice before it passed. He typed something into his terminal and then pulled back, obviously confirming Cassi's new rank.

Cassi checked her own terminal. Since they'd lost life support, the air in their pressure suits wasn't being replaced. They had portable supplies, but without the *Triumph's* processing station, their self-contained air would run out in a matter of hours.

She wasn't sure how long they would be on Dienne. There weren't any other spacecraft in the system other than the pirates. By the time anyone got to them, they'd all be out of the bottled air.

Take off the pressure suits now, or run down the oxygen supply and take off the pressure suits later? It wasn't really much of a decision.

"Yeah," she said. "Go ahead. Climb down. Take your pressure suits off."

Quinton laughed. "Alright. Ensign Requin's first official command: everyone strip down to your underwear. I like where this is going."

The cadets, Cassi included, released their restraints and dropped onto the ceiling-deck. Sijani had to help Kroyle with his helmet. The smoke from his console got sucked across his body. It had blackened the bright orange fabric on his suit, and his face shield, effectively blinding him.

It had been a good thing Bauer was qualified to step in and take over.

Bauer pulled off his helmet and tucked it under his arm, like a jock holding a football. If the crash had shaken him at all, Cassi couldn't tell. Bauer had the look of a natural leader... tall, athletic, nice hair. And he carried himself with the kind of confidence that made a lot of girls weak in the knees... at least, until he opened his mouth.

Sijani moved like she was tender, rotating her shoulder and stretching her back before sitting down. She stayed in her pressure suit, at least for the moment and lowered her face into her hands.

"Taura, are you okay?" Cassi asked.

"Fine," she said. From her tone, Cassi suspected Sijani was anything but fine. For the moment however, she had to focus on the physical. Taura Sijani was breathing, operational, and her usual brooding self. If she was pissed off at Cassi's decision to intervene with the *Lucky Bee,* well, they would have to work that out later.

Cassi retreated to the rear of the command module. She took a moment to steady herself, the way a person might before stepping off a high-dive platform. Then she undid the latch and pulled her own helmet off, this time without any problem.

The air was cool and carried scents of kelp and sand, far better than the stagnant recycled puke she hadn't realized she was getting used to. Sounds were crisper too. She could hear the cadets breathing, the scrape of their boots on the command module ceiling panels, the crinkle of pressure suits when they moved. Everything seemed fresher, clearer, as if she had transitioned into a high-definition world.

The cadets reported their injuries to Cassi: bruises, cuts, nausea, "the shakes" and general symptoms of shock, but there were no major injuries, no broken bones or sucking chest wounds. At least that was something.

Emica had a nasty gash on her left hand. Sijani used the wound glue on it— transparent paste that bonded the tissue together. Emica's hand would be a little stiff, but otherwise she and everyone else was fully mobile.

The survival pods were fine. Both flight instructors were still frozen, but all signs indicated the suspension had been sustained.

Cassi unclasped her collar and wriggled out of her pressure suit. The undersuits they all wore were tight-fitting all-purpose flight suits. Most cadets referred to them as jumpsuits, underwear, or superhero tights, but they were designed to work as full service fatigues. The fabric wicked both moisture and oil away from the skin, allowing them to be worn for days on end, like a second skin. The fibers responded to temperature, regulating it by enabling a certain amount of airflow when warm and trapping air when cold. The undersuits were rugged enough to protect cadets on wilderness survival exercises, yet reasonably comfortable.

Cassi had a stain around her collar, where some of the vomit had leeched down. She found a wet-wipe and took a few minutes to clean herself up properly. The stain was still visible, like a ring of dishonor around her neck, but she hadn't brought any change of clothing. And she couldn't worry about her own vanity now anyway.

"We need to release the flight instructors from their stasis pods," Cassi said. As cool as it might be that she had some actual command authority, they needed at least one experienced officer on the ground. Singh was badly injured and could probably sit this one out, but they needed Dodd.

Emica climbed up to the commander's pod. She had to climb up the bulkhead to open the shielding hatch on the stasis system interface. There, she tapped in the command to reanimate the *Triumph's* senior officer.

Cassi watched from underneath. *System Error: 1603. Insufficient power.*

Emica tried again and got the same response.

"Do you know what this means?" Emica asked Pelly, climbing back down.

Pelly climbed up with the ease of a spider money. He studied the terminal for a moment, hanging there. "The pod doesn't have enough power to initiate the reanimation sequence."

"Really?" Emica asked, her tone dripping with sarcasm.

"Hey, you asked."

Emica glared at him and Pelly lowered his head. "The pods draw almost no power in stasis, but the reanimation sequence requires a lot of juice. The pods need to be hooked into the *Triumph's* power grid. If they try to reanimate off the battery, it would be a slow thaw."

"What's wrong with that?" Bauer asked.

Pelly looked down at him. "Reanimation needs to be fast, nearly instantaneous. If you go slow some of your cells would start to function while others are still frozen. Your tissues would go all necrotic—then septic. You would wake up to a terribly slow and painful death."

"So we just need to hook them into the power grid." Emica looked up at panel. "How long will that take?"

Pelly climbed down from the pod hatch and scratched the back of his neck.

Emica stared at him. "What is it?"

A few of the other cadets gathered in too. Pelly looked back and forth between Emica and Cassi. "The power grid is dead."

"So we use the auxiliary power," Cassi said.

"We used most of the auxiliary power to keep ourselves from burning up," Bauer said. "I had to redirect almost everything we had into the working ramjets."

"There's barely enough power to keep AXON up," Pelly said.

Cassi thought, both trying to get a handle on the situation and generate some options. "What if we cut power to AXON? Would that give us enough to reanimate at least one stasis pod?"

Pelly shook his head and quoted some numbers. They were short by at least an order of magnitude. Even if they had ten times the power they currently possessed, reanimating either of the flight instructors was still a big risk.

"Do we have enough power for signals?" Sijani asked.

Bauer shook his head. "We have bigger problems than your radio, Taura."

Sijani crossed her arms. "Radio is *the* problem, Bauer. If it doesn't work, we can't call for help."

"Radio is *a* problem." Bauer held up a hand and began counting on his fingers. "Our flight instructors are stuck in suspended animation. We have to figure out water, food, geolocation... if you haven't noticed we're smack in the middle of an alien wilderness. There could very well be things out there that see us as lunch. Not to mention, we were just attacked by pirates. Did they survive the crash? How far away are they? You have to think about more than yourself, Taura."

Taura Sijani didn't look like she had any intention of backing down from Bauer. "Well you seem to do enough thinking about other people for everyone."

Bauer rolled his eyes.

As much as she didn't want to, Cassi stepped in between them. "We're expected back in port in about six hours. When we don't show up, they'll start looking for us."

"If a search and rescue ship enters orbit, they'll be able to see the crash site, won't they?" Kroyle asked.

Sijani shot an intense glare at Kroyle, who instinctively stepped back.

"Dienne's a huge planet," Cassi said. She wasn't sure she wanted to voice her thoughts, but instinct told her they had to get all their concerns out in the open, throw them all on the table, as much as it might hurt to look at them. "A single crash site alone won't be easy to spot." She swallowed. "Near impossible, actually."

"And that's assuming they know we landed in the first place," Sijani said. "They might think we drifted off course and burned up in the atmosphere. When a rescue comes, we need to *tell* them where we are."

"Do we have enough auxiliary power for that?" Cassi asked.

"I think so," Pelly said. "I'm not sure how long we can keep it up, but we should have enough juice for a few long-range signals."

That made Cassi feel a little better. "So that's the plan then... at least for the time being. We wait it out."

She looked around and got nods of agreement.

"Okay then. First thing, we set up a rotating radio watch... passive monitoring for any signals. When we hear something, we broadcast our rescue beacon. Worst case scenario, we have to rely on a rescue operation to triangulate on us."

"If they can," Pelly said.

Cassi nodded. "If they can. Meanwhile, Pelly, I want you and Kroyle to work together and figure out where we are so we can report a precise position."

"Aye ma'am." Both Pelly and Kroyle shuffled back to the navigational command station, seemingly happy to have a job.

Bauer placed his hands on his hips and cocked his head to the side. "Hold on. The exercise is over. We don't need to assume Requin's in charge."

"She is in charge. She was promoted. Remember?" Emica said.

"By a malfunctioning computer."

"It was following regulations." Emica sounded annoyed.

Quinton stood beside Bauer. He was almost a full head shorter than Bauer and generally followed him around like a lapdog. Whenever Bauer had an idea, Quinton was there beside him to tell everyone how good it was. "Everyone knows Bauer's the most qualified cadet in our crew."

"We should at least put it to a vote," Bauer said. "That's the best way to decide."

A vote. If leadership came down to a vote now, the only vote Cassi could really count on was Emica's. Quinton would vote for Bauer no matter what. And even though it seemed like there was little love between Sijani and Bauer, she would still vote for him. Kroyle would follow Sijani. Pelly would make up his mind independently, so he could fall either way, but even if he voted in her favor, Cassi would still lose four to three.

"We can't vote." Cassi said.

"That's the only fair way to decide on a leader," Quinton said.

She stepped toward Bauer, not at all sure she wanted to challenge him. "The Alliance Cadet Corps is not a democracy. We have operational positions. And we have rank."

"But the operation is over."

"You can't use regulations to get your way, Cassi." Quinton said.

Was she just pulling rank? Doubt crept into her mind like a tiny poisonous spider. But she had to believe that the academy instructors had seen a reason to put her in charge, even over Bauer. The decision wasn't arbitrary.

"I was the acting mission commander when Singh dropped into stasis. That makes me skipper now. That's how it works. That's how *all* of this works." She gestured around the command module, and at their uniforms, the discarded pressure suits.

"Requin's right." Everyone turned to look at Sijani, who was staring at the virtual window projected from a mobile device mounted on her undersuit at the base of her breastbone. "AXON recognizes her as an ensign. She is the commanding officer of the *Triumph*."

Quinton shook his head. "AXON's just a computer. We're talking about survival here."

"I'd be careful," Pelly warned. "Ensign Requin has ordnance authority now."

"I'm the weapons officer," Quinton argued.

"*Acting* weapons officer." Pelly looked mildly annoyed, the way he did when he felt like he was explaining something they should already know. "We didn't get field promotions when Lieutenant Singh went into suspended animation. It was only Cassi."

"What do you mean I have ordnance authority?"

Pelly held up his right wrist. All cadets wore a pair of vambrace wrist cuffs as part of their uniforms. On the non-dominant wrist, most often the left, was the *tracker interface*—a control for the individual computer and communication portal mounted on their chests. On the dominant wrist, most often the right, was the *mount*—a bracket that interfaced with the tracker and any peripheral systems on the cadet's uniform. The mount connected to and secured any number of tools, including...

"Rail guns." Quinton's eyes widened.

"You can unlock the armory?" Bauer asked.

"Of course not." But Cassi slid over to the permissions screen on her tracker. Normally it was filled with red. There were a few provisional permissions here and there, but for cadets most of the really cool Alliance tech was locked out. Or at least it was under most circumstances. Now she had authority over every system on the *Triumph,* including the armory.

The *Triumph* was an out-of-service exploratory corvette. Though the Alliance Expeditionary Fleet was not a military force, expeditionary astronauts were often a point of contact and supply for new colonies, colonies that were often fighting with each other. The standard payload included a trunk under the weapons officer's command station known colloquially as the armory. It housed a set of twenty-four K205s, each with thirty-two round magazines along with maintenance and repair kits.

"You *can* unlock the armory." Bauer read her face so easily.

He swiped over to the permission screen on his own tracker.

Quinton smiled. "Cassi... you've got to let us go outside and shoot something. Like just a tree or a rock or... anything."

Her lips, her mouth, her entire throat felt dry. Cassi wasn't sure she wanted anything to do with that kind of responsibility. Maybe it would have been better if Bauer was in charge.

Her stomach twisted again. She couldn't just let them have weapons. She wouldn't. They were all still in shock from the crash. They had other priorities. There was no need for weapons.

Or at least there wasn't, until a scratching sound came at the main entry hatch to the command module.

CHAPTER SIX

Sijani took a step back from the airlock. "There's no one else on board."

"Is there anyone else on the planet?" Emica asked. "Maybe it's a survey team that saw us crash?"

The scratching at the pressure hatch intensified. Something on the other side rattled and then pinged, the distinct sound of metal on metal.

"The pirates?" Bauer said.

"Cassi," Quinton whispered. "Open the armory."

More scratching.

Cassi cleared her throat and tried to lower her voice, not excessively so, but maybe a little, so she might not sound like a cadet. "Identify yourself."

The scratching stopped, and the cadets waited in silence. An electronic voice reported back. "Autonomous maintenance and repair robot... assigned to the AEFS *Triumph*... standing by to assist."

Bauer walked over to the hatch and turned on a little console screen at its side. A pixelated black and white image of a robot on the other side appeared. The robot was humanoid in shape with a rectangular, toaster-like head and snooper antenna, long spindly legs and lanky arms that nearly dragged on the ground.

"It's just the robot." Bauer almost sounded disappointed.

The robot was an independent machine linked into AXON that could be used for everything from spacewalk repair tasks to cleaning toilets. It was normally housed, folded up in a box near the *Triumph's* power core. With all the damage the spacecraft had received, Cassi was surprised it was functional.

When Bauer opened the hatch, Pelly jumped up. "MURPHI! Oh, man am I glad to see you."

The robot turned its head to face Cassi. MURPHI hadn't been constructed with any kind of mechanical face. It had two primary cameras where human eyes would be, and two more nested in sensory pods that whipped about its head like insect antennae. Someone had graffitied a mouth and nose on the plate covering the forward-facing surface of its head years ago, giving it an awkward, permanent marker smile. Someone else had blacked out one of the teeth. Its dark red paint had chipped off in places. Metal scars and scratches made it look like it had just climbed out of a scrap heap. MURPHI was an original piece of the spacecraft's equipment, activated when the *Triumph* was first commissioned, eighty-seven standard years ago.

"Permission to enter, ma'am."

Cassi stared at the robot.

"Cassi?" Emica prompted.

"Um... yes. Permission granted, MURPHI."

The robot strode into the command module. Its head and snooper antenna whipped around as it took in the status of the crew and assessed the damage to the *Triumph's* command module.

Then it did something Cassi had never seen it do before. It twitched, a little servo-driven spasm.

"Are you okay, Murph?" Bauer asked.

"Self diagnostic... report... damaged actuator alpha one three, tolerance violations alpha zero seven, zero nine, two two—"

"Stop report," Cassi ordered. MURPHI could spit out technical babble almost indefinitely if left unchecked. "We're in an emergency situation. Do you have any critical problems that are likely to prevent the execution of your duties in the next twenty-four hours?"

MURPHI's shoulders dropped. "Negative."

Pelly ran up to the robot and threw his arms around it. "Oh man. I figured you were scrap, MURPHI."

"I am not due to be scrapped for seven standard years." The robot twitched again and then wrapped an arm around the acting engineering officer, returning the gesture with a cold mechanical hug.

Cassi filled MURPHI in on the details of their predicament... a ship that couldn't fly, flight instructors that couldn't be reanimated, lost on an alien world, the plan to monitor the radio... the robot already knew most of the details through AXON, but Cassi still felt better explaining it.

"Your primary objective right now is keeping the cadets safe," Cassi said.

MURPHI twitched again. "Keep cadets safe. Acknowledge. Assessing operational scenarios."

"So what do we do now?" Kroyle asked. "Realistically, how long until we can expect rescue?"

MURPHI raised its snoopers, as if it had an idea.

"What is it Murph?" Bauer asked.

"Principal Source of danger: private armored transport vessel model Phoenix Mark Three, *Lucky Bee*. Status: stationary. Severe damage likely. Crew status: probability of survival: eighty-one-point two percent. Location, approximate: thirty-two kilometers north.

"Secondary source of danger: category: Dienne predatory megafauna."

Quinton rubbed his hands together. "Sounds like a good time to open the armory, Cassi."

MURPHI's attention turned to the acting weapons officer. "Please use proper terms of address for a superior officer."

"Huh? Easy there, Murph. It's just Cassi."

The robot took a giant stride, inserting itself between Cassi and Quinton. "Further breech of protocol is an indictable offence. Cite regulation: standing order 4304—protocol and discipline in Fleet spacecraft command module by uniform members. Justification: breakdown in discipline leads to inefficient actions, poor judgment, social intimidation, and increases susceptibility to psychological trauma. Offer options: comply with protocol and continue in duties, or face formal charge."

Quinton threw up his hands. "Okay. My apologies, *Ensign* Requin."

"Apology accepted. Stand down MURPHI."

The robot was only doing what it was programmed to do. And it was right. They had to keep to the discipline standards they'd been taught. But there was a fine balance between discipline and camaraderie. MURPHI's programming still interpreted the *Triumph* as the Alliance Fleet corvette it had been before it was officially decommissioned. It functioned under the assumption the *Triumph* was still a warship. While enforcing protocol was appropriate under wartime circumstances, Cassi wondered if MURPHI stepping in had made her grasp on the situation worse. A leader through enforcement wasn't much of a leader.

The pirates were a problem. MURPHI put their probability of survival at 81.2%. Did that mean there was an 81.2% chance that all of them survived? Or that about 81.2% of however many pirates had been on the *Lucky Bee* would still be alive? Cassi supposed those details didn't matter.

"You think the pirates will come after us?" Emica asked.

Bauer was already at, or rather under, his command station. He called up a Dienne map. AXON had predicted a zone for where the *Lucky Bee* was most likely to have landed and as MURPHI said, it was about thirty kilometers away.

"How long would it take to hike from there to here?" Bauer asked.

Pelly looked up at the map. "It's hard to get really specific. At a run, if the terrain is good, it might only take a few hours. But there aren't any trails. It's just wilderness. On foot, for the average person, it would take a full day. Maybe more."

"So we have time to fortify?"

Pelly nodded. "I think so. And that assumes their first priority is attacking us. They likely have other concerns now—tending to their wounded, calling for help, long term survival... the same as us."

Bauer leaned up against a bulkhead and crossed his arms. "If they're alive at all, they're going to come straight for us."

"Why do you think that?" Cassi asked.

"They attacked us. If we report what happened, whoever comes for us will either hunt them down or call in the cavalry. If we get rescued, the day doesn't end well for them.

"But if they remove us from the equation, then they can make up whatever story they want—a collision in orbit, we were in trouble and they stopped to help—if all the video evidence burned up in the crash and we're not around to dispute anything, they come out as the heroes."

Everyone was quiet.

Cassi ran her fingers through her hair. Her bun had almost entirely come out and so instinctively she pulled it out, let her hair fall, and then began winding it back up.

"MURPHI can you estimate the probability survivors on the *Lucky Bee* would predict for us having survived the crash?"

The robot twitched. "Eighty-one-point two percent."

Cassi studied the robot. Could she rely on that number? Was it just random? Now that she thought about it, it made sense that they would arrive at the same probability for the *Triumph* having survivors as they had for the *Bee* having survivors. Regardless, the specific number wasn't that important. "They're more likely than not to believe we're alive. That means we should expect them to come for us."

"Ma'am?" Pelly looked like he had an idea. "Is it possible we're over-thinking this? I mean, it will be about six hours before we fail to show up. Fleet Command will launch a search and rescue mission pretty soon after that. If you figure three hours to prepare and three hours to get here... a rescue mission should show up before anyone on foot could hike thirty kilometres without any well-defined path."

Kroyle shook his head. "That twelve hours would be an absolute minimum. It's not like the officers at the fleet dock are going to immediately declare us overdue and jump into action. The mission time has a tolerance. We could show up two hours late and still have completed it successfully. We're cadets. They expect us to get things wrong. And it takes time to mobilize a search and rescue mission, realistically. Plus, planetary extraction is a whole different operation. The first ship to get here might not have the capability of even coming down to the surface."

Kroyle turned to Cassi. "Ma'am, we could be here for several days before a rescue mission arrives."

"Days?" Sijani shook her head. "Our fourth-year placement requests are due the day after tomorrow."

The cadets erupted into questions. None of which were helpful.

"What are we going to eat?"

"What if they can't find us at all?"

"What did MURPHI mean by predatory megafauna?"

"Do you think the pirates would really try to kill us?"

"Quiet!"

Everyone looked at Cassi.

"I understand we're all feeling uncertain. We have to focus on what we know and the tasks that we have. Sijani, you're on surveillance. Kroyle, I want you to draw up a radio watch schedule. Bauer, take Quinton, Junko and MURPHI and scout the perimeter outside. Stay within sight of the ship. Pelly—you and I are going to scour the inside. We need to find food, take stock of the water, and gather up any emergency supplies for an inventory."

"What about the pirates, Requin?" Bauer didn't sound like he particularly wanted to ask the question, but they were all thinking it.

She swallowed. "We're inside an Alliance Fleet corvette. The hull is made of torronite. Unless the pirates carry the plasma cannon from their ship all the way over here, we can seal the hatches. They won't be able to get to us."

"What about the guns, ma'am?" Quinton clasped his hands together, index fingers pointed out and aimed at the now blank main viewer, one eye closed, his thick tongue poking out of the corner of his mouth.

"No guns."

Quinton's eyes popped open. "What? You can't expect us to scout around outside without the rail guns."

"Look, I know you'll feel safer with them," Cassi said. "But I don't want you getting separated out there and accidentally shooting each other."

"But—"

"The armory is locked."

"If one of us is eaten by some kind of Dienne mega-tiger, it'll all be on you, Ensign."

Bauer put a hand on Quinton's shoulder. "C'mon, man. Let's go check this place out."

At least Bauer seemed excited to go outside.

CHAPTER SEVEN

The good news was that according to AXON the *Triumph* had enough food to nourish the seven cadets for twenty-one days. The bad news was that it was all emergency rations.

Despite generations of engineering and refinement, space travel was still far from perfect. While rare, it wasn't unheard of for a spacecraft to get stranded out in the vacuum of space and have to wait for days or even weeks for rescue. Standard practice was to stock each craft with provisions to enable long term survival.

The qualification mission was only supposed to last for six hours. And because they expected to be bubbled up in their pressure suits for the duration of the flight, no one had brought any of their own food. That left them with a polymer cupboard filled with vacuum-sealed protein bars—food engineered to provide maximum nutritional value in minimal space—twenty-one days worth for the seven of them, according to AXON's inventory.

Cassi needed to check that the rations were still intact. She and Pelly climbed into the *Triumph's* mess module. Functionally it served as everything from a mess hall to a center of operations to a lounge for long flights. Right now, it looked like a tornado aftermath.

Panels were busted open, cargo netting torn, tools, wiring, spare circuit boards, and first aid supplies had all been slammed against bulkheads, ceilings and floors. Two large view screens were crushed, some carbon dioxide scrubbers had come loose and spider-webbed both of them, leaving shards of broken polymer on the ceiling. Lights flickered and a fan screeched as it tried to pump air either into or out of the module. The scent of electrical smoke hung in the air from a fire AXON extinguished on their way down.

Pelly found the wall panel where the emergency rations were kept and when it didn't open, he had to use a multi-tool to pry it off. The panel dropped and clanged off the bulkhead.

Part of the bulkhead had imploded, crushing about a third of the ration bars. A mix of gummy, nutty food-paste with the consistency of cold peanut butter had splattered over the inner side of the panel.

"Gross," Pelly grumbled.

"Turn your tracker video on," Cassi told him. "I want a record of this."

"It's just wasted ration bars. No one's going to care."

"No one's hungry yet," Cassi said, more to herself than to Pelly.

Pelly thought about it for a moment. "You think we might hoard food? Try to steal it?"

They were highly trained astronaut cadets of the Alliance Fleet. Cassi knew them all well. They were in the third year of the program. Cadets who were likely to stab the other members of their crew in the back, the ones who were likely to place their own interests over the collective... they washed out in the first year, mostly in the first month or two. "I trust our crew, Pelly. But I'm responsible for this. We need an inventory."

Having the numbers turned blind trust into a scenario where the temptation to cheat was no longer a factor.

The kid nodded. He pulled the ration bars out of their crushed storage container and stacked them in a neat pile, separating the ruptured ones from those that were still sealed. Some of those with broken wrappers were still good. They could eat those first.

"You think we might be here for a while, don't you, ma'am?"

"Someone will show up before the food runs out, Pelly. But we need to plan a long game, just in case."

When he was done with the rations, Pelly climbed through the spacecraft's fuselage, popping in and out of the mess to give her reports on what he found. The central head fared better than the one attached to the command module. They had water. That was some good news at least. Pelly confirmed the water tanks hadn't ruptured and the processing system was still functional. As long as they had some power, they could add water to the system and it would filter out anything harmful.

"It's not a major power draw," Pelly said. "But it's not negligible either."

Cassi didn't want anyone to drink Dienne water unless they could help it. Breathing the foreign air already had her on edge. Eventually they might have to shut down the filtration system to save power, but for the time being, they could filter what they needed and turn off the system when not in use.

The pirates were her next concern. She wished she had a better idea what they were up to, what they were thinking. The more she thought about it, the more nervous she got about the possibility of another attack. Was there a way she could monitor them without holding up a flag that said they survived? Maybe she could deploy MURPHI as a scout, but she wanted to keep the robot close.

The next time Pelly came back to the mess module, he looked worried.

"What's wrong?"

He took his time and sat down. "The *Triumph's* structural integrity is compromised, ma'am."

"Well, yeah. Crash landings tend to do that."

He rubbed his temples. "The hull is cracked. If anyone attacks us, the *Triumph* won't be the fortress we need it to be. All they need to do it crawl up underneath it. They'll get into the main body of the ship and they've got a number of direct routes to the command module."

"So we hole up in the command module if we have to."

"I suppose, but people who know what they're doing will be able to cut into it. It'll buy us a few hours maybe."

"Well, hopefully we won't need it. Rescue isn't that far off." Cassi tried to sound a little more confident than she really was.

Cassi's father had been a marine, a master sergeant. Though he died when she was three, she'd gotten to know him through letters and video recordings. She knew what he'd say about that plan. *Hope is good to hold on to, Cassi. But it ain't much of a strategy.*

One couldn't just hope for safety and security. One had to create them through purposeful action.

She thought through the problem out loud. "We're assuming they might be desperate enough to want to kill us—because that will keep us from reporting the initial attack."

Pelly looked up at her. "Yeah."

"But what if we broadcast a message that says we're alive and well right now?"

After asking the question, Cassi wondered if she should have said anything at all. One of the cardinal sins of leadership was appear too indecisive. But despite Pelly's young age, she trusted him to give an honest and pragmatic opinion.

From the confused look on his face though, Pelly didn't understand. "You want to tell them we're alive? With all due respect, ma'am, it's better for us if they think we might be dead."

"Don't think about them for a moment. There's got to be an Alliance or a commercial survey satellite in orbit, or an outpost monitoring station on the surface... something that will record the signals we send out."

"Sure."

"We say that we were investigating a distress call and there was an accident. We omit any hint that they attacked us, but we establish that we're now alive on the ground."

"I still don't see what good that does if no one's around to hear it."

"Someone will hear it, eventually. Anyone who might rescue the pirates would learn that we survived the crash." Cassi took a breath. "And if we make it clear the crash was an accident... it gives them a way out without a need to finish their attack."

Pelly looked up with a crooked little smile and brushed the black hair off his forehead. "It would mean the pirates couldn't attack us and get away with it. Someone would know what they did."

She nodded.

"Still," he thought out loud, "they would have to trust that we won't turn around and tell the truth later. It won't necessarily stop them from attacking."

"No," she admitted. "But it's something."

"I'm glad you're in charge, Cassi... ma'am."

That made her smile. Pelly was a loner in the crew, not overweight exactly, but soft, the kind of cadet that dragged in the physical training. His strength lay in his technical proficiencies. He was the youngest cadet in the crew, but in a lot of ways, the furthest ahead. She was glad Pelly was there too, but before she could say anything, Pelly's eyebrows lifted. "An outpost."

Cassi wasn't sure what he meant, but he certainly had the look of a cadet seized by an idea.

"Dienne's a precolonial planet. Geological survey teams have been monitoring it. They have outposts."

"There are other people on the planet?"

"Usually the outposts are automated, so probably not."

"How would that help us then?"

"The outposts broadcast to satellites. And then one of the satellites sends a drone to report back to an Alliance hub... probably at Avalon. They do it on a regular basis, once a month, I think. Legally you need to do ten standard years of geological and meteorological monitoring before you can establish a permanent colony on a planet. That's how the monitoring reports get back. If we can get to an outpost, I should be able to attach a message to the report and maybe even elevate the priority of the next transit, so it leaves sooner rather than later."

"You can do that?"

Pelly smiled and cracked his knuckles.

Cassi followed him back to the command module where he got to work at his terminal.

Sijani was half sitting, half lying back against a bulkhead, eyes down on a virtual window, legs crossed, one foot bouncing in the air. She played absently with a lock of her violet-streaked blonde hair. Kroyle was busy cleaning the soot off the face shield on his helmet and pretending to be focused on it though he kept glancing up at her. It was the kind of subtle attention that Taura Sijani seemed to draw all the time, not just from Kroyle but from 'guys' in general. Emica called it Sijani's superpower.

The cadet scrolled through a morning news feed, the social blogs, pictures of Avalon celebrities like Bright Hobbes the colony rock singer, and Jude Kissinger and Harley Casanova with a broken heart superimposed on them, some other guy with a leering gaze in the lower corner looking on.

Cassi really didn't want to say anything, but it seemed clear to her that Sijani's mind was off mission. She didn't want to make a big deal out of it, and, really, keeping everyone on task was Bauer's job, but he was out. Cassi could almost imagine Dodd listening to her through the stasis pod, waiting, his stylus tapping against his notepad.

"You're supposed to be on surveillance duty," Cassi said to Sijani.

"I am."

"You be should monitoring your command station."

"AXON will notify us if it detects anything."

"Sijani, this is serious."

Casually, the cadet began to wind her hair back into a top knot bun. "There's a lot of RF static around here, lots of white noise. It was noise five minutes ago. It's noise right now. It will be noise for the rest of the day. There's no one else in orbit."

Cassi stared at her.

Finishing her hair, Sijani sat up and got back to the terminal with a sigh. "Yes, ma'am."

And that was it. Sijani was back on task. Problem solved. Although, as Cassi turned back to the others, she couldn't shake the feeling that she'd somehow pushed Taura away, or that she'd inadvertently made a choice of hierarchy over friendship.

"Okay," Pelly said. "I think I've got something."

"Got what?" Kroyle asked.

Cassi hesitated to explain the idea. She fumbled around with specific words. "I want to broadcast an emergency message."

"That's dumb." Sijani crossed her arms. "Ma'am."

Cassi told them about the satellites and how if they made sure to avoid any mention of being attacked, that it might give the pirates a way off the planet without having to attack the cadets.

Sijani shrugged. "You're the mission commander."

"I want your input, Taura."

"Ask Bauer. He's the second in command."

"I can't. He's out there. If I radio him, the pirates might catch the signal."

Sijani's flawless eyebrows raised, as if she'd just made her point.

"It's your decision, ma'am," Pelly said. "Not everyone is going to like it, either way."

He was right. Cassi nodded. "Alright. Ready to record."

Pelly pointed, giving her a silent cue.

"This is an emergency broadcast from the AEFS *Triumph*," Cassi hesitated for a moment and then added, "Actual."

That indicated she was the spacecraft's commanding officer. Saying it felt like drinking underage, like she was breaking the rules somehow.

"Our ship collided with a commercial vessel, the *Lucky Bee*, after we deviated from our planned route to investigate a distress call. The collision was accidental in nature." She tried to emphasize that enough that it would be heard, but not so much that it would sound disingenuous. "Both our spacecraft and the *Lucky Bee* crash landed on the surface of Dienne. I'm attaching our precise coordinates to this message. If you are incapable of responding, please notify Alliance Expeditionary Fleet Command at Avalon. Thank you."

Short and sweet. Pelly replayed the message, Cassi approved it.

"I'll get Bauer to review it before we send it out." She thought that might appease Sijani, but if anything, that made her seem even more irritated.

Taura was never easy to get along with. But Cassi was beginning to sense that there was something going on with her under the surface, something Cassi couldn't place her finger on, something more than just the crash.

Pelly seemed oblivious to the tension. "Hey, there's a geological survey outpost about sixty kilometers south of us. How lucky is that?"

Sixty kilometers. That was an exceptionally long distance away, through unknown terrain, without any kind of trail. Of course, in terms of location on the planet, it was right next to them. They were lucky to land that close to one, close enough that the *Triumph's* radio could connect with its network.

Perhaps, subconsciously, as Bauer had been guiding the *Triumph* down, he had aimed for a more habitable region on the planet. Pockets of lush vegetation, moderate temperatures and a supply of fresh water would be the most likely locations for future human colonies and therefore it made sense to set up survey outposts at them. And it would make sense that Bauer would steer toward a place like that, rather than a harsh environment.

Or maybe it was just dumb luck.

Cassi allowed herself to relax a little. The shock of the crash was wearing off and if she could keep herself and her crew focused, they could all deal with any psychological trauma later. An outpost station that close was a break, maybe not much of one, but it was something, enough to suggest that they just might survive.

As Cassi let out a breath, Sijani stepped back from her station. "Um, Requin. You'd better see this."

"What is it?"

"AXON just detected this."

Sijani's terminal showed an image of the surrounding forest on the lower half of the screen, blue sky above. Hovering over the trees was a black dot, like a tiny fruit fly. But its flight path was too straight to be an insect. It was flying straight toward them.

"An air drone," Pelly said quietly.

"It's coming from the *Lucky Bee's* crash site." Sijani pulled up a bird's eye view map on her tracker and zoomed in to show their location and the location of the estimated pirate crash site. She showed them the direction the camera was pointing in. Everything lined up.

It was a pirate drone, coming straight for them.

Sijani's eyes widened. "What do we do?"

CHAPTER EIGHT

Cassi broke radio silence to call the other cadets. "Get back to the ship!"

"We're okay, Requin," Bauer replied. "There's no sign of any predators out here. A few gnats or something. Lots of driftwood on the beach, or at least, I think it's driftwood. Junko was saying that most of it is more like a hard-lattice fungus. It's like wood—"

"Bauer, there's a drone headed our way."

"We found a few flowering plants too, with berries, but there's no information in AXON about them. I have MURPHI doing an analysis to see if they'd be eatable—"

"Bauer!" her voice cracked. "There's a drone coming straight at us."

"A drone?"

"It's coming from the pirate crash site. All of you have to get back to the *Triumph*."

He shielded his eyes from the sun and tried to scan the horizon, squinting.

Bauer, Quinton, Emica and MURPHI had gone up the beach, not far, maybe only a few hundred meters or so. From what Cassi could see from the *Triumph's* optics, Quinton was up on a boulder looking around. Emica was with the robot, bent over a plant further up on the shore where the ground was thicker with grass.

"Now!"

"Yeah, okay. We're on our way. Bauer out."

The drone advanced quickly. They didn't have a lot of time.

Sijani stood and paced, twisting her neck to watch it. "If we can see it, it can see them. They know at least some of us survived."

Pelly leaned against the command station, closer to the screen, squinting. It was awkward looking at the terminals because each station hung down from above, like a technological stalactite. "Taura, can you zoom in a little more?"

The image of the drone got larger. Physically, it was about the size of a crow, with four propellers housed inside a black polymer shell. The sun glimmered off its glossy finish as it zipped over treetops.

Pelly pointed. "There, on the bottom."

A cube hung below the drone's main body. It wasn't a part of the drone. It didn't look like it had been engineered as an attachment, like an extra battery or a cargo container. Something was rigged to hang off the drone's underbelly.

"What is that?" Sijani asked.

Pelly used AXON to analyze the image. Bold capitol letters in red flashed across the bottom of Sijani's screen.

EXPLOSIVE.

Sijani swore. She checked the monitors that had been tracking the cadets. "Where's Bauer and the others?"

Cassi couldn't see them either. It was dead quiet outside. Her pulse quickened.

She grabbed the controls and swept the cameras up the beach toward the drone—no sign of them. She checked the water, the grassy knolls up on the end of the beach, the treeline, and the darkness within.

"We're back," Bauer called as the hatch to the command module opened. The three cadets climbed in followed by MURPHI. Their boots were covered with wet brown muck that stuck to the ceiling-now-floor where they stepped. Quinton looked like he'd been crawling through the stuff.

FIRST COMMAND

Bauer loped over to Sijani's display. He leaned up against a bulkhead and scanned the monitor. "You gotta see it out there," he said to Sijani.

Cassi straightened up, raising her chin. "Bauer, you were sighted by that drone. It's—"

He turned back to her flashing a smile. "Hey. How was I supposed to know—"

"I'm speaking." She glared at him.

She felt the other cadets watching her. Cassi certainly had everyone's attention now, but she waited. Precious seconds ticked down as the drone flew toward the *Triumph*.

Bauer glared right back at her, but he stayed quiet. He stepped away from the bulkhead and squared up to face her.

She waited a little longer. It was something her mother used to do.

Eventually, Bauer glanced at the ground.

"That drone is closing on us," Cassi said. "Fast."

"Am I missing something, ma'am?" Emica asked. "It's just a drone."

"It's carrying a bomb," Pelly said.

Quinton turned to Cassi. "Requin, we have to shoot—"

"Yes. We do." Cassi opened the permission screen, scrolled down to the weapons section. She quietly removed the restrictions from Bauer's profile. AXON would now permit him to use a K205.

She opened the armory. With a clunk and a whoosh, a torronite casing fell from the overhead floor in behind the mission commander's station. A small screen flashed as its independent sentinel system scanned Cassi.

Ensign Cassiopeia Requin, Commanding Officer of the AEFS *Triumph: access granted.*

Another clunk and the torronite case opened. And there they were, the rail guns. Each one would slide onto a cadet's vambrace and lock into place, moving with the forearm. They'd all used the K205s on the range back at the academy. They were all qualified on the weapons.

"Now that's what we need." Quinton said. He dashed up to the box and tried to pull one out but couldn't get it to unlock.

"Just Bauer," Cassi said.

"But…"

Cassi turned to Bauer. "Blast it out of the sky."

Bauer mounted the weapon on his forearm and clicked a magazine into place. He plucked a pair of targeting glasses out as well and slipped them on. The clear lenses darkened into a yellow tint. "Aye, ma'am."

"But I'm the weapons officer," Quinton protested.

Cassi handed Quinton a pair of targeting glasses as well. "You spot for him."

Quinton's mouth squished down into a line. He stared at her. She could have started to ball him out. Many of their instructors would do just that, but Cassi just held the line, kept her chin up and remained quiet, following her instincts. He didn't have to like it. He didn't have to be convinced her decision was correct. The only thing that mattered was that he did what she needed him to do.

Precious seconds evaporated.

Quinton nodded. "Aye, ma'am."

"You have about three minutes until that thing is in range. Go."

Sijani transferred the video feed from their targeting goggles up on the main view screen.

Bauer and Quinton scrambled through the spacecraft with all the skill of a pair of adolescent parkour masters. Outside they hauled themselves up onto the upper hull, climbing over burnt ceramic tiles, casings, sensor housings, until they got to a high point.

"Where is it?" Bauer asked. "I can't see anything up here."

"Hold on." Pelly took over at Sijani's station. "I just need to run your targeting goggle feed into... no wait, AXON's map goes into the goggle targeting algorithm. Here."

"Ugh. All I can see is a map, Pelly!"

"Give me a second. I have to adjust the transparency."

"It's getting closer," Sijani sounded desperate.

"There, is that better?"

Bauer's line stayed silent. The view from his goggles shifted about wildly.

"Bauer!"

"Awesome. Got it." Bauer slipped his goggles back on and dropped onto his belly. He extended the firing grip from its base on his forearm and clicked it into place in the palm of his hand, giving himself a trigger. Then he extended his right arm along with the mounted rail gun, locking into a classic prone firing position.

The wind picked up. Pelly's feed zoomed in on the drone. Sijani's showed it in a much wider field of view. The wind pushed it around, rocking it, forcing it to compensate after getting blown off course.

The targeting system could account for the wind, but it was only so good. Estimates of the wind speed flashed on the screen, the number constantly changing, unable to stabilize on a single value.

"That's a seventeen-hundred-meter shot," Kroyle said. "Ensign, those rail guns aren't sniper rifles."

As Bauer prepared himself, Quinton climbed over to another spot several meters away.

Pelly tried to explain what was going on. "The targeting system uses input from both sets of goggles and feeds that back to AXON. The AI uses differences in the images to establish an exact distance between the K205 and the target."

"Sixteen hundred meters," Sijani called out.

"AXON is locked on." Quinton said. "Fire when ready."

Bauer steadied his breathing, let out half a breath, paused, then squeezed the trigger.

The weapon thundered. The railgun was technically a forearm-mounted rail cannon that electromagnetically accelerated a small flechette within a plasma field.

"Miss," Quinton reported. His frustrated teenaged voice was gone, replaced by a cold, professional one. It was as if he naturally slipped into that persona they'd trained into the cadets on the range—calm, precise, extreme attention to detail.

"Wait, why did he miss?" Emica asked. "He did everything right."

Sijani updated, "Fifteen hundred meters."

Quinton: "Hold over. Fire when ready."

The gun cracked a second time.

"Miss."

In the command module, the cadets exchanged glances at each other. Cassi wasn't sure how close it had to be before the explosion from the drone would present a significant threat. The torronite hull would keep the cadets inside safe, but Bauer and Quinton were totally exposed.

It was her call to say when to pull them back into the relative safety of the *Triumph's* hull. And that was if they could get back into the command module in time. How much time did they need? How fast was the drone approaching?

Emica. "Thirteen hundred meters."

Quinton. "Hold over. Fire when ready."

The third shot missed as well.

"What's wrong, Bauer?" Cassi asked. "You're the best shot in the crew. The drone is moving toward you. You should be able to hit it."

"I... I don't know."

Was Bauer in more shock from the crash than he'd let on? As far as Cassi could tell, he seemed steady enough, but at those distances even breathing wrong could throw a shot off.

"Let me try," Quinton asked. "Please, ma'am. We don't have much time."

Cassi turned on his permissions and Bauer handed him the weapon. She half expected him to make some kind of giddy comment, but Quinton dropped into position without a word. He clicked the K205 into place, extended the handle and wrapped his fingers around it, using his other hand to steady it.

Emica: "Nine hundred meters."

Bauer cleared his throat. "Fire."

The weapon thrummed again, the sound reverberating through the *Triumph's* hull.

"Miss."

"Oh come on!" Kroyle shouted. The other cadets grumbled as well.

"I can run a diagnostic on the targeting system," Pelly suggested.

"No time for the system to go down," Cassi said. She would have to call them back.

Emica: "Eight hundred meters."

What was wrong? As the boys went through another cycle, Cassi's mind raced. If the system had been basing its calculations on Quinton as the shooter and Bauer as the spotter, then swapping the weapon over should have fixed the issue. The K205 has little gyroscopes in it to help keep it steady. Was one malfunctioning? Was the wind calculation that far off? Being on a different planet...

"Gravity," Cassi said out loud. "AXON adjusts the shot to compensate for gravity. MURPHI, what is Dienne's acceleration due to gravity?"

"Ten point seven nine meters per second squared."

"AXON, K205 firing algorithm adjustment, correct the parameter for acceleration due to gravity to ten point seven nine meters per second squared."

The computer chimed. "Adjustment made."

Bauer: "Fire."

The flechette zipped across the sky like a streak of blue lightning. The drone spun out of control and dropped out of the sky, a trail of grey smoke billowing from its tail.

"Hit."

Quinton relaxed and let out his breath.

When the drone hit the ground, it exploded.

Hard.

Light saturated the cameras.

A percussive blast smacked the hull followed by a tornado wind of shrapnel. The *Triumph* rocked, the metal in her frame grinding.

"Quinton?" Cassi called on the radio. "Bauer? You there?"

CHAPTER NINE

Both Bauer and Quinton were caught in the storm of shrapnel that followed the explosion. The blast sent a percussive shock wave out around it that tore into the surrounding trees and rocks, ripping the wood apart, spitting up stones and rocks and turned air into a curtain of sandpaper. It struck the *Triumph's* hull with a heavy thud.

As the dust, dirt and shredded vegetation settled back to the ground, the spacecraft's optical feed cleared, revealing a crater where the drone had gone down. Within a radius of about fifty feet everything was gone—disintegrated.

"I'm okay," Quinton reported as he and Bauer climbed back inside the *Triumph*. The tightened sinew in Quinton's temples, and the way he sucked air in through his teeth suggested otherwise. He limped, his right arm over Bauer's shoulders. He wasn't placing any weight on his right leg.

Thad Quinton was not okay.

Bauer had a laceration through his right eyebrow and abrasions across his cheeks and hands. His undersuit was covered with grit and soil. But he didn't have any major injuries, at least not that Cassi could see.

Quinton's leg bled freely. Blood ran from just over his knee, saturated the fabric of his pants and dribbled down his boot. A jagged shard of slivered wood, roughly an inch in diameter, stuck out of his thigh.

"Look, I'm growing a tree." Quinton held a smile, as if pretending not to be in pain might somehow make it more bearable.

Inside the command module, Bauer lay him down in front of Cassi. When he touched the floor-ceiling panels, Quinton threw his head back and grimaced. The wood shifted, threatening to break off smaller splinters that could work their way deeper into the muscle.

"Is his femur broken?" Emica asked.

Bauer stood, looking down at his friend. "I don't know."

Sijani stepped right into Bauer's personal space, forcing him to step back. "You could have been killed out there."

Bauer stood with his palms spread apart, mouth open, searching for words that wouldn't come.

Taura looked ready to tell him off, or slug him the way she was balling her fists. But as Quinton groaned, she turned her attention on him. "You have to put pressure on it." She dropped to her knees and pressed her hands hard against Quinton's thigh.

He turned away, trying not to show the tears forming in his eyes.

"It doesn't feel broken. The bone is intact. Can someone get a first aid kit?"

They were all trained in emergency medical procedures, but Taura stepped up to the plate.

"Kroyle, get the first aid kit," Cassi said quietly.

As the helm officer climbed over to it, Cassi glanced up at the main monitor. Dienne's sun was on the horizon. The blue in the sky shifted to lavender, ochre and pink. What had once been thick forest was now flattened, charred, and ripped. There were shards of glass in the sand, generated near the epicentre of the explosion. A few tree carcasses still stood, stripped of leaves, naked and covered with soot. Particulate dust hung in the air, swirling with eddy air currents. Grey smoke rose up to join it from the dozens of little pocket fires burning in the dry dead fall. The smoke was inside the *Triumph's* ventilation system and added to the static scent of steel and grease and polycarbonate that permeated the wreckage.

It was going to be dark soon. And although they'd shot down the drone, the pirates now knew they were alive.

Would the pirates wait until morning to try another attack? Would they send another drone, this one in the night? Would they come on foot? Cassi wished she knew what to do.

Sijani pulled some scissors out of the first aid kit and cut away the fabric around Quinton's leg. Aside from the blood, his skin looked raw, already beginning to get angry and inflamed. She used a squirt bottle to irrigate the wound with a disinfecting agent.

Quinton squeezed his eyes as the agent reacted with his blood, making a soft fizzing sound like when you open a can of carbonated soda. Little white bubbles formed in the blood that would kill most pathogens on the surface.

The blood kept leaking though. It wasn't an arterial bleed, at least not that Cassi could tell. In an arterial bleed the blood squirted out in jets. The fact that it was oozing was good, or at least better. But the blood was dribbling into a little puddle underneath him, and there was a lot of it.

Sijani poked at the giant splinter protruding from Quinton's leg, as if trying to get a sense of how deeply lodged in it was. Then she looked up at Cassi. "Should we leave it in, or pull it out?"

Kroyle answered for her. "First aid protocol for any impalement is to stabilize the embedded object. You have to leave it in."

Sijani glanced up at him, over her shoulder. "I know what the protocol is, Kroyle. The problem is that it's also protocol to evacuate the injured person. We're supposed get him to a hospital where they can remove this thing. But last I checked, there aren't any hospitals on this planet."

"We still have to follow protocol."

"This is one of those scenarios where we need to think outside the box. How long until the wound gets infected?" Sijani pushed her hair back behind her ears. "There was a time back on Earth, when people used to die from injuries like this."

"Not helping," Quinton grumbled.

Bauer returned the K205 to the armoury chest. Re-mounted, the system began an automated cleaning and maintenance cycle. He closed the torronite chest and the bolts slid into place with a quiet clunk. When Bauer came back, he looked tired, like he'd just crossed the finish line after running his first marathon. Still, he kept his back straight and crossed his arms. "We don't even know if anything on this planet can infect him."

"We have to treat him as if it does though," Sijani said. "I mean, if there aren't any microbes on that splinter that can infect him, then great. No harm no foul, right? But what if there are?"

"How long would I have until an infection sets in?" Quinton glanced around, expecting someone to answer, his gaze lingering on Pelly, then up at Cassi.

Cassi tugged at her hair. "I don't know. I'm not even sure if it's possible to know."

Her gut felt uneasy again. Cassi didn't like not having answers.

"The protocol is a protocol for a reason," Pelly said. He knelt down beside Quinton, opposite Sijani. "That splinter might be keeping an artery closed... like a plug. If we remove it and can't close the artery, Quinton will bleed to death."

"Great," Quinton complained. "Death by infection or death by bleeding out. You guys really know how to keep a positive mindset."

Again everyone looked at Cassi. No one had wanted her to be in charge. But now that it was time to make a tough decision, no one seemed to be clambering to make it for her.

Maybe it was just easier to pass the buck when it was time to take responsibility. Maybe, she wondered, the whole point in establishing a chain of command in the fist place was so that there was at least one person who couldn't pass the buck, one person who had to make a decision, even if that decision wasn't perfect.

"I don't think there's a right or wrong here," Cassi said. "We need to operate under the assumption that we're going to be here for a few days at least, maybe longer." She swallowed. "I think we should pull it out."

Everyone on the bridge was quiet. Cassi expected someone to challenge her, Pelly almost certainly. But he stayed silent, and she thought she even saw him nod. Kroyle seemed finished with his objections.

"Alright," Sijani pulled her hair back into a ponytail to keep it out of her face. The blood on the thin purple gloves smeared into her hair a little. She wiped little beads of sweat from her forehead on the back of her hand.

Emica knelt down beside Quinton and laced her fingers in his. It was the kind of thing she might have done if they had been in some kind of romantic relationship, but they were only friends, crew mates. Emica was just like that—a natural empath. Besides, Emica had had a crush on Bauer since their first year in the program.

Quinton had always been that annoying guy that Emica put up with to be a part of Bauer's world. Yet there she was, comforting him.

Bauer got down on his knees as well, pulled on a pair of latex gloves and took a few deep breaths.

Sijani dug a pair of syringes out of the first aid kid. "This one is an anti-pathogen agent for deep wounds," she said. "Bauer, I'll get you to pull the splinter out. As soon as it's clear, I'll flood the wound with the serum."

Bauer nodded. "What's the other one?"

"The bio-glue. It will help any damaged vessels clot and repair and... you know... glue the tissue together."

"Sounds easy enough."

"Just don't mix them up," Quinton said.

Sijani smiled and wiped her forehead again. "You ready, Numpty?"

The cadet looked around the room. His face was wet with sweat, his short hair matted to his temples. He looked pale and afraid, almost so much that he seemed unrecognizable now.

He glanced up at Sijani. "This is going to hurt, isn't it?"

"Yes."

"Okay. No point in delaying it." He took a deep breath.

Bauer pulled out the splinter.

Quinton screamed.

CHAPTER TEN

The local time was 20:17. Dienne was larger than Avalon or Earth, but it spun on its axis faster, which made its days comparatively shorter. It had an hour that lasted a standard 44 minutes and 21 seconds. The sun went down and came up faster. At the moment, twilight was racing toward them, and darkness was close behind.

They all watched as Sijani steadied her hands and tried to knit together Quinton's gaping wound with the bio glue. Quinton bled profusely. And though she didn't say anything, as it filled with blood that Bauer kept sponging up, Cassi wondered whether she'd made a mistake. Doubt clung to her like a sticky tar she couldn't wash off.

Quinton lost a lot of blood. Cassi watched his skin lose its pallor. By the time Sijani got it closed, he'd fallen asleep. His tracker monitored his vital signs. His blood pressure was down, his heart rate up, but he'd survived.

Early as it was, they let him sleep on the command module ceiling underneath the weapon systems station. Sijani unwrapped a foil survival blanket and draped it over him, the foil crinkling and cracking with any little movement. For the moment, the injured cadet seemed relatively content, curled onto his uninjured side.

Bauer was on radio watch, reading something on his tracker as he sat under the communications terminal.

Pelly found a satellite and was trying to figure out how to get it to launch a signal rocket. He'd managed to attach Cassi's message to it, and he'd figured out that it was due to go in seven days, so at least they had a rough maximum on the wait now. The rocket would execute an automatic deep space transit back to Avalon space where it would transmit the results of a geological survey, refuel, and then return to Dienne. If Pelly couldn't hack into it, they had seven days, plus however long it took to organize a rescue.

The time envelope for successful mission completion had passed. Technically, they had failed the exercise. None of them had qualified as astronauts. But that didn't matter now.

In a best-case scenario, the Alliance Expeditionary Fleet was already organizing a rescue mission. More likely, the *Triumph* was simply logged as 'delayed' and the space traffic controllers were planning to hand it off to the guys on the next shift.

Cassi kept returning to the view screen and the image of the crater made by the bomb... so much destruction on an otherwise undisturbed alien wilderness. They hadn't even been on the surface of the planet a full day yet.

CASSI HAD BEEN JUST shy of her sixteenth birthday when the Alliance Cadet Corps notification appeared in her inbox.

The bright Avalon sun warmed morning air as she walked out into the garden behind her house. Waves rolled up to the shore of the great freshwater Lake Urion in the distance. Avalon common gulls circled. A dropship launched from across the beach, on its way up to a spaceport, its engines roaring, stirring an excitement inside her even then.

Her fingers trembled as she sat on a rock in the garden, the dark stone having been warmed by the sunlight. She curled up, hugging her legs, chin on her knees and stared at the bold lettering that marked the notification on a virtual screen projected up by her watch. The device buzzed. Xan Otorro and Elsa Kinion from her school had also applied and no-doubt had their results already and wanted to either celebrate or commiserate.

An order of magnitude more people applied than Avalon's academy had positions for. Meeting the minimum requirements, or even the median scores for that matter was no guarantee of getting in.

A shadow fell over her.

Her mother, Raena Requin, stood in front of the rising sun, holding a chrome trowel, her hands covered with thick, dirty gardening gloves. The woman had the same red hair as Cassi, hers tied into a long braid that hung forward over her shoulder like a gym class climbing rope. Behind her the sun seemed like it was trying to shine, but could only manage to cast something of a soft halo around Raena.

Cassi had hoped she could be alone to read the notification. Her mouth went dry. She hadn't told her mother the notification came in. In fact, she hadn't even specifically told her mother she'd applied to the Cadet Corps either.

Lieutenant Commander Raena Requin, Alliance Expeditionary Fleet, Retired, would not have approved of it. For as long as Cassi had been alive, her mother had been an Isolationist—a member of a political activist group who opposed most human exploration of space and the colonization of new planets. As a girl, Cassi had marched in rallies with her mother every time the declaration of a new Alliance colony was announced. She remembered using scented markers to draw posters depicting humans as parasites on the galaxy. Growing up, her mother made her watch university lectures where the central themes espoused that exploration and colonization brought only interference, destruction, disease and both xenobiological and human oppression.

Her mother occasionally gave public talks to crowds of former Alliance Expeditionary Fleet personnel, mostly on the gray side of fifty, many of whom wore fragments of Alliance dress uniforms—brass collar dog pins turned upside down, threadbare berets inside out. The continuous expansion of the human race meant that humans didn't have to be responsible for the worlds they already had, or so the argument went, repeated like a machine gun with an unrelenting staccato.

But as Cassi grew up, she started questioning her mother's ideas. She read her mother's old personal logs—the declassified ones anyway—and got to know a very different Raena Requin from the one who raised her. At twelve years old Cassi got into an argument with one of her mother's professor friends about space exploration, Shuben Cakaul. After dinner he, Raena, and a few other guests sat around a table drinking wine, Cassi a soda, and Cakaul slid into another long political rant. With droplets of stray wine on the wiry hairs of his beard he went on about how descent into corruption was a direct result of the power vacuum of the continuously expanding boundary of the human populations. He'd just written a paper on it. The guy actually pulled up graphs as he went.

When he stopped to breathe, Cassi challenged him. She asked little questions as first. "How can you be against the colonization of space when we're all members of a colony?"

"Being born into a situation, doesn't mean you agree to it," Cakaul said. Her mother and their other guests chuckled at her naivety.

Cassi put down her drink. "Don't you think there's a role for leadership, Professor?" she asked. "Inherent responsibility?"

Cakaul frowned. At her mother's dinner parties no one ever really challenged anyone else. One guest would stand up and rant and the others would nod their heads like windup dolls.

"I mean, I get all that, what you're saying," Cassi went on. "There are pressures that certainly influence people, on average. But what about ownership of the problems? With effective leadership you can solve a lot of these issues that you're talking about." She went on to cite examples… how the first Mars colony led to humanity finally taking ownership of Earth's climate challenges during peak population, the management and seclusion of the quasi-sentient Primaterra bonobo population, the formation of the Alliance of Colony Republics and Territories. Humanity identified a problem and eventually someone took charge and tackled it.

Cakaul's brow lowered—a look of frustration. He didn't like his authority being challenged, but at the time she didn't quite recognize that. Twelve-year-old Cassi just kept going.

They argued back and forth until Cakaul finally pounded a fist on the table, stood up, pointed his finger at her, and called her ignorant, naïve, and made unconscionable reference to her genitalia in fit of disgruntled rage.

Her mother didn't defend her. Instead, she dismissed Cassi from the table and apologized to her guests.

Now, her mother stood over her and though Cassi had thought she'd been relatively secretive about the application, it was obvious that Raena knew.

Even if she got in, Cassi would still need her mother's permission to attend the academy. She applied anyway. A whole year of assessments, aptitude testing, letters of reference from teachers, physical training, physical testing, medical exams… just the act of submitting a completed application was a Herculean effort. And there it was, her notification, sitting in her inbox.

Cassi closed her eyes, took a deep breath, and tapped on the notification.

Her mother gasped.

Cassiopeia Requin, on behalf of Beryl West, Commandant of the Avalon's Alliance Cadet Corps Academy, and the Alliance Expeditionary Fleet, we are pleased to offer you…

She made it in!

Adrenaline surged through her. Cassi leapt up off the rock. "I made it! Mom. I did it. It's a letter of offer to the Cadet Corps."

When she turned to face Raena, her mother's stern expression hadn't changed. Her mouth remained a thin horizontal slit, her eyes cold. Her fingers tightened around the trowel.

"Mom?"

Raena swallowed. "I never gave you permission to apply there."

"But Mom—"

"You're a minor and you need parental consent. I'm not signing your life into the hands of that bureaucratic machine, Cassiopeia."

"But it's the Cadet Corps."

"You know how I feel about the AEF."

"But..."

Raena Requin turned her back on her daughter, walked back to her garden, got down on her knees and began digging through the clay-pack dirt.

EMICA SAT DOWN BESIDE Cassi. Cassi hadn't even noticed her approach. She'd been staring at the terminal, at the landscape, at the crater of sterility in an otherwise lush and vibrant ecosystem that had evolved in complete absence of human contact.

Her mother had once given a talk she'd titled *The Act of Walking Leaves Footprints (Despite One's Best Intentions)*.

"What's wrong, Cassi?" Emica asked.

"Besides the fact that we've crash landed on a planet thirty kilometers away from pirates who want to kill us, with no radio contact with civilization, few supplies and no instructors to advise us on how to survive?" Cassi took a deep breath. "I'm totally fine."

"I'm serious."

That was the other thing about command. It was hard to figure out when people were your crew and when they were your friends. Emica was Cassi's roommate at the academy, and for the last three years... her best friend.

When Cassi didn't say anything, Emica curled up, hugging her legs and rested her chin on her knees. She sat in silence for a while. Sometimes Emica had a way of just being present that was comforting.

"I wish we could just stop the simulation," Emica said. "Call it a night, go back to the room, shower and figure out what to do from the comfort of the bunks. While eating chocolate."

Cassi smiled.

"Intrepid Twins," Emica said. She held out her fist.

Cassi bumped it with her knuckles. "No trouble too to tough to be trounced by truffles."

Emica smiled broadly, eyes nearly closed. Cassi wanted to keep that smile on her face, but she knew she couldn't.

"We have to move." Cassi kept her voice low so only Emica would hear. She wasn't sure she wanted to announce it to the other cadets yet. But she'd known for a while now. That was why she told Sijani to pull the splinter out of Quinton. He would have to move too.

"Are you sure that's a good idea?"

"No. But the drone attack was the second time that the pirates tried to kill us. They know we're alive. They want us dead. They're going to come again."

"The *Triumph* can protect us. You said that yourself."

"That was before we knew they could do that." Cassi motioned toward the image of the crater. "The *Triumph's* hull is broken, Emica. All we really have is the torronite shell around the command module. That's something, but there's nowhere to fall back to if they breach it."

Bauer got Kroyle to take over on signal watch and then joined Cassi and Emica, standing beside them, hands on his hips. "You ladies having a private conversation?"

Neither of them answered.

"Okay... just asking."

"No," Cassi answered finally. "It's fine."

She was going to have to tell Bauer sooner or later. And she was going to need him to go along with the idea. She was going to need everyone to go along with it, and Bauer was the key to that.

"I'm thinking about abandoning the *Triumph*," Cassi said. She told him what Pelly told her about the hull, how vulnerable they really were.

"So we make sure they don't breach the command module," Bauer said. "We can set up obstacles, traps. And we have weapons."

"It's one thing to shoot down a drone." Cassi looked straight at him. "Do you think you could you shoot a human being?"

She expected him to shrug it off. To toss out some off-hand comment. *Just one*? Or *Line 'em up*. But Bauer took his time to process the question. "I don't *want* to shoot anyone, Cassi."

"I didn't say that you did." She realized in the moment that she might be shaking his confidence. As far as she could tell, there was a very real chance that they might need to engage the pirates in a fire fight, and if that happened, she didn't want Bauer doubting himself, hesitating or wrestling with ethical dilemmas.

Leadership was hard.

"For the record, I have every confidence that you can," Cassi told him. "If you have to. But I think the point here is that we need to do everything we can to avoid it."

Bauer nodded. "The sun is going down. You want to leave in the dark?"

"Not really. But I don't want to wait here either. Our best guess is that they can get here from their crash site in about six standard hours. If they left shortly after the drone crashed, well… that's about four hours from now."

"Ensign," Emica said. "If we're talking about this, can I suggest we talk about it as a group?"

Cassi noticed that most of the other cadets were watching her now. They were turned casually away, staring at their trackers or their command stations, but they were all watching her.

"Okay—everyone on me."

The cadets quickly gathered around. Cassi wished she could present them with a better plan, something coherent even. Somehow, she felt as if she was letting them down with uncertainty. But there was a time to hide uncertainty, and a time to be honest about it. She decided to go with honesty.

"If we leave the ship, where are we going to go?" Sijani didn't seem at all excited about abandoning the spacecraft. "I mean, I get your point about being trapped here. But out there… we really have nothing."

"There's an outpost," Cassi said. "It's a survey station, and it's not far away. We'll be able to make the hike in a couple of days."

"Do you think that will really be easier to defend?" Sijani asked.

Pelly called up the map and showed them all on their trackers. "Probably not. In fact, given the choice between there and here, this is probably the better spot for a last stand."

Sijani looked up from her tracker. "So we should stay."

"Well, no. For one, they might not track us at all if we're at that survey station. There's a chance of evading them completely.

"Second, even if they do track us, it buys us time. If they come tonight, they'll be here in a few hours. If we stay ahead of them, we make a stand there, in a couple of days. And maybe a rescue ship shows up in the meanwhile."

Taura still didn't look like she was buying it.

Bauer rocked his head back and forth, cracking his neck. "Third, right here we're clustered together. If they take out one of us, they take out all of us. Out there, we can scatter. They don't know how many of us there are. They might engage some of us, but that could give the others a better chance at survival."

"You don't have to be faster than the bear, you just have to be faster than the slowest person in your group." Kroyle tried to laugh at his own joke, but it didn't come out genuine.

Quinton was awake at that point. A few people glanced over at him, but no one said anything. His leg was stretched out straight, the tissue glued back together. But no one knew how mobile he was. He hadn't walked anywhere yet.

Sijani looked back down at a virtual window projected from her tracker. "That outpost is sixty kilometers away."

"We've done survival hikes longer than that," Bauer said.

"With supplies and proper equipment. And Pelly got medevaced off the last one." Sijani took a breath and turned directly to Cassi. "Look, I'm not trying to be stubborn here, but we have to be adults about this and that means that we have to consider all the foreseeable consequences of this decision."

"You're right," Cassi said.

"And what about the flight instructors?" Sijani turned back to everyone else. "Commander Dodd and Lieutenant Singh are stuck in the survival pods. We can't carry them. If we leave, we're abandoning them. We have a responsibility to protect them."

"Right again." Cassi felt as if her arms and legs were chained to two separate horses pulling in opposite directions, and her body was nearing its breaking point.

Everyone was staring at her.

"We power down the spacecraft. We turn everything off and scuttle it."

"And just hope that the pirates don't find the two survival pods? You can't be serious." Sijani stepped back shaking her head.

Quinton rolled onto his side, his eyes open. "We can bury them."

More cadets turned toward him.

"The earth up on the beach is pretty soft. We dig down, bury them in the mud, mark their positions and hide them under a pile of driftwood or something. Then come back once a rescue shows up."

"What if they still get found? What if we don't make it back?" Pelly asked.

Cassi bit her lip. "The pirates won't know to look for them."

"But what if they search the perimeter, looking for us?" Pelly insisted. It was clear he didn't like the idea of leaving the flight instructors.

"Even if they find the survival pods," Emica said, "they can't activate them any more than we can. Dodd and Singh are as safe as they can be in them. If we bury them, it'll give them a chance."

"If the pirates find them, they could power the pods down," Kroyle said. "They would thaw and die."

Cassi let out a deep breath. She wasn't sure she wanted to say what she had to say. "If they're going to do that, us being here and dying before they do it isn't going to stop them."

She could tell they knew she was right.

"I don't like it. But that's the reality of the situation. Our best move is to hide them as best we can and get out of Dodge."

"What about surveillance?" Kroyle asked. "If a rescue mission shows up, we need to be able to broadcast."

Pelly stepped up to answer that one. "We've already sent out a rescue message, so whoever gets it will know to look for the crash site. If anyone does show up, MURPHI will be able to communicate with them. And he's already backed up AXON's database as well. So we're not losing that either."

Cassi looked at Bauer. "Yeah, let's do it."

Then to Emica. "Of course."

Kroyle stared down for a while, as if he didn't want to look at Cassi, but eventually he did. He nodded.

"It's the best of some pretty bad options," Pelly said.

Sijani's arms were still crossed. If she dug her heals in, Kroyle might renege and support her. "I don't think it's the best plan."

"Do you have a better suggestion?" Bauer asked.

She glared at him, and opened her mouth as if to speak, but hesitated.

"So you're in?" Cassi asked.

"Fine."

"You have to be all in, Taura." Bauer said. "We're a team. This only works—"

"I'm in. But I'm not going to break out the pompoms about it."

"Alright." Cassi accepted that. Sometimes to function as a team, individuals had to bury their personal feelings. And that could be hard when you felt strongly about something.

"MURPHI?" Cassi asked. "Are you in?"

"Clarification required."

"Do you concur with the decision to scuttle and abandon the *Triumph*?"

MURPHI twitched. "Affirmative."

"Quinton, what about you?" Cassi asked. "Can you walk?"

"I'm fine. We're bringing the rail guns, right?" He peeled the foil blanket off and stood up.

And then fell over after placing a little weight on his injured leg.

CHAPTER ELEVEN

Cassi pulled the plug.

Once she made the decision to move, she had to move the crew quickly. Time was a predator stalking them in the shadows.

After Pelly wiped AXON's database from the spacecraft servers, Cassi initiated the *Triumph's* scuttle sequence—a leftover from the ship's time as a military corvette. It wasn't as flamboyant as she expected. The explosions were small, little micro-charges that flash-melted integrated circuits and fried the spacecraft's neural networks. Puffs of silicon smoke wafted up from under panels. The constant hum from little fans and pumps dissipated into silence. Lights dimmed then winked into darkness.

The survival pods remained operational. Little colored diodes on their panels indicated they still had power and were functioning properly. Each one was capable of sustaining a human being for more than one hundred years. Cassi had once heard that the hundred-year limit was more like a 'best before' date, that in theory they could go on almost indefinitely even with a total loss of power, but it was best not to keep a person in stasis for too long.

Bauer, Kroyle, Emica and MURPHI took to digging. MURPHI was able to claw at the alien soil, digging through it like a dog. The cadets used twisted metal from the wreckage to help scoop it up. They worked quickly and efficiently and fortunately they picked a soft section of the beach where they got down about three feet—wide enough to place the pods side by side, like a pair of shallow graves. With the robot's help, they hauled the survival pods out and dropped them in the ground, then filled in the hole.

As Quinton suggested, they gathered driftwood and piled it on the overturned earth. They tried to make it look as natural as possible, carefully placing the logs on top that were coated with fine blue lichen so it would appear as if they'd been there long enough for the lichen to grow and eat away at the wood.

It was a good idea and even though it ate up more time, it provided the concealment the flight instructors needed.

Before leaving, Cassi knelt down and placed a hand on the log pile. She wasn't leaving them for dead, but she was leaving them. She only took a few moments, and she wasn't entirely sure what for, maybe to wish them luck, maybe to reassure herself she was making the right decision.

"They've got the easy job," Bauer said when he came to get her. "They can sleep through all of this."

She wanted to ask him if he thought she was doing the right thing, but kept quiet. They'd given themselves a six-hour window for contact with the pirates. She'd used up three of those hours digging and preparing.

Bauer held out his hand and pulled her to her feet.

Back inside the *Triumph*, Cassi issued every cadet a firearm along with three magazines, a maintenance kit, and a pair of targeting goggles. MURPHI could not fire any of the weapons, it was illegal for artificial intelligences to execute any lethal actions, but she had it carry four spares and the rest of the ammunition. The rest MURPHI destroyed, twisting the metal with its mechanical hands. Cassi had no idea what weapons the pirates had, but at least she could ensure that they didn't acquire any more.

Because MURPHI carried AXON, he also housed the target tracking and ballistics software. In order to use the weapons to their optimal effect, they had to be in radio-contact with MURPHI.

Without it, they could still override and fire the K205's like old-fashioned handguns, aiming by eye, but that would reduce their combat effectiveness substantially.

Pelly said he could re-route the program so that the cadets would have a self-contained algorithm on their trackers, but that would take time. And quite possibly, the pirates were only a couple hours away.

They cannibalized the *Triumph* and sorted out the survival gear and supplies on board. Within each pressure suit was a water bladder with a filter that could be mounted in a survival knapsack. The helmets had removable flashlights and batteries that could serve as spares for their trackers and they could mount flexible solar cells on the knapsacks as a means of trickle-charging their electronics. The pressure suits were rolled up and compressed. They could serve as sleeping bags, a second set of clothing for if they had a chance to wash their undersuits, and foul weather gear. The survival kits also contained synthetic wool toques that could both stave off hypothermia and any chance at a date. Each cadet had a personal multi-tool, and they added some basic tools to their packs from the maintenance and repair caches, in case they needed to make any modifications to the survey station either to get in, or defend themselves. To that they added the survival supplies: matches, ripcord, a couple knives, survival blankets, first aid supplies, a handful of toilet paper squares, and of course, the ration bars. Quinton even packed the small fishing tackle kit even though it wasn't clear whether any fish they could catch would be edible. Overall, their impromptu gear wasn't ideal for a multi-day expedition on an alien world, but given that they had embarked on what was supposed to be a six hour space mission, they were reasonably well outfitted.

Cassi had Bauer independently go through each cadet's kit to second check everything. She wanted to make sure the weight was evenly distributed, and that they weren't forgetting anything because one person thought someone else was bringing something. There was a certain finality to embarking. Once they left, they wouldn't just be able to come back if they realized something critical was missing.

That was a good move, but it ate up even more time.

Outside, Cassi paired everyone up in teams: Kroyle with Pelly, Sijani with Quinton, Bauer with MURPHI, and she partnered Emica with herself. At no point was one person supposed to be out of earshot with her or his partner. Preferably they would all stay close as a group, but if they did get separated, she didn't want anyone operating alone.

"We need a sign-countersign," Quinton said.

Sijani rolled her eyes. "Why?"

"What if there's someone else out in the darkness? How do we identify each other if its dark and the trackers don't work?"

"Um... what about, 'Hey Taura, is that you?'"

Quinton blushed.

"He's right," Cassi agreed. Sijani scowled at her but didn't say anything else.

"Everyone remember the dormitory rooms from our first year?" Cassi asked. "Challenge with Drade, respond with House. Got it?"

The cadets nodded.

"Drade," she whispered.

"House," the cadets whispered back.

"How's the leg, Quinton?"

"Fine." He grimaced when put his weight on it, but now that he'd figured out how much weight he could tolerate, he seemed able to keep his balance and hobble around.

They both knew he wasn't fine though. And Cassi wasn't sure what was worse, the fact that he was lying to her, or that he was lying to himself. But it was too late now anyway. The *Triumph* was scuttled. And the pirates were coming.

They had to go.

The cadets stepped out of the *Triumph* and climbed down into the wilderness. The sun was setting quickly. It was already kissing the horizon. Their shadows stretched out behind their bodies, long and thin making them seem like giants setting foot on the alien world.

Pelly and Kroyle led. They moved quickly, a human canter of a pace, not quite a full run, but faster than a quick hike, probably top speed for Quinton. Everyone was full of nervous energy and though they all knew they'd have to conserve it, that they'd be walking for a long time, Cassi also wanted to take advantage of it.

Cassi wished she would have had more time to appreciate the significance of setting out over the alien terrain. She'd spent her entire life on Avalon, and she'd expected that touching down and exploring Dienne would be exhilarating, and even life-changing, the way the cadets who had qualified as astronauts described it, and not full of desperation and trepidation. Still, that intimate contact with the ground carried a solemn gravity, as if she had just become a part of this world.

Interspersed through the round rocks on the beach, a yellow-brown freshwater kelp grew in globular clusters and squished underfoot, squirting out little jets of water and oil over the rocks, making them slippery and difficult to stand on.

Up from the beach, the ground grew soft with a kind of fungal carpet, and that was easier to walk on. It compressed like a pillow under each step, inflating behind them as they passed, erasing their tracks. Cassi stopped to look back, wondering if they were leaving a more subtle trail that might be more obvious in the light of day. Any disturbance in the land could give them away.

They kept quiet. Cassi hadn't specifically ordered them not to talk, but they all knew that a single word might carry and give away their position. Every few hundred meters or so, one of them would put up a hand and they would stop, crouch down, and listen.

The alien woodlands made all kinds of hushed noises. Life. Any given sound was exotic, odd, and yet in chorus they combined in a way that seemed familiar, the way intonation and feeling carried through a conversation spoken in a foreign language. Insects, or at least insect-like creatures swished by with whispered Doppler zips. Lake water lapped at the shoreline, muffled by the irregular clusters of kelp scattered through the rocks. A shrill cry screeched across the land, something that reminded Cassi of a seagull, but lower, more ominous.

As they moved under a canopy of trees, little balls of dandelion-like fluff fell on their shoulders like a quiet snow, and then twisted and scuttled when the cadets tried to brush them off—like tiny spiders.

They seemed harmless enough. Cassi couldn't even feel them through her undersuit. Still, there was something unsettling about dozens of little life forms crawling all over her, lightly brushing the skin on her neck or her the backs of her hands like feathers. It was as if the planet's biome was conducting a kind of tactile search, mapping out the humans, investigating them.

In the absence of chatter, Cassi's mind ran free, and in directions it probably shouldn't have. She wondered if they were going in the right direction. Every time MURPHI twitched, she wondered if his navigation systems were damaged. The compasses on the trackers were supposed to be independent, but the trackers were so tightly integrated with AXON, it wasn't inconceivable that the robot might be propagating a navigational error through all of their electronics. So she studied the night sky and paid attention to their vector as they moved.

Cassi wondered about the predators on this planet. On Earth, humans were the apex predator and at least on an evolutionary scale, quickly wiped-out megafauna like mammoths and sabre-toothed tigers wherever they showed up in history. But no one had wiped out anything on Dienne. Were there any monsters lurking in the shadows, watching them, waiting for an opportunity to strike?

Quinton's wound continued to bleed. The gauze dressing quickly soaked through again. When they paused, Sijani pointed to it and the ground. She was worried Quinton was leaving a blood trail.

More than once the entire squad stopped because of a sound, a crack of a branch, an animal call, a rustle in the dead leaves… then they all whipped up their K205s, the little targeting cross hairs rendered on their goggles scanned the darkness, trying to identify an enemy. More than once Cassi patched the view in her goggles to MURPHI, using his snooper optics to see into the infrared portion of the spectrum.

They had been hiking for about an hour when the unmistakable sound of an explosion cracked through the alien trees.

CHAPTER TWELVE

"What was that?" Pelly asked, his voice hushed. It was the first thing anyone said in a long time.

Emica pointed to the tracker on her wrist. Pelly typed out the same question on his tracker. To avoid broadcasting it with radio waves and signaling the pirates, he used the line-of-sight optical communication option. The camera system identified all trackers in the vicinity and then sent out low light laser pulses to pass on the signal. It was a modern system of speaking Morse code with flashlights.

Bauer: *It came from the* Triumph.

Quinton: *Pirates attacking.*

More explosions percussed the still night air. The shock of each blast hit Cassi in the gut. Had they found Dodd and Singh under the driftwood? Dug them up? Even if they hadn't, she remembered the massive crater the drone had left. Would the pods survive that kind of explosive force, even buried? The probability was there. The stasis pods were tough, and the earth on top of them provided extra insulation from a blast.

The fact that she couldn't do anything else to protect the flight instructors ate at her. She clenched her teeth and flexed her fingers into hawk-like talons.

At least she'd been right to get the squad away from the spacecraft wreckage.

Cassi counted heads. She'd been doing head counts since they left, every ten minutes or so. Counting the cadets was reassuring. Everyone was with her. Everyone was safe.

Bauer: *Need to pick up the pace if we want that 10 km cushion.*

Cassi looked back at him. Bauer was searching the forest behind, peering into the darkness over his shoulder as if he'd heard something. When he turned his attention forward again, Cassi nodded in agreement. They did need to go faster if they could.

She tapped Kroyle on the shoulder and pointed forward. They'd been following some kind of game trail, a rut where the larger shrublike fungi had been pushed aside by something large, saplings with broken stems, grass crushed and flattened, but no distinct footprints that Cassi could discern, no sign of scat. Though the trail let them move relatively unhindered, it was a gamble sticking to it. On one hand they may have been following the Dienne equivalent of an elephant, large and docile so long as it was left alone. On the other, it could have been made by something akin to a Tyrannosaurus rex.

They pressed on, Kroyle and Pelly leading the way. Bauer and MURPHI brought up the tail.

Quinton struggled. He'd picked up a walking stick and was using that to bear some of his weight. It helped him hobble a little faster, but his leg looked stiff, like he was fighting to work it through its full range of motion. Sijani stuck with him, breaking trail for him, helping him navigate rocks and little creeks, pockets of black mud and uneven ground fungus. She offered him a hand or a shoulder when he needed it. At first Quinton insisted on doing things on his own as much as possible, but they'd been moving for a couple of standard hours now. Everyone was tired. The initial adrenaline of the exodus had worn off. He needed to lean on someone.

Pelly: *HALT.*

Cassi put up her hand and the whole squad stopped where they were and sunk to the ground. Though no one said anything, from what she could see of their expressions no one was happy about squatting in the darkness.

Cassi: *What is it?*

Pelly: *Did Kroyle circle back?*

Cassi: *No.*

Cassi spoke. "Kroyle?"

The cadet didn't respond.

She listened for breaking branches, the rustle of deadfall in the darkness, something. Wind rushed through the forest. Some of the fungal shrubs gave off an eerie kind of bass vibration that resonated on her scalp, a note of warning. It was so dark that in some directions all she saw was void.

A fluff spider crawled across her neck and up her earlobe before she flicked it off with a cold shiver.

She stared at the trees and shrubs and tall fungus, knowing that wasn't *exactly* what she was looking at. They were tall with wood-like trunks and leaves and roots that pushed down into the earth. Whether a xenobotanist would call them trees or Dienne megaflora or give them some other label didn't really matter.

What mattered was Kroyle. He knew better than to wander too far away. That was something Bauer might do, or Quinton if his leg wasn't so gimped up, but not Kroyle. Kroyle played by the rules.

Cassi moved up with Emica and nearly tripped over Pelly, crouched in a little clear patch next to a tree with translucent leaves.

Pelly pointed forward, the direction Kroyle had gone off in.

Cassi called out in a directed whisper. "Kroyle? Kroyle, where are you?"

The wind answered with a cold gust.

Emica placed a hand on Cassi's shoulder. She looked unsteady, nervous.

Cassi tapped back into MURPHI's infrared and an image popped up on her goggles. With the robot behind her, it was difficult to orient herself. She was looking at her own back side. But she quickly counted off everyone in the troop... except Kroyle.

Even with infrared, there wasn't much she could see up ahead. That was where he'd gone though.

She brought the crew in closer together and then they advanced together, as a team. Bauer and Quinton had their rail guns up, but Cassi waved them down. She didn't want them to accidentally shoot Kroyle.

She told herself Kroyle had just wandered up a little too far. Maybe he needed to pee or something and didn't want to make a production of it. A good commanding officer was supposed to trust those under her command to make independent decisions that were consistent with the mission's goals, and she trusted Kroyle.

"Kroyle?"

When there was still no answer, she invoked the challenge. "Drade?"

Nothing.

She moved a little further into the darkness, her boots swishing through knee-high wet grass, the ground uneven under her feet. Her call came out louder now, sharper, a whisper with a hint of voice. "Kroyle!"

A curious odor wafted through the air, a putrid fermentation scent that stung her nasal cavity. The Dienne forest was full of strange smells, but this scent was different from the baseline, as if there might be a corpse rotting close by in the darkness.

MURPHI's infrared showed something warm up ahead.

Then a whisper, "Requin? Help."

On the ground she caught a glimpse of moonlight reflecting off of his face. Kroyle was bound up.

The ground looked like a web of curly dark grass. But it tugged at her feet. Spaghetti noodle blades shifted under her, not passive like normal grass, but active, like a thousand skinny snakes.

Cassi jumped.

The ground held her feet in place. The grass criss-crossed around her boots with purpose, weaving her to the ground. She fell over backward, her feet stuck in place.

"Get back!" she shouted, warning the other cadets.

Cassi clawed at the soft dirt behind her. She twisted, but the living grass pulled at her boots. And now that she was down, it slithered up around her calves and shins. She kicked and crawled only to be pulled deeper.

Bauer dropped down beside her. He pushed her face first into the ground. "Hold still," he whispered.

Instinct drove her to thrash against even him, but something in his voice carried just enough confidence that she managed to override her impulses.

Cassi stopped struggling.

"Just be still," he said.

"What is it?" she asked.

"I don't know."

The grass blades wormed along her legs, up her thighs. They clung to her uniform fabric like burrs or living Velcro.

"Perfectly still," Bauer said. "Breath shallow."

That was easy to say. Her heart was racing. But she took in a few deep breaths. The Cadet Corps taught all cadets how to quickly center themselves... to take deep breaths, in through the nose, hold, out through the mouth, hold. Deep to shallow. Still.

The grass blades stopped pulling against her.

"You don't move. I'm going to move you. Don't even nod, just relax."

Cassi lay still and tried to do her best impression of a rock on the cold ground. But even with the shallow breathing exercise it was hard. She was trembling with a mix of cold and fear.

Bauer was on his hands and knees. He studied the ground carefully.

"We can cut them out," Pelly whispered.

Bauer looked back and shook his head. Then, as if to argue by example, he picked up a stick and placed it on the patch of living grass.

No reaction.

Then he pulled it away with a sudden jerk. The blades responded whipping around it like a little cyclone of snakes. They wove an intricate pattern around the stick and Bauer let go of it just before the blades wormed up to his hand.

He tried again with another stick, this time pulling away gently, with only gradual changes in pressure. The grass stirred in response, but far less aggressively. He was able to pull it free.

What was she caught in?

Carefully with the stick, Bauer nudged a few of the grass blades from around her knees. It took some skill to tease them off, sharp little fibers clung to the undersuit fabric and even poked through, prickling her shins and calves, like little mosquito bites. As Bauer swept them off, they fell away slow, seemingly more concerned with the movement of the stick than her still legs.

Squinting into the darkness, leaning out over the grass, Bauer worked more of them off her, all the while whispering to her not to move, his voice low and calm. He kept going, lifting off each blade with surgical precision, until her legs were free. Then he pointed to a couple more sticks.

Emica and Pelly grabbed them.

One at a time Bauer slid the sticks down the outsides of her legs.

Emica and Pelly each took an arm.

"On three, one... two... three."

Cassi tightened her abs, lifting her boots gently up over the grass. Bauer pressed down on the sticks, roughly replacing her weight. The living tentacles snaked around and tugged at her legs and boots, but only with a strength in proportion to her movement. Bauer moved the sticks, confusing the tentacles, getting them to give up the legs for the movement. Pelly and Emica pulled her arms, dragging her backward through the dirt until she was clear of the living grass.

"What is that?" Emica asked, maybe a little louder than she should have.

Bauer wiped the sweat off his brow with the back of his hand, then shook his head. "I think it's a Dienne land anemone."

"Is it an animal?"

Bauer stared at it. "More like a predatory plant. Although I don't know if there's quite the same divergence between plants as animals on Dienne as there is on Avalon."

Cassi sat up. Her legs were itchy and raw, but the undersuit was intact. It did what it was supposed to and formed a barrier between her and the anemone. And her boots were fine. A single slender tentacle still lurked in the darkness, caught in her laces like an inchworm, torn from its base. She flicked it off even though it no longer presented much of a threat. "Thanks Bauer."

He nodded, already focused on Kroyle.

Cassi had only been trapped to her ankles.

Kroyle was buried in that nest, still alive and almost completely cocooned.

As her eyes adjusted to the darkness Cassi noticed carcasses of other animals buried under a blanket of living fiber, the strands piercing their scales, skin and fur as the anemone dragged them across the ground.

Kroyle was slowly suffocating within a living haystack.

CHAPTER THIRTEEN

Kroyle managed to keep his head out of the slurry of little blade-like tentacles, but they wove up and around his neck, a thousand little fingers each searching for his pulse.

His eyes were flushed pink. "It hurts," he whispered.

"Bauer's right," Pelly said. He'd been reading something on his tracker. "The tentacles ensnare the prey and tangle it up to immobilize it."

Kroyle sucked in a deep breath through his teeth. He squinted, keeping his eyes shut the way guys did when they were trying not to cry. He was trying to lie still, but his chest kept heaving up and down. "Why does it hurt so much?"

Pelly sent around AXON's file on the creature. Each tentacle had micro-spires on it, like tiny razor thorns, or teeth. At the tip of each spire was a pore that secreted digestive enzymes. The tentacles would snag the prey and the spires would pierce it. The spires dug into the skin. In addition to the enzymes, they secreted a cocktail of hormones and steroids that kept the prey alive, so it wouldn't rot.

Extremely slow and painful death, were the precise words in the file.

Quinton studied the images on Pelly's link. "Can we shoot it?"

"It's living grass, Quinton." Sijani answered.

"I know. But a sea anemone has like a mouth and a body and everything... the tentacles are just part of it. If it has a heart, we can kill it, right? A brainstem? Something central?"

Pelly read a little more, scrolling on his tracker and then shook his head. "It doesn't say anything about a heart or other organs."

MURPHI twitched, a sudden powerful jerk, much more dramatic than the others. The robot stumbled like a drunk.

"You okay, MURPHI?" Pelly asked.

The robot twitched again. "Drone detected."

Cassi looked up to the sky, at the pin prick stars. There were millions of them. She listened, but couldn't hear the whir of propellers.

But the word 'drone' made her shiver.

"There's nothing in the—" Quinton started to say.

"There." Sijani pointed.

It was almost indistinguishable from the night sky, but when it dipped low, it silhouetted against a backdrop of tree-like fungus, and that lit up the targeting system on Cassi's goggles.

Quinton dropped into a shooting position.

"Wait," Pelly whispered. He grabbed Quinton's shoulder. "It's not coming at us."

The drone was moving perpendicular to them, not toward them.

"It's a search pattern," Sijani whispered.

She was right. Cassi had no idea how long it would be until the drone spotted them. If it had infra-red imaging or sensitive audio, it would pick them up sooner, but it was probably just a cheap exploratory drone.

It spooked Sijani, though. She looked straight at Cassi and whispered, "We have to move. Now!"

Cassi motioned her head toward Kroyle. They couldn't just leave him there.

Bauer crouched at the edge of the anemone and drew a utility knife. He grabbed a handful of the spaghetti tentacles, lifted and sliced.

A shock wave rippled through the anemone.

Kroyle grunted as it squeezed him tighter.

More tentacles stretched out and attacked, coiling around Bauer's wrist, stretching, reaching. They wrapped around his fingers and the knife blade. He twisted and pulled back, wrenching the blade around, cutting and tearing until finally he fell back into the dirt beside Cassi.

His chest rose and fell with rapid breaths. Little droplets of wet oil glistened on his hands. It smelled like pepper and mold. He quickly wiped it off, clenching his teeth. The oil was filled with the digestive enzymes Pelly had talked about and by his reaction, Cassi could tell it burned.

She'd been lucky it hadn't got through her boots or the fabric of her undersuit, at least not much of it. Her legs itched.

Kroyle was enduring it as he lay there, trying to hold still as he cried in quiet agony.

Cassi felt balled her fists with helpless rage. Willister Kroyle was her friend. In the academy, back when they'd been studying for first year exams, she remembered folding little paper airplanes with him and tossed them off a balcony in the library, competing silently to see who could get the furthest. In second year, they argued relentlessly about colony politics, and in third year Cassi was the one Kroyle quietly admitted his crush on Sijani to.

"We can circle back for Kroyle later," Sijani said, keeping her voice low. Her eyes were wide and she shifted, like a nervous dog in a thunderstorm. "Right now, we have to get out of here."

Cassi shook her head. They still had time. The drone might veer off or follow something else. She wasn't going to leave Kroyle to die.

Quinton knelt down beside Bauer and stretched out his wounded leg. His bandage was still mostly iodine yellow, not too much blood had seeped through. But he winced as he got down.

"What if we burn it?" Quinton suggested.

Sijani shook her head. "Are you insane?" She pointed up at the drone then at her eyes, indicating that would give away their position.

"We could control the burn," Pelly said. "We surround it and gather up dirt to toss on it if it gets out of control. Then we slowly burn the tentacles until we can get to Kroyle. Keep the flames low, put it all out as fast as we can."

"If that drone sees it, you know what happens," Sijani said.

Bauer glared at the anemone. "I think that's our only chance... Kroyle's only chance."

Sijani shifted anxiously from side to side. She glared at Cassi.

Cassi opened her tracker to the contour map of the local area and marked a position two kilometers ahead—the south end of a little pond. Then she tagged it with the text: *RP*—rendezvous point—and sent it over line of sight to the cadets. They might have to move fast and split up.

"Burn it," Cassi ordered.

Bauer, Emica and Pelly grabbed dry sticks, all hoping that the wood they seemed to be made out of was similar enough to wood on their home world.

Sijani didn't say anything else. The muscles in her face tightened. She glanced up over her shoulder at the drone, but with a deep breath, she joined in the work, part of the team.

"Gather round," Bauer said. "Make a human curtain."

He ejected a round from his K205 and Cassi authorized him to fire. Placing the muzzle against the tip of the stick, he squeezed the trigger.

The weapon made a loud pop and zip. The scent of hot ozone wafted up from the weapon. A purple flame leaped from the muzzle and singed the stick. The end instantly blackened, but then... a flair and an orange flame.

When Bauer touched the burning stick to the tentacles they recoiled with a sudden, violent jerk, the way people pull their hands away from a hot frying pan after burning a finger.

Pelly, Emica, Sijani, Quinton and Cassi all picked up sticks and lit torches off of Bauer's. They tried to shield the flickering light from the drone by keeping their bodies between it and the flames and they circled around the perimeter of the anemone—about twenty feet in diameter.

"Now," Cassi ordered.

In unison the cadets touched their flames to the anemone. The tentacles sizzled and the creature recoiled. The oil fizzed and boiled. A putrid burning odor filled the air. The tentacles didn't so much burn as they charred and cooked. They folded and retreated back. Other tentacles stretched out, searching for an escape route.

Bauer moved around, shifting with nimble, nervous energy. "Pin it in."

Cassi waved her makeshift torch about, trying to keep the tentacles from creeping around her. She didn't want to burn it. Every time she held the torch close, every time a tentacle touched the flame, it spasmed and sizzled. The smell was almost unbearable.

"Let go of him," Emica urged, as if the anemone could understand her.

Kroyle coughed. His face flushed pink. "It's squeezing!"

Bauer inched his way in, torch in one hand, knife in the other, slashing and burning at the living grass. As he tread inward, the tentacles he hadn't burned crept around him in an enveloping pattern.

"The drone," Sijani said. "I think it sees us."

The machine looked like it was flying toward them now.

"Quinton, can you shoot it?" Cassi asked.

"A little busy right now."

He had streams of tentacles on either side of him and was waving his flame around wildly. Some of the dead fall began smoldering.

"Keep it contained," Pelly said.

Sijani held her section at bay, using a more aggressive approach. Rather than just the tentacles on the edge she waved the flames at as many of them as she could reach, using the heat to keep them down and away rather than directly burning them.

"Sijani, you'll have to take the shot," Cassi said.

"What? I suck at marksmanship."

Nearing Kroyle, Bauer moved as quickly as he could. But the drone was gaining ground too. No one said anything, but they all knew there was a reasonable chance the pirates had armed this drone with explosives or some other kind of weapon. Quinton and Bauer had been lucky to survive the last encounter.

Cassi broke into her command voice. "Sijani," she snapped. "You're a cadet in the Alliance Expeditionary Fleet Cadet Corps. Un-suck at marksmanship and nail that drone."

Sijani shot her a look that dripped with venom, but then drew back from the grass, got into a kneeling position, and turned on her targeting system.

She hit it with the first shot—1123 meters.

The drone exploded.

The percussive shock, heat and grit washed over Cassi and the others, but it was too far away for any significant shrapnel.

Sijani leaned back. "I hit it."

"Taura, your boot," Quinton shouted.

Sijani squealed. Her foot was wrapped in the black spaghetti tentacles, almost up to her calf. She pulled and tired to wrench herself free, just like Cassi had, triggering the organism to fight harder to hold onto her.

In a panic, she whipped her K205 around and started firing shots wildly into the grass, screaming.

"Sijani!"

Cassi tackled her to the ground and used the heat from her torch to burn the anemone away from Sijani's foot.

"Get off me!" Sijani growled.

"Focus," Bauer called.

Cassi rolled off into the dirt as Sijani stood and backed up away from the anemone.

Bauer reached Kroyle.

"Easy," Emica coached. "Don't burn him."

Kroyle rocked under the pressure, as if the anemone had somehow decided that if it were going to die, it would take him with it. "Burn me if it'll get this thing off!"

Slowly the tentacles peeled away under the heat. Bauer was quick with the knife. He slid the blade down Kroyle's neck and slashed the fibrous tentacles, using the flame to drive them back.

Cassi circled around. With its grip on Kroyle waning, their goal shifted from keeping the anemone from running off and dragging Kroyle into the darkness, to keeping its tentacles from encircling both Kroyle and Bauer like a crab pincer.

Kroyle broke loose with a scramble.

Bauer looped an arm under his chest and dragged him back to the safety of the dirt where they both collapsed, Kroyle falling back on Bauer.

Kroyle's uniform was torn, his exposed skin red with welts and blemishes where it was already reacting to the oil. His chest heaved up and down. He sucked in air as if he'd just been pulled up from underwater.

"Everyone up," Cassi said. "We have to move."

Kroyle looked up at her. "We can't. We can't see those things, Cassi. If we move, one of us is going to walk right into one all over again. Or something even worse."

CHAPTER FOURTEEN

Cassi weighed her options. Even in the darkness, Kroyle's skin looked angry with a reaction to the anemone enzymes.

Sijani opened the first aid kit and gave Kroyle an analgesic. She also dug out some anti-inflammatory ointment. She smeared it on his welts, circling it into the skin as gently as she could. The cadet hung his head forward and chewed his lip to fight through the pain.

Kroyle was right. If they pressed forward in the darkness, they might just march right into another land anemone, or something even worse. On the other hand, Sijani had just blown the second drone out of the sky. In doing so she tacked a pin on a map, telling the pirates their precise location. The dice could come up bad either way. There wasn't a good option.

"Kroyle," Cassi said. "We can't stay here. We can't defend this position. We need you to move."

"What about—"

She cut him off. "We know to look out for them now."

"We could put MURPHI in the lead," Pelly said. "The robot can scan for thermal emissions from... its digestive process."

Cassi glanced at MURPHI. The robot stared back at her in the darkness with its stupid, care-free smile painted on its head. "That'll eat up more of MURPHI's power, but I think it's a wise use of it. Bauer, you take the lead with MURPHI."

"Aye, ma'am."

"Kroyle, can you move? Can you make it work?"

When he looked up at her, his face hardened. They both knew it wasn't a question.

The cadets forged ahead with MURPHI and Bauer on point.

As the first rays of an indigo dawn stretched over the horizon, Cassi realized a deep fatigue was setting in for all of them. Emica looked like she'd aged five years overnight. It wasn't just that her hair was out of place or that Dienne dirt had worked its way into her skin. Emica walked as if in a zombie-like meditation, her focus several feet in front of her. She had stopped looking around, no longer startled by the odd noises that haunted the dark foliage they were trekking through, apathetic to the snap of a twig or the warning hiss of translucent snakes slithering underfoot.

Exhaustion even weighed on Bauer. His uniform shirt was wet with sweat. And though he fought it, snapping his head around, widening his eyes with purpose, his steps were sluggish, and he tripped and stumbled more often than he should have.

They'd traveled more than a marathon distance in the night, cross-country, with no set path. Her crew had every right to be tired.

Cassi was tired too. More than once, when they stopped and waited for Quinton to close the gap, she caught herself leaning against a tree, or sitting on a rock, closing her eyes for longer than blink. Cassi had pulled a few all-nighters in the academy. As much sacrificing sleep was frowned on, sometimes there was just too much test material to know, too much project work to get done, too many plans that needed to be made. And all of that was on top of keeping personal uniforms clean and pressed, rooms organized, kit operational... the life of a cadet was a constant fight against the clock.

A few months ago she stayed up through the night because Emica had been on the verge of quitting the program.

For Emica, it hadn't been one single factor that made her doubt herself. Rather, it had been an accumulation of factors. Every cadet in the academy came into the program used to getting very high grades and out-performing classmates in standard educational programs in just about every assignment or physical challenge. When they passed through the bottleneck of academy acceptance, most became average, and everyone dealt with that a little differently. Emica struggled on the exams. She always passed, but she struggled. She struggled to keep up on a lot of the physical training, not because she was out of shape, but she'd been a champion figure skater. Cadet training emphasized team-oriented sports and raw physical conditioning through calisthenics, weight training, running, and swimming.

The stress of continuous assessment wore on every cadet, and everyone had their brush with a breaking point. That night Emica had been hit with a triple whammy. She had just passed another test by the skin of her teeth, the senior cadets were throwing a party that she'd wanted to attend but no one had invited her, and her boyfriend from back home broke off their relationship. Cassi stayed up crying with her, listening to her, eating chocolate truffles, and trying to convince her to stay in the program.

Cassi still wondered if Emica had stayed for herself, or if it was because Cassi admitted she didn't think she could get through the training without Emica.

If she had quit, Emica would have been home on Avalon right now, top of her class, popular, training for some skating competition, safe.

Cassi's gut quivered as she wondered whether she'd dragged her best friend into this disaster.

Up ahead, MURPHI twitched and cocked its head to the left.

MURPHI: *Sub-audible alert. Footsteps. Human gait.*

That caught Cassi's attention. She waved the squad to keep going, to create the impression they hadn't noticed the pursuer.

MURPHI's snoopers were up. The robot projected an estimated position behind them... less than two hundred meters away, through a grove of towering, stilt-like trees that whipped around in the wind like inverted pendulums. The terrain was covered with feathery grass, sulfur bogs and moss-coated, granite boulders. The wind whispered and whistled, the grass rustled, little creatures skittered about unseen. It was a wonder MURPHI could detect anything like human footsteps that far off.

Cassi tried to remember what she could about ground defense tactics, but what she knew was limited to one or two classes worth of survival training, and the occasional video game. Alliance Expeditionary Fleet officers had a lot of things to know. In her mind ground engagement tactics were stored in some dusty file marked "other."

But her mind locked onto the problem with a lockjaw bite. Cassi spread her team out, directing Quinton and Sijani out on the left flank, Pelly and Kroyle on the right. Spread out, her crew could still concentrate fire on a single position, while whoever was approaching would have to spread out their fire, lowering the probability of any cadet casualties. Cassi swung the squad around to start climbing a hill. It moved them off course from the survey outpost and slowed them down, but climbing gave them the advantage of an elevated position.

As the footsteps came closer, Cassi's pulse quickened. Her fatigue slipped away, replaced by a renewed surge of fear-induced energy that bordered on panic. A firefight in a video game was one thing, but there a low score was the only consequence.

Cassi really didn't want to get into any kind of fight with the pirates if she could avoid it. With guns, even if you played exceedingly well, the consequences of even a minor mistake could be absolutely devastating. The thought of losing someone from her crew, anyone, made it difficult to breathe.

Bauer: *Good spot.*

He pointed to a location in the terrain that offered some natural concealment. The ground was covered with more of that featherlike grass that was easy to slip into and hide in. Underneath was a floor made from metamorphic rock that made the terrain uneven and could provide solid natural shielding if the pirates started shooting. It was as defensible a position as they were like to get in the coming minutes.

Cassi halted the cadets and texted her order. *Dig in.*

She dropped into the wet grass and, with the others, turned her weapon directly toward the footsteps MURPHI was tracking. The sun was over the horizon now and the extra light was welcome, but there were still a lot of shadows in the trees that mixed in with bright rays of light as the foliage shifted in response to the wind. White fluff spiders fell though shafts of light like a gentle snow, dropping onto mushroom-like leaves then skittering about before leaping back into the air. Translucent snakes hissed in the trees, oblivious to the plight of the humans below.

With a tap, Cassi released AXON's weapons lock on every firearm they had. A faint green outline that surrounded her field of view through the goggles shifted to an ominous red, indicating her system was active—she and everyone else in the cadet flight crew could now shoot to kill.

Cassi pressed herself into the ground. She sunk into the grass and pulled it up in front of her to hide her position. She leaned against a boulder, cold hard rock, hoping that it was strong enough to defend her against whatever the pirates threw at them.

Emica dropped down close to her.

"Remember to cover your buddy," Bauer spoke just loud enough that the other cadets could hear him. "One of you is always ready to fire down range. Watch your arc of fire. If you change position, call it out."

Bauer was a natural commander for this kind of thing. Cassi just wanted to lie there and wait and hope that MURPHI was wrong and that what it identified as a human was actually some harmless Dienne unicorn trotting through the woods.

The proximity estimate shrank... two hundred meters. The pirates should have been close enough to see. Cassi strained her eyes, studying the shadows, the trees, the movement in the feather-like grass, for anything that looked human.

"I don't see them," Emica whispered.

"Patience," Cassi told her.

Bauer: *Rules of engagement?*

Cassi hesitated. Ethically, it wasn't as easy as telling them to shoot anything that moved. Alliance protocol dictated that they had to be under an imminent threat of death to independently engage an enemy with lethal force. By activating the K205s, she had effectively authorized her crew to kill. That decision had to be accompanied with rules of engagement.

And she didn't have time to dither.

Cassi [to the entire squad]: *Fire only if fired upon, or on my direct order.*

Quinton pointed into the darkness. "I have a lock."

Cassi followed his indication and saw movement. "Hold," she ordered.

Would hesitating too long get someone on her crew killed?

A lone human emerged from the shadows at a run. He carried a Tek rifle, a much more powerful version of the forearm-mounted rail guns the cadets carried. His shirt was damp with sweat and his knees were brown from crawling through mud.

Quinton had a clear shot. Sijani locked onto him too.

All Cassi had to do was give the order.

It seemed like he was alone and easily exposed.

MURPHI's snoopers were still only picking up a single audio source. When they were further away, the system hadn't been able to discern numbers, but now, the footfall sound pattern was isolated... a lone human... an adult... and as he came into view, he looked frightened.

Cassi: *Warning shot.*

Quinton's K205 barked, discharging a round that slammed into a tree not twenty feet in front of the mysterious man. The trunk exploded into a plume of yellow splinters and the tree buckled under its own weight. It fell, long leaves trailing it like streamers and coming to a rest like relaxing cilia.

The man halted and looked around, his eyes twitching, head curled low, his shoulders in a tight shrug. A professional soldier would have fired back, dropped, rolled and come up to observe in a different spot. It looked like this guy didn't know whether to shoot back or raise his hands.

Cassi held her breath.

The man looked as though he might bring the Tek rifle to bear on them. The muscle in his arms tightened. But then, holding it across his torso, he raised it up, like a sacrificial offering.

Was this a trick?

Cassi called out her crew. "Keep alert for peripheral movement. Pelly, keep a bead on him. Bauer, Quinton, your teams need to provide flanking security. I don't want anyone sneaking around us."

She lowered her voice in an attempt to sound older, more authoritative.

"Drop your weapon!"

The words came out sounding... like a girl trying to pretend she was more than she was. They came out shrill and desperate.

But the man did as he was told. He gently placed the weapon on the ground in front of him.

"Step back. Ten paces." Cassi wasn't sure how far back he needed to go, certainly far enough that he couldn't dive for the weapon.

He complied as he looked around, into the grass, squinting. Cassi realized he couldn't see any of them yet.

Emica made a twirling motion with her finger.

"Turn around," Cassi ordered. "Face the direction you came from."

Again, he did as he was told, showing them his back. Cassi checked his waistline, looking for any obvious bulges in his pockets, other weapons. Nothing stood out.

"Hello?" the man called back over his shoulder.

"Face the direction you came from," Cassi ordered. "We're armed and authorized to use lethal force." That sounded like something an Alliance officer would say, didn't it?

"Understood."

Cassi flipped over to MURPHI's optics. The robot's periscope-like sensor arrays rose up over the grass allowing it an unobstructed and enhanced view of the surroundings. She searched the maze of tree trunks, dead fall, grass and darkness, but saw no sign of other humans.

She turned to Emica. "Cover me."

Carefully, Cassi crawled out from behind her rock. When she poked her head over the grass, it was slow and deliberate. If there was anyone in the darkness, waiting for her to emerge, that person would have a clear shot her now.

"I'm alone," he said.

Cassi let out a hesitant breath. After a few more seconds, she rose and approached the man. She kept her weapon ready and made sure not to cross a line between him and Pelly or Emica. As she stepped closer, she kept glancing out into the surroundings, looking for some sign of a trap.

"You can relax," he said. His head began to turn.

Cassi shot the ground, the K205 bucking hard on her forearm. The shot kicked up dirt between his legs. She'd intended the shot to be a lot further away, another warning shot, but between her nerves and the uneven terrain the shot came too close.

The man swore.

"Don't think I can't aim higher," she said.

He turned his head away. "I told you I'm alone and—"

"You have K205 kinetic rail cannons coupled to an autonomous artificial intelligence targeting system trained on you. Stay quiet. Answer my questions only. Do you understand?"

He swallowed. "Yes."

She waited.

"Ma'am."

Cassi picked up the Tek rifle and slung it over her shoulder.

"Name?"

He swallowed again. "They call me Maverick."

"I don't care what anyone calls you. What is your legal name?"

"Mason Lapoint... ma'am."

"Were you a crew or passenger on the *Lucky Bee*?"

He coughed but didn't move to cover his mouth. "Crew."

"Where is the rest of your crew?"

He shifted uneasily. "I don't know exactly... they're out searching for you... and for me."

CHAPTER FIFTEEN

Mason Lapoint had the emaciated build of a man who spent a lot of time in the absence of gravity. The top buttons on his uniform were loose, offering a view of the deep indented notch over his sternum. His upper ribs and collar bone stood out under loose skin. He had long, slender fingers and bony elbows. A few grey hairs were set in amid his dark curls and frosted his goatee.

When Cassi finally permitted him to turn around, his eyes widened at the sight of the Alliance Cadet Corps insignia on her shoulder. "You're a cadet. Where are the qualified astronauts from your spacecraft?""

"I am an Alliance Mission Commander. Mr. Lapoint, you said your crew is searching for you. Why?"

He shifted again, glancing over his shoulder. "Give me back my rifle, kid. We're wasting time."

Cassi kept quiet and calm, the way her mother always had when Cassi had a guilty conscience. Instilled silence and patience had a way of drawing the truth to the surface.

"That's going to take some time to explain... ma'am. Look, I'm no threat to you."

"You were carrying a Tek rifle."

"That's not to use against you." He swallowed again. "It's to use against *them*."

Cassi waved at Bauer and MURPHI to stand down. Even though that exposed her flank, she was pretty sure that if anyone was out there and planning to use Lapoint as a distraction to make a move, they would have done so by now. Bauer's physical presence might make this guy take her more seriously.

Bauer was half a head taller than Lapoint, and probably had twenty-five to thirty kilograms on him. "Permission to ask the prisoner why the hell they attacked us, ma'am."

Lapoint didn't seem intimidated by Bauer or the robot at all. He just shook his head. "I can't tell you that."

Bauer lifted his K205. "Don't think for a second that I'll hesitate."

"Easy, Bauer," Cassi said. "Give him space."

Bauer had his chest puffed out; his jaw thrust forward. Posturing as if daring the older man to challenge him.

"We need to get moving," Lapoint said. "They know where we are. They're coming."

Cassi glanced into the alien forest. Even though it was getting brighter by the minute, she still couldn't see anything other than tree trunks and that weird feathery grass. But her instincts told her the threat was out there somewhere.

"Why did you attack the *Triumph?*" she asked.

"We have to go." He took a step to move around her, as if to call her bluff that any of the cadets would shoot him.

"MURPHI, arrest Mr. Lapoint."

The robot twitched and for a moment Cassi wondered if it might just break down right there and let Lapoint walk free. But its servos whirred and by his second step the maintenance robot grabbed him, yanked him off balance, and snapped him over an extended leg with a hard and powerful robotic rendition of a judo throw.

Lapoint cried out.

"You are under arrest by order of an Officer of the Alliance," the robot stated.

Lapoint struggled, but the robot turned him onto his chest and wrenched both arms around his back until it looked like he was in such a tight hammer lock his tendons might snap.

MURPHI pushed him face down into the grit, its arrest program applying pressure to the man's arm in direct proportion to the resistance he put up. After a few seconds and some colorful language, Lapoint had to stop.

"You need to listen to me, Cadet, Ensign, whatever," he said, his chest rising and falling. "They're coming."

"We're not going anywhere until you tell us why you attacked the *Triumph*."

MURPHI turned its head toward Cassi. "I cannot apply pressure to force the prisoner to answer." It twitched. "Mostly."

"I don't know why you were attacked."

"How can you not know?" Bauer demanded.

Lapoint struggled a little more but relented with a groan as MURPHI jacked up the pressure on the tendons in his shoulder. He took a few deep breaths.

"Something's happened to my flight crew. They went all crazy... like psychotic. If they find me, they're going to kill me. If they find you... they'll kill you too."

"Why would they want to kill you?" Bauer asked. "Did you betray them, break a pirate code or something?"

"Pirate code? What are you talking about, kid?"

Cassi knelt down to get closer to him. "Usually, people don't just spontaneously decide to kill other people. It sounds like there's more to the story."

"I told you, they went psychotic. Look, I'm happy to fill you in on the details. But we've got to get moving. What part of 'They're coming to kill us,' are you having trouble with kid?"

"The proper term when addressing this Officer of the Alliance is 'ma'am' or 'Ensign Requin,'" MURPHI stated.

"Alright, they're coming to kill us... ma'am."

Cassi's instincts told her to just trust the man and get moving. Glancing around, she could see the other cadets felt the same way. They had all been sure the pirates were coming for them before and everything Lapoint told them only confirmed that. It was true they could move and talk, or move and question this guy later.

But she didn't want him calling the shots. There was a still a possibility he could be routing them toward a trap.

"I need more detail," Cassi said.

Lapoint turned his head to the side and took a couple deep breaths. "We were freelancers, hired to survey this continent for rare metals. There were six members of our team... three flight crew and a payload team... me and two others... we're private geological surveyors. Or at least, we were. A few days ago, we were busy setting up a seismic sensory array. The flight crew took off to explore. While we were working, I fell off one of the server domes and injured my arm."

Lapoint tried to roll a little to display a purple bruise that ran up the side of his right arm. It was too old to have been caused by the scuffle with MURPHI.

"Misha, my team leader, ordered me to go get it checked out in the *Bee's* medical bay. While I was in there, the flight crew returned to the landing site, but something was different about them."

Lapoint paused as if searching for words. Cassi noticed little tremors in his fingers. "The flight crew murdered my team. Ma'am."

"Murdered?"

"I was in the medical bay. I saw it all happen through a window. When the flight crew came back Misha and Nalan were still working, just pegging down a tarp. Our skipper picked up a hammer and just..." Lapoint paused. "He came up behind my team leader and... he killed Misha."

"Nalan tried to run, to get back to the *Bee*, but our flight engineer, Beja, caught him and tackled him to the ground. Beja held him there while Captain Hondo bludgeoned him with a crowbar."

Lapoint took a few more deep breaths. If he was lying, he was certainly a good actor. But that seemed like a rather detailed and unnecessary story for a lie.

"I tried to get an emergency communication rocket off, but the flight crew got back on board the *Bee* fast. They didn't even try to hide the bodies. I hid in the ship's trauma tank."

"But you were in orbit when we found you," Cassi said.

Lapoint twisted a little and glanced over his shoulder, not at MURPHI, but back into the forest. "Can't I explain this as we move?"

Cassi had to make this man understand that she was in charge. To do that, she had to convince him that he wasn't going anywhere until she heard what she needed to hear. That's what Commander Dodd would have done.

Her captive swallowed again, his Adam's apple shifting under the skin on his neck. "They left the bodies, got back into the spacecraft and we launched.

"I was in that trauma tank for six days. I survived on intravenous plasma. From inside I had access to the ship's systems, so I knew when you showed up. At first, I was happy. I was hoping that an Alliance spacecraft might help."

"Then you attacked us," Bauer filled in.

"They attacked you. I was in the tank."

"You said you had access to the *Bee's* systems. You couldn't send us a warning of some sort?" Bauer asked.

Lapoint looked at the ground. "If I had, they would have known I was on board. They would have *killed* me. And I didn't know you were a bunch of cadets. Your spacecraft was an Alliance corvette. I thought you would be rescuing me."

Cassi looked at Bauer, wanting his assessment. It was clear from the furrow in his brow that Bauer still didn't trust him.

"Look, I know it's not exactly an easy-to-believe story, but you don't have to trust me. We just have to get moving."

Bauer turned to Cassi. "What if they're tracking him? We could send him left and go right. That would split up their search effort."

Cassi thought for a moment. "MURPHI, scan the prisoner for RF emissions. Locate any source and superimpose it on Bauer's and my targeting displays."

In a half second three red icons popped up. Bauer pulled off Lapoint's watch, his wrap-around glasses, and removed a small tablet from his pocket.

"Come on. You're gonna take my tech?"

Bauer tossed it all on the ground, took the Tek rifle from Cassi and crushed each item with the butt, destroying all of it.

Lapoint shook his head. "Oh, that's great."

Cassi watched the red emission icons wink out and then scanned Lapoint again. Nothing.

Lapoint clenched his teeth and looked skyward. "Have you tried using your radios out here? Ma'am? There's nothing but noise on this planet. You can't get a signal more than forty feet away from anyone. It's even worse where we are right now."

It was likely he was telling the truth. He was right about the noise. A network of static masked just about any radio signals on the planet's surface. But still, she didn't want to take any chances. "This way we know for sure they're not tracking you," she said.

Bauer nodded his approval.

"Bauer, MURPHI, I'm assigning you to prisoner watch. Mr. Lapoint is not to be more than five meters from MURPHI at any time. If he attempts to flee from custody... shoot him."

Lapoint turned up his palms. "I'm not a threat to you, Ensign. In fact I'm probably the best chance you have at surviving."

"We'll see, Mr. Lapoint" she said.

As she waved the squad up and they started walking, Lapoint shook his head. "What's that supposed to mean?"

MURPHI walked beside the man, Bauer behind him, carrying the heavy rifle, following Cassi's order to keep Lapoint close, but not so close he could try something like making a grab for the weapon.

They found their way to another inland lake, which was fortunate. Though the lake itself was an obstacle, the shoreline made for relatively easy travel, as the terrain was relatively even, sandy, and aside from the occasional jam of driftwood, free of obstacles. That helped them make up some time and log a few more kilometers.

Lapoint fought to keep up.

At first Cassi thought he might be purposefully dogging it, but the man was sweating profusely and breathing hard whenever she checked on him. Alliance cadets had a challenging fitness regimen that kept them all in a physical condition that rivaled professional athletes. They were all used to running an average of ten kilometers a day, cross country, and maintaining a minimum pace. Cadets had to keep up with the physical training standards to remain in the program. They also swam, lifted weights, played team sports like avalanche (handball on a climbing wall), underwater hockey, paint ball and rugby, and trained in combative sports like judo. And since the cadet diet was largely established by nutritional AIs, by the end of their first year at the academy, cadets were usually very close to their peak physical condition.

Lapoint simply did not have the same conditioning or drive as the cadets.

"Do you want us to carry you, Mr. Lapoint?" Bauer asked.

The geologist shot him an angry look and picked up his pace.

They made good time, getting all the way around to the far side of the lake as the sun was coming down.

The cadets had covered nearly fifty kilometers since sunrise and now there was no sign of the *Bee's* survivors other than Lapoint. To his knowledge, they were out of drones and pursuing the cadets on foot. She sent Pelly and Kroyle to scout for a good position to ground for the night. Everyone needed a rest, and she didn't want another anemone attack resulting from them racing through the dark.

Rest in the darkness, move in the light. It seemed like a good enough idea.

Unfortunately, as the sun touched the horizon, the Dienne megafauna attacked.

CHAPTER SIXTEEN

They had six stilt-like legs, about thirty feet tall, maybe taller if they were stretched out, yet each leg was as narrow as Cassi's own. Their bodies looked like a kind of plate mail exoskeleton covered with a fuzz of white dandelion-fluff that could have been an independent biome of those little spider-like creatures living on it like parasites. At eye-level, the legs looked like the slender trees the cadets had been walking through. A head hung from the underbelly, on a long, trunk-like neck. Mandible pincers extended from the sides of the mouth—natural crushing machines.

Cassi couldn't see any eyes.

They moved with long, purposeful strides, must faster than humans could travel, even at a sprint.

They cut across a lake, sinking deep in the black water, but not so deep they submerged.

"MURPHI, what are those things?" Cassi asked.

The robot twitched. "Dienne forest striders."

"You wanna give me back my Tek rifle?" Lapoint stared out across the water at the striders.

"We don't know they're coming for us." Sijani said. "Maybe they'll just pass us by."

Pelly studied them. "They're heading straight toward us."

Cassi's heart picked up. Instinct told her to run, but there was no way she or any of the cadets were going to outrun those things.

"How many are there?" Quinton asked.

Bauer counted through the Tek rifle's scope. "Half a dozen, maybe."

Sijani pointed off at a ninety-degree angle. "There's more that way."

Another five moved through the treetops, their motion smooth and fluid across the uneven terrain, their gait robotic and precise.

"They're flanking us," Pelly said. "Their natural prey must be some kind of herd animal. There must be something about us that they're picking up on that's making them mistake us for what they normally hunt. Maybe if we spread out, walk in a different pattern or something..."

Lapoint laughed. "Are you for real, kid? It's not that complicated. Flesh is flesh."

Quinton was already targeting the closest one, his railgun arm outstretched. Bauer had the Tek rifle up. The others began targeting the alien forest striders with their K205s as well.

Cassi didn't want to turn this into a shooting gallery if she could help it. Alliance Expeditionary Fleet standing orders dictated that all forms of life were to be treated as humanely as possible. They couldn't just shoot something because it looked menacing.

Still, the forest striders were clearly predatorial. And advancing on them.

Cassi texted the crew: *Easy everyone. Be still. Quiet.*

They took cover in the piles of driftwood on the beach. Little beetle-like crab-bugs crawled out of the sand, over the logs and over their uniforms. Bird-like insects that reminded Cassi of either giant mosquitoes or narrow hummingbirds hovered over the driftwood as well, zipping through the air and stabbing at the beetle-bugs with sharp beaks. Tiny black dot insects jumped up and swirled over patches of fungal grass amid the rotting wood.

Cassi held as still as she could. The black dot insects swarmed around her hair, picking at it. One of the hummers zipped past her head, close enough that she felt the beat of the air against the back of her neck.

The striders ambled closer. The first one stopped about ten meters away, its feet still in the lake water. It had five normal legs. The sixth stopped about halfway down and dangled like a pendulum, swinging back and forth in the air trying to compensate for the creature's shifting balance as the angle of its mandibles changed, like it was searching.

Cassi still couldn't see anything that looked like eyes. Did it hunt by sound? Smell? Heat?

Another came closer, this one at least ten feet taller. The bony plates underneath its fluff carried something that shimmered in the light, like chrome. It was a silverback. The smaller ones scuttled out of its way.

The silverback strode directly over top of the cadets and stopped. A head, or at least a mouth connected to its long neck dangled over them. Powerful musculature flexed and bony mandibles spread. Black lips peeled back revealing a mouth nearly a meter in diameter, full of shark-like teeth, some as large as Cassi's hands, and glistening with saliva.

"Bauer, fire."

The Tek rifle let out a roar of a shot.

Cassi expected that to be the end of it. She expected the strider to go down and the others to back off.

Instead, it recoiled, taking a couple steps back, but its mandibles flexed and snapped in defiance with a sharp clack. It let out a shrill call that rang though Cassi's spine.

It stepped in closer, lowering its mouth toward Bauer.

He fired again. And again. Each hit forced the strider to stumble back.

"Quinton," Cassi commanded. "Fire."

Quinton delivered two shots, one right into its mouth.

The strider screeched again.

"Squad! Three round burst! Fire!"

BANG! BANG! BANG!

The high velocity rounds broke through the monster's exoskeleton plating. Green fluid oozed out, running down two of its legs like warm syrup.

"Warning! Warning!" MURPHI called out.

The five-legged one crept around and dropped on Lapoint, snatching him up with its mandibles.

Lapoint screamed.

Cassi turned and pumped six rounds into the smaller strider. She had a clear line on its long neck, and she took it. The rail gun kicked against her forearm with each shot. Her instructors would have unleashed hell on her for firing with a person so close to her line of fire, but taking the shot was the only option she saw for a chance at saving Lapoint. Those mandibles could crush him.

The five-legged strider recoiled and let him go. It limped back into the water.

Lapoint dropped into the sand from about twenty feet up and his body made a muffled crunching sound. He writhed, screamed, and cursed.

The silverback took a few more steps and then fell backward and landed in the water itself. Body fluid leaked from its wounds, spilling into the water like a fluorescent green oil slick. Its legs kicked and spasmed, forcing cadets to drop into the sand to stay out of the way.

It straightened out in one final spasm, the plates grinding against each other, the dandelion fluff whirling about in a cloud of confusion.

And then its body slipped into the darkness below the surface.

Its legs relaxed.

Lapoint crawled through the sand. "Shoot them! Shoot them all!"

"Hold." Cassi ordered. Her voice sounded so high and timid compared to his, but no one fired another shot.

The other striders had spread out around them, but were holding back, as if their main purpose was to herd the humans together and keep them from running. But now that the largest of them had fallen, they shuffled about, as if unsure what to do next.

Cassi tried to assess the numbers. All seven members of the squad fired three shots into that strider to stop it, plus their initial shots. There were still over a dozen striders surrounding them.

The cadets didn't have enough ammunition to kill all of them.

CHAPTER SEVENTEEN

"What are you waiting for?" Lapoint shouted. "Gun them down! Gun them all down!"

He hadn't stood up yet. Even from fifty feet away, Lapoint's right ankle looked broken.

"Only fire if you need to." Cassi tried to be loud, but to keep the emotion out of her voice. "Conserve ammunition."

Bauer called out. "Movement on the right flank!"

The cadets shifted to face a new threat. Another strider approached, the dark plate armor underneath the network of spiders flashed glimmers of blue and cyan. The mandibles on this one seemed larger and they made a series of sharp clacks that made the others stop and lower their stature. Some of the smaller striders shifted about as if the sound made them nervous.

Cassi wanted to shut the sound out of her ears. It had the kind of grating edge to it that resonated in her bones. She wanted to run.

Instead, she recorded the sound on the tracker. As she did, she moved closer to Pelly.

"Do these things have a weak point?"

Pelly looked down at his own tracker but kept glancing back up. He shifted his gaze from one strider to another and then back at the virtual window projected in front of his chest. His lips quivered. "I... I don't know, ma'am. I'm not a xenobiologist."

Sijani and Quinton were in a thatch of waist-high sedge and surrounded by logs. Both could drop down, out of sight to anything human-sized, but to the striders, they must have looked like little minnows trapped in a tide pool.

Sijani kept her gun arm up, waving it around as her targeting system shifted from one strider to another. "They have to have some kind of brain, or nerve center or something. But I can't tell if that appendage on the bottom is just a trunk, or a head on a neck. Can anyone see eyes?"

Quinton steadied himself and fired a careful shot. It struck a shoulder joint on the blue back strider. The dart tumbled through the joint, shattering it from the inside. That leg suddenly dropped limp, causing the strider to stumble. But after only a couple awkward steps, like a baby calf learning to stand on fresh legs, it resumed its advance as if nothing happened, dragging the limp leg behind it on stretching sinew.

The brain, if Cassi had to guess, was deep inside the body somewhere. That meant in a worst-case scenario each kinetic dart had to penetrate the exoskeleton armor of unknown thickness and then travel through maybe three feet of flesh or so before it got to the brain, and not get knocked off course.

No wonder the striders could take so much damage.

The strider with the half-leg, the one that had grabbed Lapoint, climbed out of the water. The network of fluff spiders was gone from its body and its plate armor glistened in the sunlight as lake water ran down its legs.

What did it take to kill those things?

As it advanced, the cadets all started shooting. The repeated concussive blasts sounded like a giant machine gun. Cassi lost track of the number of shots.

Unperturbed by the hail of kinetic darts, the five-and-a-half-legged strider climbed out of the lake and stepped over piles of driftwood, its mandibles clacking and grinding.

The two largest striders, the blue back and the five legged one, charged forward. The rest of the striders—now more than a dozen—parted for each of them. The cadets may just as well have been throwing stones at the creatures.

The half-leg turned with a sudden jolt. Its feet slipped on the gravel, but it recovered and broke into a full on five-legged gallop.

It pounced on the larger blue back!

The neck-trunk whipped about and shot down, mandibles striking with a lethal crunch as it bit into the back of the blue strider. The armoured plates made a sickening crack. Green slime erupted from inside, spattering the assailing creature.

It struggled to stay on top as the blue abandoned its advance to shake the other alpha off.

The half-leg's mouth and neck-trunk slithered inside the exoskeleton as the blueback jumped and spun and bucked like a rodeo bull. A muffled, sickening snap came from inside, like a tree trunk cracking underwater. The bottom strider dropped into the sand, lifeless.

The half-leg jumped off, landed upright, and turned to the others in a low aggressive crouch. Its mandibles snapped with an eerie, low, clack, clack, clack.

"Did that just happen?" Pelly asked.

Quinton had his K205 up in a firing position, tracking the half-leg strider, still searching for weaknesses. The half-leg was terribly wounded, and it looked even worse with the green sludgy blood from its victim dripping off of it. There were cracks in its armor, and though Cassi didn't understand much of the xenobiology of this world, she would still bet money that strider didn't have long to live.

"Is it defending us?" Sijani asked.

It loped forward and pounced on another of the striders. Forelegs came up like lances, but the half-leg was a split second faster and more powerful, even despite its injuries. It wrestled the other to the ground.

On its back, the other strider flailed. The half-leg dipped and snapped, ripping into its plating. The bottom strider kicked and let out a series of desperate clacks and shrieks that hurt to hear. The screech forced the other striders to back off. With an angry strike, it plunged its mouth inside the victim and crunched whatever vital organ lay inside it.

The other striders broke into a retreat as the half-leg unmounted its victim and pursued.

The other cluster out near the water lingered a little longer, as if deciding what to do.

"Quinton," Cassi said, keeping her voice quiet. "That one that's standing in the water... can you hit it in the knee? At the waterline?"

"I don't think that will do much—"

"Just do it."

He rolled his head, steadied himself, aimed and made the shot.

As with the others, the sudden loss of a limb made it stumble, but it recovered. Rather quickly. If anything, the injury just angered it.

"Well that was a waste of a shot," Quinton grumbled.

"Hold on. Watch it."

When Quinton hit it, the strider stumbled and the puncture wound dipped below the surface, well into and under the water. It shivered and stumbled about, splashing as it recovered its balance.

The necks of the others whipped about, perhaps sensing one of their pack members was injured.

"Wait for it," Cassi said.

Quinton hadn't taken his weapon down. "If you know something, Cassi, let us in on it."

She spoke softly, to herself, or to it, as if it might hear her sub-vocalization. "Don't fight it. Just let it in. Surrender. Let it in."

The injured strider turned away from the cadets. Its mandibles made a shivering set of clacks, light, rapid, a pattern they hadn't heard before.

The other striders spread out, shuffling nervously away from the stumbling strider.

"Come on," Cassi whispered.

"What's happening?" Bauer asked.

A full minute passed and most the striders either took a few steps back or remained motionless.

"They're preoccupied with something," Bauer said. "You think we should try to run for it?"

"Hold," Cassi answered. She didn't want their sudden flight to trigger some instinct in the predators to pursue. The striders weren't attacking right now. The cadets could wait.

Another stumble.

Two minutes since the wound was exposed to the water.

The strider relaxed. Its body expanded and contracted, as if it were out of breath. The neck hung down like a pendulum.

Another minute.

It stretched its legs, drawing itself up to it full height. Then after a final shuddering spasm, the injured strider attacked, turning on its own pack.

Legs kicked and thrashed. The monster leaped and pounced. The others recoiled and countered, bucking and wrestling against it, legs thrashing.

"Let's move," Cassi said. "Everyone up. I'll explain on the way."

Lapoint shook his head. "Sorry, ma'am. That's a negative on movement."

With all her attention on the aliens trying to eat her crew, she'd forgotten about him. Lapoint's ankle was swollen and bent at an awkward, unnatural angle. "I'm not going anywhere."

Bauer dashed over to Cassi and turned so that he faced away from Lapoint. He kept his voice low. "Those things are only going to be distracted for a moment. We have to move."

Bauer was always a challenge to read, but his cocky arrogance was gone. He looked tired and scared, not like a kid, but like a soldier who'd just survived combat and was wrestling with shock and bewilderment and twenty other emotions swirling around inside his mind like a psychological hurricane.

But she knew what he meant.

Bauer was suggesting they abandon Lapoint.

CHAPTER EIGHTEEN

Quinton and Sijani were already edging away from the fighting striders. There was a grove of thick trees just to the north of them, thick enough that the striders might have a hard time moving through them, but not so thick it would hamper the cadets.

Kroyle and Pelly lay in a little indentation in the ground, as if they'd been under fire, as if the small ditch might have protected them against the giant striders.

Lapoint crawled closer to them, his white teeth clenched together, eyes narrow slits as he dragged his broken foot through the sand and gravel.

Lapoint wasn't a member of her crew. Cassi still hadn't completely ruled him out as a pirate. He was bleeding and shivering, his lips purple-black.

Bauer was waiting for an answer. They had to move, and they had to move fast.

Cassi scratched the back of her neck. "MURPHI?"

The robot turned its head toward her.

"Pick up Mr. Lapoint and carry him."

The robot twitched. "Acknowledged, Ensign. I must inform you, however, that my power supply is at half capacity. With the added mass, the probability of me successfully reaching our destination without recharging is only twenty one percent, ma'am."

"Understood."

"We *need* MURPHI to survive," Bauer whispered.

"I know."

"We don't need Lapoint."

"I know."

He stared at her, expectantly. The striders were still wrestling with each other, the zombie strider surrounded by the others. It clacked and screeched as it postured, then attacked those around it. Their window to escape wouldn't stay open forever.

It would be physically easier to just leave Lapoint. They could give him back his weapon, but even if Cassi wanted to believe that he had the grit of a survivor, the reality was that if she turned her back on him now, she might as well just shoot him in the head and get his death over with.

"MURPHI, execute my order. Crew, move out."

She could deal with any fallout from Bauer, and MURPHI's waning power supply, later.

THEY MOVED FAST, CASSI keeping the pace as quick as they could manage. And with a finger to her lips, she reminded them all to remain quiet.

The cadets hiked into the thick grove and wound their way through grassy swamps and dense thickets of sharp, brittle shrubs that on occasion forced them to back track and circle around. Temperature in the late afternoon climbed and some of the swamps smelled of thick sulfur and methane, enough that Pelly, Sijani and Emica reported headaches.

And since the encounter at the lake, no one touched their water.

Cassi assumed that the striders hunted either by scent or sound, which was why she ordered them all to remain as quiet as possible as they moved. That made the travel even more difficult. On one hand they had to move fast, but every snap of a twig or rustle of grass had the cadets glancing back over their shoulders, looking for those monsters, or something even worse.

It felt like she was trying to drive a herd of cattle through a stream without making a ripple in the water.

The hot afternoon quickly gave way to a tepid evening.

The combination of Dienne's short days and the intensity and desperation of their situation gave Cassi a kind of temporal disorientation. She had to rely on her tracker to tell her how long the cadets had been hiking through the alien wilderness and when they should take breaks.

Quinton's leg had stiffened up even worse, but he still managed to walk on it. Just about anyone else would have collapsed and given in to the pain, but Cassi suspected that Thad Quinton would keep going until his leg fell off.

Almost three years ago, Quinton had walked through the Iron Gates of the Alliance Academy with his nose broken and little speckles of blood on the gaudy white dress uniform that all new cadets were issued. The nose job had been a parting gift from his little brother. Though Quinton had never explained the details behind it, Cassi suspected that it had something to do with the family situation Quinton was escaping, a situation that his little brother had to go back to. Quinton's mother hadn't been there to see him enter the academy. Quinton didn't have a biological father, or at least not one that he talked about. Occasionally he complained of an endless stream of low-life men that shacked up in his mother's place and then disappeared. Because of that broken nose, Quinton had spent the first hours of academy indoc in the school's medical infirmary and though that was only a few hours, when he finally did get assigned to their crew, he was one step behind everyone else. And even after years, it seemed like the guy never quite caught up.

Still, Quinton managed to make it through the rigors of the program. He excelled physically. He stuck close to Bauer who helped him with his studies, always just enough to pass, just enough to make the cut, rarely more. The last Cassi had heard, Quinton was dating a town girl... Larissa, Marissa, something... though Cassi wasn't sure if anyone had actually ever seen his mystery girlfriend. It always seemed to her as though, unlike the rest of them, Quinton wasn't in the program to earn his stars and become an astronaut. For him, it was more like the program was a way out of something else. But even that didn't make much sense. If his life at home was so bad there were other, easier, ways to change it.

She never had been able to figure Quinton out, but she was sure about one thing. Even if his leg turned black, Quinton was the kind of guy who would survive by cutting it off with a pocketknife.

It was Lapoint who slowed them.

For a spacecraft maintenance and repair robot, MURPHI was doing an exceptional job carrying the injured surveyor. The humanoid robot could bend forward and hold its torso parallel to the ground, bending its head up and thighs forward, modifying its gate to keep its torso that way, without any complaint or reduction in operating efficiency. This enabled Lapoint to mount the robot like a horse.

Lapoint's right leg was broken just above the ankle, and without a medical facility, there wasn't a lot Cassi or anyone else could do for him. She thought about trying to get MURPHI to set the bones, but it wasn't programmed for that and there was a chance the robot would do more damage if it applied traction the wrong way. Sijani and Bauer splinted the ankle with sticks and triangular bandages from the first aid kits.

As it predicted, MURPHI's power supply drained quickly under the added weight. On board the *Triumph*, MURPHI was never more than a few hundred meters from a charging station. Its batteries could last for about three days on a single charge, but that was its specification sixty-three standard years ago. And it was meant to operate in the absence of gravity.

When they stopped shortly after the sun set, Pelly reported that MURPHI's batteries were down to thirty-three percent.

That night Cassi put the squad to ground. Despite the challenges, they'd put over a dozen kilometres between themselves and the site of the strider attack. She wanted it to be more, but she also didn't want a repeat of the land anemone incident. So, she had everyone eat some rations, wrap up in survival blankets and try to sleep.

No one really slept, except for Lapoint who they had to keep poking because his snoring threatened to attract unwanted attention. But most were content to rest at least.

When Cassi had watch, Bauer came and sat down beside her.

He stared at MURPHI, crouched in a power-saving hibernation mode. "Thirty three percent?"

Cassi nodded.

"You think it's aware that we're going to have to leave it?"

The debate about whether AI units were self-aware had been going on for centuries and it was one of those philosophical issues with no clear or objective resolution. Most people just came down on one side of the fence or the other. Some people anthropomorphized the machines, believing they were no different from humans, even to the point of holding rallies for AI rights. Others treated them as no different from a toaster. Bauer was asking what side of the fence Cassi was on.

"We don't know that yet, Bauer."

"At some point we'll have to undock MURPHI's head. We can't let the power get below ten percent. We'll need some juice to detect and signal to a rescue."

Implicit in the question was a reality that Cassi wasn't sure she had the guts to deal with. If MURPHI couldn't carry Lapoint... then what?

"I'm just being pragmatic."

"Well, don't."

He turned away, his survival blanket crinkling with his movement. The air had a chill to it that night. They'd been fortunate that they hadn't crashed in a region of the planet that was not too cold or too hot, but Cassi had a chill now and she tightened her own blanket around her. Her breath crystallized in front of her face.

Bauer poked at the ground with a stick, like they should have been sitting by a fire. They had discussed a fire. It would have improved morale, but it might also attract either the rest of Lapoint's crew or some other monster.

"So, what happened to that strider back there?" By the way Bauer asked the question, she could tell he'd been thinking about it for a while.

Cassi hadn't said much about it because she was working on a theory. But it was just a model of an idea. She didn't have all the facts she needed, and probably never would.

"I don't know."

"But you have a guess."

She sighed. "Just something Lapoint said. If we take it that he's telling the truth, his flight crew went for a swim. What if there's something in the water? A parasite or a germ or something, and if it gets into your bloodstream, it—I don't know—makes you..."

"A homicidal maniac?"

"Something like that."

Bauer poked at a rock. "But what's the point of something like that? I mean, from an evolutionary standpoint."

"What if there's something they might normally prey on in the water? Those striders are pretty brutal. I bet those mandibles could crack through steel plating if there was a meal on the other side. They're fast and agile. If their prey are going to survive, they either survive by numbers, which can be a challenge when you're a big animal, or you develop some kind of alternative defense."

His brow furrowed. Bauer looked like a dog trying to figure something out. Then he laughed.

"It's not a bad strategy, really. Get your predators to fight against each other. Then you avoid conflict altogether. I'll have to remember that when I make captain some day.

"You think that's what happened to Lapoint's crew?"

"I don't know. It fits though."

"Yeah. I suppose. I think I liked it better when they were just pirates though."

She was too tired to ask him why, but he must have caught the question from her facial expression.

"It makes the ethics a lot more straight forward when you're up against a bad guy who's just bad for the sake of being bad. When you've got a normal person who's actually sick..." Bauer hesitated as if unsure what to say next.

Cassi didn't say anything. He was right.

He shifted about, his blanket crinkling more. "Hey, there's something I've been meaning to ask you, but there just hasn't been a good time to bring it up."

"What's that?"

Bauer looked into her eyes. "You got a date? You know, for when we get our stars?"

Cassi's face flushed with heat and her breath caught in her throat. A date? When they got back, when all of this was over, assuming they passed the mission, as third year cadets at the completion of their program they would go through a graduation ceremony of sorts, have gold stars pinned on their uniforms, designating them as qualified astronauts. The after-party was a big deal too. You didn't need to bring a date, but most people did. Her lips quivered. She was glad it was dark out, glad that he couldn't really see her. "Wha... um... no... not really."

But Bauer couldn't ask her on a date. Dating within the academy was permitted, but not within a crew. In fact, he was her direct subordinate now that she had actual rank. Not only was a date frowned on, but it was also illegal. A date with Bauer could get her kicked out of the program.

"Well, you know Saul Duschene in Three Crew..."

Who?

"He's on my avalanche team. He was asking."

Saul Duschene?

Cassi let out a little laugh. "He doesn't get any points if he doesn't ask in person."

Bauer looked up at the sky. "Yeah. He's kind of a doofus that way."

Cassi looked straight at Bauer.

He shrugged. "Hey, I figured you two would have something in common."

She hit him in the chest as he stifled a laugh.

"Ma'am."

That made her laugh.

In that moment, Cassi realized that there probably wouldn't ever be anything between her and Anson Bauer, nothing in a romantic sense anyway. And that was okay. They were friends.

She leaned up against him, and for a moment lowered her head onto his thick shoulder. She closed her eyes and tried not to smell the days of sweat on him. She listened to him breath, to the gentle crinkling of their survival blankets as his shoulder gently rose and fell.

He leaned his head on hers. It was just for a moment, barely long enough for her to realize it happened, like a pleasant dream in the five minutes before you have to get out of bed.

"It'll be light soon." Cassi lifted her head. The first rays of the morning were already lighting the sky. "We should be able to make it to the survey site by the afternoon. We need to wake the squad and get ready to move."

"Good luck with that. I gotta piss." He stood and walked into the darkness, leaving her alone.

CHAPTER NINETEEN

That morning the cadets drank the last of their water at breakfast. Emica collected samples of Dienne water from a brook. Using a flashlight's protective polymer window as a slide, she spread out a drop of the potentially pathogenic water and linked her tracker to the robot's optics. Because MURPHI's optics were designed for inspecting integrated circuits, its cameras could act as microscopes. Emica took dozens of still pictures, tomographic images and cine loops of the samples and then ran them through an image-search to identify microorganisms present in the water.

She built and lit a fire and boiled a sample of water in a metal flashlight casing which they used as test tube. Then she compared the boiled sample against the unboiled sample. As the cadets prepared for the hike ahead of them, Emica showed Cassi the results.

"I boiled it for five minutes," Emica said.

MURPHI's images showed that the boil killed ninety-eight percent of the visible microorganisms, including the unidentifiable ones. That was good. But ninety-eight was not one hundred.

"You sure you didn't contaminate the samples?"

"This isn't a clean lab, Cassi."

Cassi stared at the results, holding her chin between her thumb and forefinger. Boiling water was supposed to denature the proteins that made up just about any living organism, which meant nothing should have survived. Did Emica accidentally get something on the slide, or were there thermophile microbes on this world that could survive that kind of extreme heat? Was the boiling point of water that different on Dienne? And if they had survived, were those the microbes that turned people psychotic?

Emica ran the images of the surviving bacteria through MURPHI's copy of AXON to see if the AI could identify them, but the results were inconclusive.

Cassi had to make a decision. Drink the local water and risk turning into psychotic killers, or avoid it, and try to complete the hike without anyone passing out from dehydration.

A bat, or at least something bat-like, fluttered over head. There were others about, flying through the trees, chasing little insects that were confined in pockets of opaque air. The bats were not attacking each other. In fact, aside from the striders, all animals they'd encountered so far hadn't been influenced by the pathogen, at least, not so far as Cassi could tell. Were most sources of water safe? Or did it have to enter through the blood stream, meaning only people who were already wounded would be infected? There were too many unknowns.

"Alright," Cassi said. "We should still avoid the local water for now."

Emica was already putting her flashlight back together. "We can't go without water for long."

"I know." Cassi squeezed her shoulder, trying to reassure her physically, then doused the fire and circled the camp to check in with the other cadets.

She found Pelly working on a contraption of wood and rope cord. It almost looked like a bridge at first, something a child might build.

"It's a knee-crutch." Pelly glanced up at her with a wide grin. "Mr. Lapoint can bend his knee to ninety degrees and tie this cord around his thigh and this one at the back of his knee, this one to his ankle. It can transfer his weight directly onto this foot, so he doesn't have to put pressure on his broken ankle."

"For Mr. Lapoint?"

He nodded. "It's not perfect, but it should make him ambulatory. I can't think of anything to help Quinton though."

The knee-crutch worked. By the time the full circle of Dienne's alien sun rose, the cadets and Lapoint were on the march and moving at a reasonable pace thanks to Pelly's jury-rigged crutch system. Despite the harsh terrain, they arrived at the geological survey site just after noon.

"That's it?" Sijani dropped her backpack and pulled her hair out of its ponytail, doing little to mask her exasperation.

The bastion where the cadets planned to hold up until rescue came down from the heavens... was nothing more than a few dome tents.

Polymer fabric stretched out over graphite ribs provided shelter from the rain and moisture in the atmosphere. Rudimentary climate control systems kept their internal temperature at an ideal operating condition of fifteen degrees Celsius. But they were so packed with equipment, there wasn't even room for a single cadet to crawl inside.

"We came all that way for this?" Sijani turned to Cassi. "Leaving the *Triumph* was your idea. We could have been back there, with shelter, without bugs crawling all over our skin, living grass trying to ensnare and digest us, giant spiders trying to eat us... and instead we have four pup tents and a handful of computers."

MURPHI stepped between Sijani and Cassi. "You need to address the mission commander via proper protocol."

"Screw your protocol."

"Cadet Sijani, you are charged with—"

"Stop, MURPHI." Cassi stepped in front of the robot. "Cadets are free to express opinions colloquially, for the moment."

MURPHI's shoulders fell. Its snoopers drooped. It took a step back.

"You think that's going to make up for this?" Sijani's teeth were clenched together.

Emica came to Cassi's defence. "We all heard the explosions from the *Triumph*. We could have been there when they blew it up, but we weren't. Because of Cassi."

"We could have defended it. Is a rescue even coming?"

"Keep your voice down, Taura," Bauer said.

"Why? The *Bee's* crew are probably back in their ship right now, eating rations with their feet up. They've probably just written us off for dead. And you know what, when rescue comes, they'll probably be right."

MURPHI twitched. The robot was down to twenty three percent power. But its snoopers snapped up.

"What is it MURPHI?" Cassi asked.

"Warning." The robot twitched again, then returned to a default resting position, snoopers down.

The cadets all lowered into crouches, even Sijani and scanned the treeline canopy for any sign of striders, but no one reported anything. Cassi only saw jungle.

"What are you warning us about, MURPHI?" Cassi whispered.

The robot took a couple of steps, spasmed and then paused. "Warning? Which warning are you referring to, Ensign?"

"You just said 'warning.'" Bauer looked around and stood up, stretching his back.

"I did not."

MURPHI twitched again.

Pelly approached the robot. "I think we should take it offline," he said. "The combination of low power and structural damage is adding up."

"There is no problem with me. My diagnostics are... are..." it twitched again. "May I be of some assistance, Ensign?"

"Sleep MURPHI," Cassi ordered.

"Hibernation mode..." the robot's head lowered, its snoopers drooped, and it curled into a tight, fetal ball.

"Now that you have no machine backing you up, maybe we should revisit the issue of Mission Commander," Sijani said.

Bauer stepped right in front of her, right in Sijani's personal space, and not in a pleasant way. He was a full head taller than Taura and loomed over her. "Requin is the Mission Commander."

Sijani stepped back, mouth open.

"It's okay," Cassi said.

"It's not okay." Bauer glanced back at Cassi, but then turned back to Taura. "This sucks. Sure. But you know what makes it suck worse? Listening to people bitch and moan."

Sijani looked like she had venom dripping from her teeth, like a cobra backed into a corner, waiting for an opening to strike.

That's when the robot pounced.

A robot, not MURPHI, but a larger, newer machine. It had four legs crab-like legs and two steel maintenance arms. It emerged from a thicket of twisted shrubs and tackled Sijani. She didn't even have time to scream.

"MURPHI, activate!" Cassi ordered. "Protect Cadet Sijani!"

The quadruped machine rolled on top of Sijani into a classical fighting mount, one hand down, around her neck. The servos in its joints whined as it worked to crush her throat.

MURPHI sprang up from its hibernation position and with two great strides jumped on the centaur. They rolled in a twisting, writhing mass of metal, the quadruped still clutching Sijani in a death grip.

Bauer raised the Tek rifle and ambled toward the fray but kept his finger off the trigger.

"I can't get a clear shot."

The squad watched, paralyzed by the sudden ferocity, all circling around, facing inward.

"Defensive circle!" Cassi barked.

Emica turned to her with a questioning look.

"Bauer, help Sijani. Everyone else, down, search the tree line and canopy!"

As they spun and dropped, Emica caught sight of another black steel machine jumping through the trees. "There!"

Emica marked it with her targeting system. That relayed the relative three-dimensional coordinates through AXON, which rendered a full model of the threat and painted it on the goggles of all the other cadets. This second robot moved more like a giant lizard, complete with a long mechanical tail.

It slither-waddled though the trees and leaped, launching itself at Emica.

Crossfire erupted.

Cassi, Pelly, and Quinton all hit it with round after round, their lines intersecting, at the machine. The high velocity kinetic darts chipped at the torronite chassis and tore shielding panels.

It fell to the ground, but kept driving forward, taking hit after hit.

Emica screamed. "There's another one!"

Cassi's pistol jammed. A translucent error warning flashed in the periphery of her goggles.

Behind her, Emica fired at the other robot.

MURPHI wrenched the quadruped's hand off Sijani, sacrificing its own legs in the process. Metal strained and scraped and one of MURPHI's hip joints popped out of place.

Cassi ran through the immediate action drill for her K205, snapping open the port, clearing the jammed round, loading in the next one, then closing the port.

By the time her error message cleared, she lost track of the robot closing ground on her best friend. It only took her a second to re-acquire it, but it was already on top of Emica. Its tail coiled around her neck.

Bauer scrambled over to Emica and the lizard-machine.

It opened a set of powerful crushing jaws, and just as it was about to close them around Emica's skull, Bauer leveled the Tek rifle and fired.

The point-blank shot ruptured the shielding on its central processing unit and scrambled its inner circuitry. Bauer rolled with it, under it, as the machine spasmed and dropped into some preconditioned defensive mode. The cadet managed to roll over, pin it and unleash a series of shots, one of which shut it down completely.

Kroyle pumped shots into the third robot, his super-heated rounds ricocheting off its armor and up into the sky.

Quinton and Cassi joined him and together, they pinned it down and fired until their magazines emptied and the mechanical monstrosity frazzled in the dirt.

Sijani lay on the ground, clutching at her neck, her face flushed red, welts from the attack swollen and angry on her neck.

The targeting cross hairs on Cassi's field of view cut out and she gave her goggles a tap.

She'd lost connection to AXON.

MURPHI lay still in the dirt, both of its arms twisted, its right leg severed from the rest of its body. It twitched with seizure-like spasms.

MURPHI's memory housed AXON. For all intents and purposes, MURPHI was AXON, or all that was left of it.

But the quadruped stood on MURPHI's head and the little LED readouts within a now open access panel winked out.

MURPHI was dead.

And so was AXON.

CHAPTER TWENTY

Bauer spent the remaining rifle rounds on the quadruped robot. From a kneeling position he took careful aim and nailed the machine with a series of critical strikes that knocked it to the dirt and ruptured the armored plating around its head.

When the Tek rifle ran out, Bauer charged forward and screamed as he swung the butt of the weapon at the machine, knocking the head back, busting servos in its neck. The robot crumpled and fell over backward.

Bauer fell to his knees in the mud, his shoulders rising and falling rapidly. Even though the attack had only lasted a couple of minutes he looked overwhelmed with the fatigue of a prolonged fight. His hands shook and he pushed them into the soft ground to steady them.

Emica scrambled over to Sijani. She was struggling to breathe, the air passing through her throat with a wheeze every time she took a breath. She held her neck and rolled onto her side.

Quinton's leg was bleeding profusely now, his wound having split open during the melee.

Kroyle eased his way out of the grass, like it was infected with plague. His skin was raw. Some of his wounds were blistered and leaking a straw-colored puss.

Pelly knelt over MURPHI, shaking his head. He opened an access panel and kept flicking switches and punching buttons, as if the right combination might restore power to the thing.

And Lapoint lay on the ground, shaking his head. "They won't stop, you know."

"What were those things?" Cassi demanded.

"Robotic crew from the *Bee*."

Cassi cleared her weapon. "They attacked us. But they're artificial intelligence machines. Robots can't attack humans."

Lapoint sat up. "Well, they just did, kid."

"AI units have deeply rooted programming and redundant safety programs that keep them from being reprogrammed for criminal action," Cassi said.

"The world doesn't always work they way we think it does, Ensign."

Cassi glared at Lapoint. She really didn't like the way he talked down to her.

Bauer handed Lapoint the empty rifle. "Your flight crew must have figured out how to hack the core program. How many of those units did you have on board?"

"I don't know."

"Make an educated guess."

Lapoint sighed. "Well, the one with the tail—that's our hull unit. The other two are the loaders. We have a maintenance robot too, a KONG."

Bauer looked at Cassi. "So there's one more, at least."

Cassi nodded. The robots did not specifically attack Lapoint. She didn't say anything about it and wouldn't for the time being. But she couldn't have been the only one who noticed.

Emica knelt on the ground beside Sijani. Cassi dropped down next to her. "Taura? Are you okay?"

Sijani coughed and took a few rasping breaths. "I hate this planet."

Pelly looked up from the robot. "I can't fix MURPHI."

"Yes you can," Quinton said. "You're a genius. You can fix anything."

"MURPHI's power supply is fried. So is the auxiliary supply. I can't build a power supply out of alien mushrooms and rocks."

Quinton limped over to Pelly. "But you have to, Pelly. I mean, that's our only ticket off this rock. If we lose AXON, we're screwed."

Pelly blinked. "We *have* lost AXON."

Suddenly the combination of everything—the robot attack, the injuries, Lapoint... it all faded away. The cadets fell silent. And they all looked at Cassi.

Even Sijani.

Bauer rolled his head. "Well, we survive for however long it takes. There will be people on this planet sooner or later. It could be years before we're discovered, but we'll run into someone eventually. We just have to survive for as long as we need to."

"Years?" Pelly asked.

"We're not going to last five days," Sijani said. "Take a look around. This planet is hostile. We've only lasted this long by the skin of our teeth, and frankly, some of us aren't doing so good."

"Easy, Sijani," Bauer grumbled.

"Not to mention, we've got psychotic pirates trying to hunt us down with killer robots."

"That's enough!" Bauer glared at her.

Sijani glared back, leaning forward, fists balled, like she was ready for a fight. But Bauer remained stern in his stance.

Sijani turned away first, but she went straight to Quinton. "You should tell them."

"Tell us what?" Bauer asked.

Quinton clenched his teeth together. He took a deep breath, as if speaking the words pulled him into a reality he didn't want to enter. "I think my leg's infected."

Without antibiotics or some kind of antiseptic treatment, the probability of Quinton's immune system fighting off a septic infection was very low. He wouldn't last years. No one could say how long he had, but it was likely a matter of days before the infection rendered him immobile. And though no one said it out loud, if he didn't get medical treatment, he might not survive at all.

"So what do we do now?" Pelly asked.

Cassi took a deep breath. "Is there any way to use the tech in the survey station to send a communication rocket? Some kind of signal? You thought you might be able to do that before."

"That's when I thought it was a habitat. This is a remote station. It monitors and records environmental data. It's basically a weather station, ma'am."

"But it sends a signal, doesn't it?"

"I needed MURPHI to hack into it." Pelly shook his head. "Even if I could, the information only gets stored in the satellite relay. We've already broadcast a message on there. I can't hack into the programming from here."

Emica spoke up. "But what if there's a rescue ship in orbit right now? Could we use it to send a crude SOS or something?"

"I can try." Pelly's expression didn't appear all that hopeful.

Cassi crossed her arms. "Mr. Lapoint, did the *Bee* still have operational communication systems active after the crash?"

Lapoint's brow furrowed. "What are you thinking?"

"Did it?"

"Well, yes. I think so. I never really had a chance to test them though."

Bauer glared at Cassi. In fact, everyone in the squad was staring at her and they all wanted to hear the idea running through her head. But it wasn't formed yet. It had to incubate. She didn't want to expose it prematurely.

The sky was getting darker. "Pelly, if there's anything you can do, do it now. Kroyle, I want you to help him."

Kroyle reached around his back and scratched, then forced his hands down. "I'm pretty useless with electronics."

"You're an Alliance Cadet. Just because you're not perfect at something, doesn't mean you don't have some basic competency."

Kroyle looked like he was about to voice another objection but stopped himself. He tugged at his shirt. "Aye, ma'am."

CHAPTER TWENTY-ONE

Cassi allowed herself some sleep. Wrapped in a survival blanket, under the vestibule of one of the server tents, she closed her eyes, tried to ignore the gnawing pangs of hunger in her gut and the growing dehydration headache slowly building tension in her skull like a winding rubber band. Sleep crept up on her. When Kroyle tapped on the vestibule polymer, Cassi woke with a start.

The sun was coming up outside already. Emica hadn't woken her for her watch.

"Cassi?"

"Yes."

"You gotta see this."

She crawled out from under her survival blanket and tried to ignore the greasy feeling of the undersuit against her skin, clothing that hadn't been washed in days. Even though the fabric of a cadet uniform was designed to wick away sweat and the oils that came off human skin, she'd been in that same uniform for close to a Dienne week now. She felt gross and desperately wanted to just retreat into a hot shower and wash this planet's grime from her body.

Outside, tiny bioluminescent organisms zipped around in the early morning light, skipping over the tips of knee-high grass blades. The air had cooled over night, but the ground was still warm. Moisture rose off if it, generating a rolling fog that encircled the survey station. Something large moved through the grass in the distance. It was maybe half a kilometer away, several dark humps, too distant to distinguish through the fog. They made Cassi think of a bison or a cow, quietly moving across the planet, peaceful.

Pelly showed her the display on his tracker.

Cassi rubbed her eyes. "Okay. What am I looking at?"

He didn't need to explain. She recognized the orbital traffic control map. It plotted everything in orbit around Dienne, and there, circled in green, was an Alliance frigate.

Cassi rubbed her eyes again to make sure that she wasn't just seeing what she wanted to see.

Pelly smiled.

Cassi hugged him, as if he had made it appear. "Wait. How are you getting this feed?"

"Oh, well, the survey station has a direct link to one of the relay satellites. It's not a high-level encryption, because, like, who's going to hack into it from here, right? So I linked the feed to my tracker. I can see what the relay satellite sees."

"Can you send a message to the frigate?"

"Yup... I mean, yes, ma'am."

Cassi linked her own tracker to Pelly's and into the satellite. They called Sijani over and she helped to initiate the hail. By the time it went through, the entire squad had gathered around her.

The tracker emitted a quiet hail. D*eedle-deedle-deet... deedle-deedle-deet.*

An image of the frigate's bridge popped onto the screen.

Cassi felt like her heart was going to explode.

The software tagged the frigate's commanding officer as Commander Zignew Bolton—square-faced, with tight, box-cut hair, Bolton frowned at the screen. He identified himself and the frigate as the AEFS *Endurance*. The signal paused and rendered in broken, blocky pixels. "With whom am I speaking?"

Cassi wiped the coalescing moisture from her eyes and took a deep breath. "This is—Ensign Cassiopeia Requin of the Alliance Expeditionary Fleet Spacecraft *Triumph*. We crash landed on Dienne."

In the wide-angle view of the screen a few of the *Endurance*'s crew smiled, but Bolton remained stone-faced, his brow furrowed. He squinted at the screen. "Ensign? There weren't any ensigns on the *Triumph*'s manifest."

Bauer pushed into the conversation. "Our flight instructors are injured, sir. They're in stasis pods. Ms. Requin was issued a field promotion."

Bolton's nostrils flared a little, as if attempting to sniff out some truth.

Someone off screen confirmed it.

Cassi swallowed. "Sir, Commander Dodd and Lieutenant Singh are still with the wreckage. We are approximately one-hundred-and-twenty kilometers northeast at a geological survey station.

"All cadets are accounted for, but we have some wounded... a leg laceration, which I believe is now compromised with a xenoinfection, a bad skin reaction to a land anemone attack, lots of superficial wounds, and... we've picked up a survivor from the crew of another vessel. Mr. Lapoint has a broken ankle. We're okay, but we need a medical evacuation as soon as you can arrange it."

"Medical evacuation... acknowledged. We... entering the atmosphere shortly. We're glad to hear that you're alright. There are a lot of people on Avalon worried—"

"Commander," Cassi said. "I have to warn you. There's a—"

"Hold on," Pelly said. "I think the screen froze."

"Commander?"

"... abou... you..."

Cassi tapped her tracker, as if physical agitation might bring the signal back. But the image was still and blocky, stuck at low resolution. Red text scrolled over the screen. *Signal lost.*

"I thought you said you had a good connection," Quinton grumbled.

Pelly got defensive. "I did. It's not on our end." He issued a few more commands on his tracker and lines of white computer code rained down against a black background. He showed it around to the other cadets. "There's radio noise all over now... some kind of natural phenomenon."

Lapoint coughed. "Or the *Bee's* crew are jamming the signal."

"Why would they do that?" Pelly sounded like he was fighting to keep his composure. "That doesn't make any sense. Commander Bolton knows we're here now."

"I don't think they're playing that game," Cassi said.

"Huh?" Pelly looked confused.

Cassi licked her lips. "Remember what happened with that strider? They're running on an instinct to disrupt and kill."

Bauer looked up at the sky. "It doesn't really matter. They'll just land that frigate, and we'll climb on and go home. The Alliance can send actual medics to help the *Bee's* crew... or a platoon of armored marines."

"But how are we going to tell them where we are?" Emica asked. "Dienne is a big planet. They know we're here. They know we're at a survey station. But do they know which one?"

"I was trying to relay our coordinates," Pelly said. "But we lost the signal before I could get them out."

"Fires," Cassi said. "We build signal fires. The biggest fires we can, place them in a triangle and that will give away our position."

"Would they be able to see fires?" Bauer asked.

"If they're looking, and if we make them big enough."

Cassi put the squad to work hauling dead fall from the surrounding forest. They lit a single pilot fire, built it up and then lit two more each about one hundred meters away. After a couple of hours, they had each burning hot, with flames three stories high and columns of smoke that rose into the morning sky.

Now all they had to do was wait and watch.

They were going home.

CHAPTER TWENTY-TWO

When Kroyle broke out the last of his rations, Cassi's gut instinct was to tell him to stop. They weren't off the planet yet, and even something as straight forward as a touchdown extraction could have a million things go wrong with it. But they were all ravaged by the kind of hunger that carried with it weakness, irritability, and irrational thought.

And they would all have a real meal soon.

So she suppressed her instinct and allowed everyone to eat breakfast to give them strength for the ride home.

Cassi found Sijani sitting in front of Lapoint. She had his splint untied. She pressed each of his toenails, watching the color underneath change from white to pink, making sure his blood was still flowing well through the break.

"Cassi?"

Cassi crouched down beside her.

"Don't worry, my foot's not going to fall off," Lapoint joked.

Taura Sijani looked at the ground. "I just... before we get back, I wanted to apologize. I know I challenged your leadership when I shouldn't have."

That caught Cassi off guard. She knew there was some kind of social code that dictated she should now brush it off and tell Sijani that it was all okay, make some excuse about how they were under duress and she would have done the same, but going through a song and dance like that felt disingenuous. Sijani challenged her command and made some poor decisions that could have jeopardized the squad. Cassi didn't want to downplay any guilt that Sijani might be feeling.

"Thank you," Cassi said.

Sijani's perfect eyebrows lowered. Her smile shrank into a small, level slit. Clearly, she'd been expecting a little more of a reaction from Cassi, though Cassi wasn't sure exactly what that was. A part of her desperately wanted Sijani's friendship, or at least her allegiance. But she couldn't just roll over and pretend a quick apology made everything okay.

Cassi took a deep breath. "We move forward as a crew, right?"

"Agreed."

"Hey, I've got a lock on the *Endurance*," Pelly announced.

Cassi was glad to have a distraction.

Pelly had made a little technical nest for himself inside one of the survey stations. On a server tower next to another old monitor, he'd flipped up a maintenance screen on which he had a low-resolution map of Dienne rendered with a green icon marking the *Endurance's* position.

"Do you think they saw our fires?" Cassi asked.

Pelly nodded. "Oh, yeah. Absolutely. They probably saw them a while ago, but it was too late to initiate their descent, so they looped around. They should be ready to enter the atmosphere any minute now."

Emica joined them. "How will we know if they start a descent?" The view Pelly had up was a two-dimensional map. It didn't show how high the frigate was over the surface.

"Oh, we'll know."

Cassi studied the coordinates. Math had never been her strongest subject, but there was something about being completely immersed in the moment that made it all the more tangible. A problem written out on a white board was just that—an abstraction meant to be solved with other abstractions. But a real problem made things different. She used her own tracker to orient herself to Dienne's true north and then figured out the angle, rotated around and shielded her eyes from the sun. "About there."

Emica looked up. A few of the other cadets followed her too.

There. It was too far to see much detail, but a line of white vapor condensate and light from the atmospheric entry tore across the blue sky.

Cassi used the cameras on her targeting goggles to zoom in and enhance the image. The familiar outline of an Alliance spacecraft popped onto a virtual window the tracker projected at arm's length in front of her chest.

She made the window available for the other cadets to see.

Kroyle and Emica started whooping. Quinton and Bauer joined in. Pelly remained a little more reserved, fixed on his own tracker, but smiling broadly. Even Sijani stood up and started jumping around in a display of joy Cassi didn't think she was capable of.

"You okay?" Pelly asked Cassi.

"Yeah, sure."

That's when Cassi realized she was crying.

"When I get back," Pelly said. "I'm going to take a long hot shower... the kind where you just get lost in the water, you know? I'm sure they'll give us a couple personal days. And I'm going to spend an afternoon eating ice cream and playing video games..."

"Sounds nice," Cassi said.

Like a ruck sack that she'd been carrying for a long time, Cassi was anxious to drop the weight of command, to go home and feel responsible only for herself. It wasn't that she didn't like command, but having a brief respite from it, some time to not have to worry about everyone else... it was going to be wonderful.

"I can't wait to take a dump in a real toilet again," Quinton said. Then he looked around. "What? Oh, come on guys. You have any idea how hard it is to squat in the bush with a leg you can't bend?"

"You'll have to excuse me if I don't want to high-five you, kid," Lapoint grumbled. But even he was smiling.

Pelly's smile slipped away; concern furrowed his brow. "What's that?"

Something shot up from the surface, from the general vicinity where they had crashed, from where the *Bee* was.

"No. No! NO!" Pelly cried.

Cassi felt shackled to the ground, unable to do anything but watch as the little rocket sped toward the *Endurance*.

"They'll see it," Bauer said. "That's an Alliance frigate. It's got state of the art threat identification and tracking systems... countermeasures..."

"They have to be on to work," Pelly said.

"They'll detect something moving at them that fast. They have to," Kroyle said. "It's basic navigation."

"Why do you have rockets on the *Lucky Bee*?" Cassi asked, standing over Lapoint.

"I don't know. They didn't tell us anything about military rockets. It's a survey ship, or at least, it's supposed to be."

"It could be something hacked together," Pelly suggested, "like a communications rocket with some explosives in it, like what they did with their drones."

That would explain why the *Endurance* wasn't trying to avoid the rocket. They may have assumed it was an attempt to communicate. With the radio cut off, if Cassi had to get a detailed message to the *Endurance* she might have sent a rocket... maybe... if she'd had one.

"Can we signal them?" Sijani asked. "Smoke signals or something?"

They only had seconds to impact. Not enough time.

Pelly opened an audio channel on his tracker. "AEFS *Endurance* from stranded cadets on Dienne surface. There is a rocket headed straight at you. Evade! Evade! Evade!"

"We don't have a connection," Bauer said, his voice calm and low.

"Maybe they can hear us," Pelly said. "Evade!"

The two objects in the sky drew closer.

Emica squinted and pointed. "There. They see it. They're rolling out of the way."

"The rocket's adapting," Pelly reported.

"Come on..." Cassi muttered.

The *Endurance* turned hard, pulling the kind of maneuver that would have blacked out anyone not wearing a pressure suit.

They were moving too fast to spit out countermeasures... at that velocity anything without added propulsion spit out from the front of the spacecraft would slow and tear at their hull as they raced through it.

The impact came quick. The rocket slammed into the *Endurance* and the two white vapor trails erupted in a flash of light and smoke.

"It's still in one piece," Pelly said. "They survived."

"Right on Alliance engineers!" Bauer shouted.

But the *Endurance* rolled, flying in a corkscrew pattern. It was the kind of flying Cassi had seen at air shows as a kid, the kind of spiral that made kids look up in awe from their ice cream on a hot summer day.

It arced toward the ground, nose first.

Bauer swore.

The *Endurance* flew right into bedrock and erupted in a second explosion. Little pieces of the spacecraft shot up into the sky like little model rockets fired in different directions. A rolling ball of orange flame rose up like a giant devil climbing out of a hole to hell. The heat flash from its core meltdown stung Cassi's face. The pressure wave smacked into her body.

Bird-like life forms rose out of the tree canopy, squealing and calling, scattering into the wind to escape the foreign blast of heat.

Cassi flexed her fingers. It felt as if victory, even survival, had been torn from her hands.

Quinton covered his mouth and coughed. "Well. There goes that plan."

CHAPTER TWENTY-THREE

They had to drink.

Cassi had put off the water issue long enough. She couldn't allow the cadets to get any more dehydrated than they already were. Thirst would weaken them, and they would start making poor decisions. If Cassi started making poor decisions, even one, even a paralysis of indecision at a critical moment, it could get them all killed.

And with the wreckage of the *Endurance* smoldering in the distance, the matter of minutes or hours left on Dienne had now reset. Days? Weeks? The certainty of rescue crumbled through her fingers and now she was left facing an entirely different set of priorities.

Water was now at the top of that list. They could no longer put off drinking the Dienne water.

Emica volunteered to drink first.

"I can't let you do that," Cassi said.

"Why not?"

Because you're my best friend and I don't know if I'll survive this if something goes wrong. But Cassi couldn't say that. The mission commander had to make decisions based on cold logic, what was best for the mission.

Right now, what was best for the mission was Emica drinking the water.

"Okay."

Sijani brought water from a river that ran near the survey site. She and Emica boiled and cooled it, and Emica tested it again. She removed one of MURPHI's optical sensors and connected it directly to her tracker to re-construct her microscope. Still the best she was getting was about 98% contaminant free, but the contaminants had to be environmental. It wasn't biology that killed the pathogens, but physics. At the temperature required to keep the water at a boil the molecules needed for any kind of life just couldn't hold together. Their atomic bonds ruptured.

Cassi couldn't help but think about thermophile bacteria—microorganisms that could survive temperatures over 100 degrees Celsius. They were rare on Avalon and on any world humans had colonized, but they existed.

Would boiling the water protect them from the pathogen? Cassi hated not knowing for sure, but at this point survival was all about calculating and managing risk, not eliminating the risk. It was now a given that they were going to have to drink the water eventually.

Emica turned over her K205 to Cassi. They all watched her as she filled her water bottle and then took a long drink, about 250 mils. She wiped her mouth and looked around at everyone with enforced confidence. "I'll be fine."

Bauer quietly armed his weapon.

They waited for two hours, the seconds passing slowly. Cassi watched Emica intently, the sweat that beaded on her temples, the movements when she shifted her weight, what she looked at, what she said. All the while Cassi sweat herself, viscerally aware that she was using her best friend as a guinea pig.

It had only taken a few minutes for the microbes to infect the striders. And Lapoint said that the *Bee*'s flight crew weren't gone for an hour. So they had decided on two hours as a safety threshold.

At 2:00:00 after Emica had taken her drink, Cassi's tracker chimed.

"That's good enough for me," Quinton said. He held his water bottle over the makeshift pot they'd made out of a metal server box, and dunked it, the bottle releasing large glugging bubbles just under the surface.

Cassi walked up to Emica and embraced her tightly. Maybe that wasn't what a mission commander was supposed to do, but she needed to hold her friend. She closed her eyes and held back tears.

"I'm fine," Emica whispered.

Cassi couldn't let go of her.

"Cassi. I'm fine. I'm okay."

Cassi trembled with some kind of psychological hypothermia. She couldn't stop her muscles from shivering. The weight of her own K205 attached to the undersuit vambrace on her right arm felt like a shot put, like she couldn't hold it up.

"So, are we okay to drink the water then?" Kroyle asked. When Cassi looked up at him, she saw the pain that he was in. His eyes had sunk back into his skull and his skin seemed to have shriveled, showing creases where it wasn't inflamed from the land anemone. He had barely complained, but he was hurting.

She glanced at Quinton and his blood-crusted leg. He was hurting too. And it was her fault. All of this was her fault. All she'd had to do was stay the course, do what was asked of her and they would all be back on Avalon right now, probably at the Sky Guy Pub n' Grill celebrating the successful completion of their mission. Instead, they were here.

She looked at Emica, okay for now, but she'd just rolled the dice on her best friend's life. And she'd been ready to shoot her.

Cassi pushed Emica away. "I'm sorry."

"Cassi?"

"Just... I need a minute."

"Can we have a drink or not, ma'am?" Pelly asked.

"I don't know." Cassi turned and threw down Emica's weapon. She tore off her own K205 and threw it on the ground.

"Well, that helps," Sijani grumbled.

Cassi balled her fingers into tight fists. The urge to scream boiled in her gut. Instead, she turned and ran.

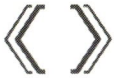

SIXTEEN-YEAR-OLD CASSI stood before Lieutenant Balachandar Singh in her cadet fatigues. The left arm pocket was unzipped, her right pant leg wasn't properly bloused around her boot, her beret sat on her head like a partially warmed marshmallow. She dropped her duffel bag on the tarmac and presented herself with as much confidence as she could muster.

"Sir, Cadet Cassiopeia Requin, reporting as ordered."

She was the twentieth cadet in a line of sixty. The academy had them out on the spaceport tarmac, formed up into long lines in the order they got off the shuttles, standing, carrying with what little personal gear they could each fit in a duffel bag. Lieutenant Singh and the other instructors sat behind little portable tables. One by one, they interviewed the cadets and formally admitted them into the program... right there where they were still close enough to feel the heat radiating off the shuttle engines.

There'd been a problem with the seventh cadet in Cassi's line. A tall, lanky kid with neatly combed hair and ears like radar dishes saluted the lieutenant in a manner that suggested he had no idea what he was doing. He answered every question as if he were on a battlefield, loud and sharp, despite the lieutenant's instructions to relax. Cassi and the other cadets watched in tense silence when Singh stood up, hands on his hips.

"Son, is this a forgery?"

The cadet glanced around. His face flushed pink. He swallowed. "No. Sir."

Singh glared at him. The ice in his eyes chilled Cassi to her core, despite the dozen cadets between the instructor and her. "If this is a forged acceptance letter, that's a serious offense. In that uniform, you're subject to Alliance Expeditionary Fleet Act regulations and the Cadet Code of Discipline—whether you're actually admitted to the Cadet Corps or not. If you admit the forgery now, I can have a flight arranged home. You'll only have to reimburse the Alliance for the cost of flying you out here."

"Sir, it's not—"

"We have a database, Son." He showed the cadet a virtual window. "This is your file right here. You didn't score high enough on the mathematical aptitude, and it looks like your psychological evaluation was marginal. You were not offered admission to the academy."

"Sir, I've wanted to get into the fleet my whole life—"

Singh held up a hand. "Sorry." He pointed to a covered waiting area off to the side and didn't say another word until the cadet hung his head, threw his duffel bag over his shoulder, and did as he was told.

Two more joined him before Cassi reached the lieutenant.

She stood in front of him now, throat dry, sweat collecting inside her fatigues in the hot sun. Singh skimmed through her file, checking over her scores and assessments. That reassured her a little. Her tests were legitimate. Cassi had earned her spot.

It wasn't until he got to the permission form that he paused and looked up at her.

"Is there something wrong, sir?"

Singh pinched the bridge of his nose with his thumb and forefinger.

"Cadet, this form is fourteen years out of date. Look, it has a section about Wallace House assignment. Wallace House wasn't even a possible assignment when I was a cadet."

Cassi swallowed. She'd prepared for this as best she could. "Sir, my father was a master sergeant in the Alliance Spacemobile Marines. He... he died when I was three years old. In combat. When he was still alive, he filled this out for me, because it was a dream of his that I join the fleet. I could have given you my mother's signature, but I was hoping, for sentimental reasons, that this would suffice."

It was true of course, that her father had died in battle. But there hadn't been a form. Cassi had carefully dug through archives and found an unused digital form from the brief period where she and he had both been alive. She electronically forged his signature.

Singh pursed his lips together. "Yeah. Well, it checks out. It's just odd." He smiled, flashing white teeth. "Welcome to the Avalon Alliance Cadet Corps Academy, Cadet Requin. I'm sure you'll do your father proud."

She forced out her own smile, the kind that emerged from genuine joy, mixed with the guilt and stress of knowing that whatever she could build here would rest on a foundation with at least one loose stone that could roll at any moment.

After a month of fighting about it, begging her mother to sign her into the academy and getting nothing but shut down, Cassi moved out of her mother's house two months before the academy training cycle began. She packed up her things and left a written note on the kitchen table for her mother to find one evening when she came home from her job at the university.

Cassi lived on her own for two months—sixteen years old, earning money for rent and food as a freelance programmer, all the while preparing for life as a cadet, studying or training every spare minute she had.

Her mother never came to visit her once.

CASSI FOUND A CREEK a few hundred meters from the survey station. She stopped on its rocky bank and fell onto her hands and knees. Her breath quivered. She wasn't sure whether she was going to vomit or not, or if her body even had enough fluid left for that kind of thing or if she'd be stuck dry heaving. She looked at her reflection in the alien water, all distorted by ripples on the surface. Her skin was covered in grime and blemishes from not having properly washed in however many days it had been. Tears streaked through the dust on her cheeks.

She couldn't take this anymore.

Something rustled the rocks beside her, and she didn't even look. Everything on this planet wanted her dead. It was just another threat and at this point, she wished something would just grab her and kill her quickly. At least then she wouldn't be responsible for anyone else anymore.

Emica sat down beside her and crossed her legs.

"What do you want?"

Emica picked up a stone and skipped it over the water. "Bauer told everyone to take a few minutes for themselves."

She offered Cassi her water bottle, stretching out her arm in silence.

Cassi sat back on her heels and all of a sudden felt ridiculous. She wiped whatever was left of her tears on the back of her sleeve and then sat back beside Emica.

For a long time the two of them said nothing, they just sat and watched the water rush by and shimmer in the sun. The river reminded Cassi of the mountain rivers back on Avalon, white water racing over sedimentary slate rock. This was also cold glacial runoff. It was clear enough she could see to the bottom, at least three feet down. Shoelace-like fish slithered through it, flashes of shadow and light.

"This is what it's all about, you know?" Emica said. Her voice was so quiet, Cassi wasn't sure if she'd actually heard it, or if she was just imagining it. "We're training to become explorers, to push the boundaries of the human envelop. It's not supposed to be easy.

"But then... this. A river, out in the middle of this alien world. I mean, sure, there's probably something in it that will eat us, but it's not like there weren't crocodiles back on Earth. There's a beauty to it that we haven't really had a chance to appreciate. After jumping across light years of space, almost burning up in this planet's atmosphere, getting attacked by pirates and monsters... we get to be the first humans to see what parts of this planet are like, naked and untouched."

Cassi sighed, grabbed the water bottle and drank, allowing Dienne water into her body.

It tasted so refreshing. She downed almost the whole bottle and then realized she was taking too much and handed it back.

Emica smiled. "Here, I've got something."

She fished open her pack and inside opened a little tinfoil wrapper. A pair of chocolate truffles.

"I was saving these for when we got back, but hey. Maybe now is a better time?"

Emica picked one up and held it out. "Intrepid Twins?"

Cassi smiled. "No trouble too to tough to be trounced by truffles."

Warm, buttery chocolate melted over her tongue, flooding her blood with sugar. The truffles were Emica's personal recipe. Cassi had once asked her what was in them and the cadet simply smiled and said, "chocolate."

They both savored the treats as they dissolved in their mouths. Cassi even savored the aftertaste and waited a long time before rinsing it away with the rest of the water.

"You don't have to get it perfect, you know."

Cassi wasn't sure whether Emica was talking about the mission or the truffles. Maybe both.

"You make the best decisions you can in the moment and then you do everything you can to make them work."

"Sure." That sounded like something Cassi would say.

The trembling in Cassi's fingers steadied, at least a little. The headache was still there. Dehydration headaches didn't just disappear when you had something to drink. They could take hours to ebb. But the psychological stress of thirst was gone. Maybe it was replaced with the uncertainty of the water supply, but that, at least, was manageable.

Water was solved. And Cassi was still in charge. She had to move down the list to the next greatest threat to her mission crew. But she didn't know what that was.

Emica looked down at her wrist. "The battery on my tracker is getting low. It's at twenty five percent."

Another problem. The trackers were both their connection to the archives of human knowledge, and each other. If a cadet needed to look up how to start a fire or how to build a shelter, it was just a few taps away. Without their trackers, the dynamic out here would shift. That advantage would be ripped out from under them.

"Do you think Pelly might be able to rig up some kind of charging system, you know, now that he can cannibalize the survey station?"

Cassi thought about that for a moment. "I'm sure he could."

"Should I tell him to get on that?"

Cassi took a deep breath. "No."

Emica raised an eyebrow.

"I'm not sure about putting that on his shoulders right now."

"What do you mean?"

"Pelly's fourteen years old. I worry about over-burdening him, even if he is a prodigy." They needed the trackers, but they needed Pelly more. He'd been resilient so far.

Emica nodded. Cassi could read in her face that she hadn't thought about asking too much from Pelly. "Maybe I could try to come up with something."

Cassi stared at the stream. She wanted to peel off her undersuit and slip into it, to submerge and scrub off the days of sweat salt and dirt that worked into her skin. There was something ritualistic about cleansing. But that water was still a big question mark. The boiled water was safe enough. But could they bathe in a river?

She'd been nursing a theory that the pathogen had to get into a person's bloodstream directly to take effect. Only the injured striders turned on the others. But what was safe? Did a minor scrape on the skin make someone susceptible?

Rubbing her temples, Cassi stared down at the water as it flowed past. The bottom was smooth with polished little stones in a bed of sand. It dropped off quick into a dark murk beneath the shimmering surface. She listened to the soft rush and babble. She breathed in the scent of mud and turned earth and… something else.

A heavy footstep crunched pebbles behind her.

When she looked up Emica stood in front of her frozen, mouth open.

"What is it?" Cassi mouthed.

A shadow stretched over her, and she felt air pressure build across the back of her neck and shoulders.

Slowly Cassi turned.

The creature behind her was about the size of a horse, its skin thick and crusted, plated with armor on the back like an ankylosaurus dinosaur, and its body covered in yellow-grass-like shag. Four mandibles like bony scythes protruded from the sides of its skull. It stared at Cassi with thousand-year-old black eyes, paralyzing her with instinctual fear.

"What do we do?" Emica asked. Neither of them had their weapons.

Mandibles the size of Cassi's forearms quivered. It crouched down, the muscles in its rear legs tensing, tendons and sinew tightening under its skin.

"Dive," Cassi said.

She dodged a predatory attack, the mandibles scissoring shut with a snap. It cut at the air just above her as she hit the water and dove into the fastest flowing current she could find. She dove deep and kicked hard, and crawled through the water as streamlined as she could make herself.

Emica followed.

When she came up for air the monster was after them, charging through the water, a thousand of pounds of muscle and armored plating all barreling down, splashing, on the attack.

For such a massive creature, it moved with surprising agility, bounding over the rocks.

When Cassi came up for air, its mandibles snapped at her head, so close she felt the movement of air across her face.

Emica slammed against a rock, dunked under in a spray of white water, and then rolled up on an exposed boulder like a landed fish. The predator slowed and turned its attention on her.

Cassi clawed her way out of the flow, and forced fingers numb from the cold to pick up a six-foot-long driftwood branch. Shivering, she climbed onto the rocks, wound up and slammed the branch against a bony ankle joint so hard the wood snapped.

The strike did enough. The massive predator had been balanced precariously on the river rocks and the strike acted like a foot sweep, knocking the monster's hind legs out from underneath it.

Its weight shifted back, and it fell into the current.

Cassi hopped over the rocks and helped Emica up. Together they broke into a sprint, back up the riverbank, over thorny shrubs and through sedge grass.

"Quinton! Bauer!" Cassi cried forcing her voice as loud as she could make it.

The beast clawed its way out of the water and let out a shrill cry, snapping its mandibles.

"Over here!" Emica cried.

CRACK!

A K205 round zipped through the bushes and landed right between the four mandibles. Then another. And another. Blood splattered as armored plates cracked and the beast recoiled.

CRACK! Four.

It ambled toward Emica.

CRACK! Five.

It crouched and backed a few paces.

CRACK! Six.

The predator turned and scurried into bushes, disappearing within the foliage.

At the same time Bauer came running out of a fungal grove, Quinton ambling behind, their weapons ready.

"What's going on?"

"Cassi?" Quinton huffed. "You okay?"

She couldn't stop shivering. The combination of cold water and adrenaline sent her into hypothermic shock. Her teeth chattered and she suddenly realized how cold she was.

Bauer scanned the bank for any sign of the creature, or anything else predatory.

Emica, shivering too, could at least talk and managed to describe what was going on.

Quinton hugged Cassi.

It took her a few minutes to realize he was trying to transfer his body heat to her. "Easy, Cassi," he said. "You're hypothermic. You need to get warmed up."

As uncomfortable as it was, as hard as it must have been for Quinton to wrap his arms around her, he didn't flinch. He used his gross pit-stained undersuit top to towel her off and then hugged her. And for a long time, Cassi didn't say anything. She just warmed up.

THE SUN WAS STARTING to set before Cassi could speak coherently again. The cadets put her and Emica in their pressure suits and Taura filled their water bladders with heated water that they then used to raise their core temperatures.

As they did, Cassi gradually became aware of the noises around their camp.

"It's the haelocron," Quinton said. "It knows we're here and it's circling, waiting to strike."

"When will it go away?" Sijani said.

"I don't think it will," Pelly answered. "They're predators. They won't give up on a meal that easily."

"I can deal with it," Quinton said.

Sijani stared at him. "You're injured and half delirious with fever."

"It's going to come back," Quinton argued. He swallowed. "I know how to hunt. We need food."

"I'm a vegetarian," Sijani said.

Quinton stood up, grimacing with the weight on his leg. "I'll go with him," Pelly said, standing too.

Bauer got to his feet as well and brushed himself off.

"Bauer..."

It was the first thing she'd said in a while. She still wasn't fully recovered. "Stay."

"But I'm..."

She glared at him. In her mind the logic was reasonable. Kroyle was a mess with his skin still reacting to that land anemone. Emica and herself were still recovering. Taura had moved into the role of nurse and though qualified, would probably hesitate to shoot a haelocron unless it was gnawing her leg off. And Cassi still didn't fully trust Lapoint. The sun was going down. She needed someone close who she could trust to picket.

Or did she just want Bauer close?

Quinton and Pelly reloaded their K205s and disappeared into the fading light.

Was that the right decision? It seemed to rub just about everyone the wrong way.

NOISES CRACKED IN THE dark.

Bauer snapped up and aimed his weapon into the darkness. He tapped his targeting goggles and squinted.

"What is it?" Cassi asked.

"I can't see anything."

More rustles. Crisp dead grass crunched.

Cassi's tracker showed that he armed his K205.

She looked up. It was dark now. The sky was full of stars, but Dienne's moons were on the other side of the planet, casting the terrain in a deep black void. The river rushed in the distance, bathing them in soft white noise. Dienne insects chirped and buzzed, all invisible to human eyes.

"Something's out there."

Kroyle armed his weapon as well. "You think it's that haelocron?"

"Drade," Cassi called out in a projected whisper.

"House."

Pelly stumbled out of the darkness, staring at a virtual window. When he noticed the cadets, he wiped the window away. "Am I glad to see you guys."

"Pelly, where's Quinton?" Bauer asked, looking out into the darkness.

"I don't know. He turned off his tracker to save battery power. I lost track of him. For a guy with a wounded leg, he moves fast."

"Pelly!" Sijani said. "The last time you lost someone..." she trailed off.

"It's not my fault. Neither of us thought it would get that dark. I tried to look for him for like an hour, but then I figured if he lost me, he would have circled back here."

"We should look for him," Kroyle suggested.

Cassi's gut turned. She was still in her pressure suit, finally warm. "Not in the dark. We'll be out there with weapons, unable to see each other, with a haelocron and who knows what else hunting us. We need to wait for the light."

Sijani was tucked up beside one of the modular server stations, hugging her knees, her pressure suit draped over her shoulders like a cape. "Cassi's right. Quinton knows how to take care of himself. It'll be light in a couple hours. Until then, we should stay where we are."

Bauer was clearly agitated. He was agitated by the fact that she'd made him stay in the first place, and now that his friend was out there in the alien wilderness alone, he couldn't sit still. He just peered out into the void, as if his eyes might adjust a little more and offer some hint to Quinton's whereabouts.

Cassi tried to sleep more, but like all of them, she couldn't. Sijani boiled some water and tried making a tea with a hairy crimson lichen that AXON was able to identify and had been cataloged as a potential source of carbohydrates. The tea turned into a kind of pasty soup that tasted like spaghetti squash. As she dished it out, Pelly perked up.

"Did you hear that?"

Cassi couldn't hear anything but the river.

A K205 cracked quietly in the distance. The sound distorted, warping as it traveled across the uneven foothills. Bauer glanced at a virtual screen and then pointed, having tracked the source of the sound with audio software. "That was a K205 for sure. The tracker identified it by the report signature."

More cracks.

Then silence.

It was still too dark to set out. Cassi looked to the horizon, willing the sun to come up. Was that a call for help? Was Quinton stuck in a bog somewhere? Tangled up in a land anemone? Captured by Lapoint's crew or another robot they'd sent after the cadets?

Emica came over and sat beside her. "We'll find him."

CASSI WAS JUST SLIPPING her backpack on when Pelly jumped up.

"Thad!"

Quinton came limping over a hill, hunched forward, his pressure suit tied around his back like a partially inflated parachute. Blood ran down the sides of his undersuit. He was limping and leaning on a walking stick.

His white teeth beamed through the grey mist, a hundred meters away.

"Is he carrying a head?" Sijani said, wiping stands of hair out of her face.

Pelly tapped his targeting goggles. "Looks like the head of a haelocron."

Sijani's face twisted in disgust. "What's he doing with that?"

"Guess what I killed?" Quinton called out. "I mean... uh... House."

No one had challenged him. He snickered as if that was some kind of joke in his version of reality.

"Where were you all night?" Bauer demanded, his voice carrying equal parts frustration and elation.

In the camp, Quinton dropped his pack and the monster's head rolled. He'd hacked off the mandibles, leaving a thick, bony skull.

"Quinton! You didn't have to decapitate the thing," Sijani complained.

"Yeah. I did."

Sijani bit her lip but couldn't hide the anger in her eyes. Quinton looked away from her.

He sat down and stretched out his injured leg. Sweat damped his short hair, drawing it together in natural spikes. He took a deep drink of water, the last in his canteen before Emica filled it up again for him.

"It was hunting us," he said, referring to both himself and Pelly. Then he pointed to his leg. "Sorry, I had to ditch you, Pelly, but it wasn't safe. It was tracking my blood trail.

"I climbed up an escarpment and hid in the rocks. It came sniffing in the night. I had to wait until it was on top of me. I lay there shivering on the rocks for like an hour, but when it came, that was it. I shot it through its open mouth.

"It still took four shots to kill the thing."

"But why'd you bring back the head?" Emica asked. "There's not much meat on that."

"No. There isn't. But I think there's something else."

CHAPTER TWENTY-FOUR

The haelocron's head smelled awful. Hair hung down in matted dreadlocks about eight to ten inches long making it look like a giant mop with bony plating protecting the top of the skull. A pair of bloody sockets with severed tendons dangling out of them remained where the bone-crushing mandibles has been. Dead black eyes stared up at the sky. A million little bugs jumped out of the hair and zipped around in circles and then disappeared again. The monster's head was its own biome.

Quinton poked at it with his fingers. In an odd way he reminded Cassi of a biology professor. "Dienne haelocrons are the result of an evolutionary process that has seen multiple cycles of water-to-land transitions and adaptations."

He pulled back some of the animal's hair. A new and even more foul scent rose up, as if simply touching it released some pent-up gas. The wound underneath was wet with a black, greasy slime. The slime was all over Quinton's shoulder from having carried it, all over his undersuit and mixed with blood.

Cassi's stomach tightened. It was empty enough she wasn't too worried about puking again, but she still had to step back for some fresh air, to keep from dry heaving.

"The head's full of natural triglycerides." Quinton cocked a half smile. He turned to Lapoint. "Didn't you say that there were a lot of natural nitric acid pools around?"

The geologist's eyebrows lowered. "Yeah."

Pelly crouched down and wrote out some chemical equations in the dirt and then scratched the back of his neck, staring at them.

Quinton underlined the sodium hydroxide. "We can boil some hardwood ash, scrape it right off the top."

Pelly tucked his chin into the notch between his thumb and forefinger, but then nodded.

Bauer looked around. "What?"

Sijani rolled her eyes. "He's talking about making an explosive, Bauer."

"Wait... you can do that?"

Lapoint nodded. "It's not impossible."

As Quinton took some time to rest, Pelly, Emica and Bauer got to work extracting the haelocron oil. They boiled it down to flaky white cake as Sijani, Kroyle and Lapoint roamed up the rocky hillside on mining detail. Using their trackers and Lapoint's geological expertise they were able to find a nitric acid pool in a cave about a kilometer away.

After spending the day on the project, the cadet crew had created a crude but relatively stable chemical explosive. Taking apart some metal batteries, they fashioned a set of rudimentary bombs.

Bauer and Quinton also went back to the site of the kill. They quartered the haelocron carcass and brought back meat. They cooked it over a small fire, providing a protein-heavy compliment to Sijani's tea-soup. Quinton also managed to dry some of the meat into jerky.

As they worked, Cassi made up her mind on what to do next. The idea had been there for a while, since they'd first seen the survey site really. But like any bold idea, she'd needed to digest it first, think it through, consider if from different angles and work through the repercussions. The more she thought about it, the more it seemed like their best option.

Sijani's reaction was predictable. "You're insane, Cassi. You're dehydrated and that's completely obstructed your capacity for rational thought."

Cassi put her hands on her hips. "I'm fine."

"That is what an insane person would say," Lapoint said. He smiled smugly and then looked around at the cadets staring at him. "I'm just saying it out loud."

"How are we supposed to commandeer the *Bee*?" Pelly asked. He didn't look at all impressed with the idea. "Just because we've completed a few live-fire exercises doesn't make us soldiers."

"We go around them," Cassi said. "Only engage as a last resort. The point is, if we can get into the *Bee*, we can lock them out. Everything they have is inside that spacecraft. Their hull's not compromised like ours was."

"We'd still be under siege," Kroyle said, "Assuming we can even get inside in the first place."

"We're going to be under siege out here anyway. I mean, we're already more-or-less playing every move like they have us under surveillance." Bauer stepped up beside Cassi and turned his attention straight on Sijani. "Would you rather we dig holes and sharpen sticks?"

"We can set up a minefield, at least."

"We have a dozen bombs," Bauer argued. "And we have to ignite them by fuse. That's not really enough to establish much of a mine-based defense. With Cassi's plan we get a torronite hull between them and us."

Pelly cleared his throat. "Ma'am, how much are you depending on me to hack the *Bee's* security systems? I mean, I'm good, but... depending on the system they have..."

"We shouldn't need to hack anything," Bauer said. He nodded toward Lapoint.

"He has the access codes," Cassi explained.

"As of about three days ago," Sijani said. "They might have changed them by now."

Cassi nodded. "Look, I understand the trepidation here. I didn't even want to propose this as a possible course of action. But they won't be expecting a crew of cadets to go on the offensive. We can sneak up to their perimeter. If it looks like it's really going to be that bad of an option, we sneak out. With any luck, they won't even know we're there until we're inside and secure."

"Maybe we should vote," Sijani suggested.

"No." Bauer crossed his arms. "This is not a democracy. We have a chain of command."

"It's okay, Bauer." Cassi spoke softly. "It's not a democracy. But I'm not going to order anyone into an assault against their will either. If we go, it's a unanimous decision. So.... all in favor?"

She and Bauer put up their hands.

Emica backed Cassi pretty quickly.

Quinton glanced around, looked at his leg, then his K205. "I'm in."

Kroyle shivered. His condition was getting worse. The welts on his skin were bright red, with patches of milky white, and weeping in places. His body was fighting whatever foreign toxin that anemone introduced. There was a chance that at some point, the irritation would be too much to bear and he'd drop to the ground writhing in agony. For the moment he held it together. There would be medical supplies on the *Bee*. There, they could sedate him if they had to. He put up his hand.

Pelly looked down at his tracker. "The probability of success is not as high as I'd like, but I don't think this is something we can look at in absolute terms. It's a relative choice. Cassi's proposal has a higher probability of success than a defense of this survey station, by at least a factor of two."

"So you're in?" Bauer asked.

Pelly put up his hand.

That left Sijani. "Well I think it's a risky, stupid idea. We don't have to dig in here. We can keep moving, make ourselves impossible to find."

"But if rescue does come, how will they find us?" Kroyle asked. "How will we even know when they arrive?"

"I'm just pointing it out."

Taura Sijani had always been a popular girl. Good-looking, smart, from a rich family. Even at the academy she had a cohort of other girls who followed her around like lapdogs. She wasn't used to being the odd person out. Those she kept close to her usually agreed with just about anything she said out of some kind of beta instinct.

"I didn't say I was out." Taura put up her hand, though not without some reluctance.

"Well, that's it then. We're doing this." Bauer sounded a little less sure than Cassi would have liked.

Cassi pointed to Lapoint. "You get a say too."

"How kind of you."

"Are you in?"

The man sighed and looked down at his ankle. "I don't know how much help I'm going to be."

"You know that spacecraft... all the little things that we can't look up or figure out through observation or that you might remember from training. We need you."

"Yeah," Lapoint said. "Sure, kid. I'm in."

CHAPTER TWENTY-FIVE

As dawn broke the next day, the cadets filled their water bottles again and began the long march back in the direction they'd come.

It took them six Dienne days to make the trek back to the wreckage of the *Lucky Bee*. They could have made it in less time, but Pelly managed to pinpoint the site of the *Endurance* crash, so Cassi decided they needed to scout it out, in the event anyone survived.

"I really don't think anyone could have survived that," Lapoint complained, as he limped along with the cadets. "They were in a nosedive and supersonic speed. And you saw the fire ball."

Cassi knew he was right. The probability of anyone having survived such a crash was extremely low. "We have to look," she said. "I know the odds are against it, but if anyone did survive, maybe they could use our help. Maybe a dropship managed to get out at the last second... and now they're on the ground trying to figure out what to do. We have a duty to look."

The old geologist rolled his eyes. But Cassi kept walking and Lapoint kept following, limping along behind her, trying to keep up.

Cresting a hill, the trees opened to a view of the smoldering crater. Thin columns of smoke rose from fires that hadn't yet burned out. The ground was charred, black like a god had sprayed it with a massive flame thrower. Wreckage was strewn out over a three kilometer radius. Their trackers didn't pick up any signals.

Cassi sent Emica, Sijani and Bauer into the crash site to investigate closer, but they came back empty handed.

"We couldn't even find the flight data recorder," Bauer said, shaking his head. The sun was going down on them. "There's a chance the Bee's flight crew will guess this move and look for us here, so I don't want to spend any more time crawling around that wreckage than we need to."

Cassi nodded.

"There weren't any signs of life," Emica reported. "Like, it's so bad down there, we'd be hard pressed to find DNA samples."

"It's that bad?" Pelly asked.

All three scouts nodded.

"Right then. We keep moving." Cassi got to her feet and hoisted up her pack.

"It'll be dark soon," Lapoint said.

"That's why we need to move. We're taking a risk being this close to the wreckage." That wasn't to mention her walking wounded had had some time to rest. Instinct told her that sticking around the wreckage was a bad idea. Or perhaps it was just cold fear of something Cassi didn't want to confront. The deaths of dozens of astronauts on the *Endurance* who were only trying to rescue the cadets haunted her, like ghosts now living in the alien soil.

So they moved.

Though not far. Even the healthy cadets were fighting a battle against dehydration and hunger.

By the third night away from the outpost, it was clear Quinton had a fever. His hairline was constantly wet with sweat and his skin grew so pale that he looked like a walking corpse. They kept him hydrated and Sijani kept the gash in his thigh as clean as she could to slow the progress of the infection. But as the days wore on, Quinton took on a stiff-legged limp. And worse, the fatigue of the constant internal battle wore on him.

A couple of times he wandered away from the squad. Sometimes he was hunting. Sometimes they had to use up time searching for him, and when they found him, he seemed distant. His answers to questions took longer than usual and he kept holding his head and staring at the ground.

And that placed another issue front and center. Losing MURPHI meant they also lost AXON, and AXON was their weapon interlock system. As mission commander, Cassi could instantaneously lock or unlock the K205s, effectively authorizing lethal force. But with AXON offline she had to leave each system unlocked. That handed full responsibility for the weapon over to each individual, which on the face of it was fine. Legally there was no problem with that. They were under threat of violent attack and when the Alliance issued a weapon to one of its officers it was placing full trust in that officer to wield it in accordance with Alliance doctrine and spirit.

But at what point would Quinton's fever compromise his ability to make reliable decisions? She had to constantly assess and re-assess whether she would need to take his weapon away from him. But Cassi had no clear guidelines, no litmus test to ensure he was competent enough to carry the K205. It wasn't like she could base a decision on whether Quinton could name Avalon's Colony Premiere. While he might eventually lose enough of his faculties that he could no longer be trusted with the rail gun, Quinton was her best shot in the absence of the automated targeting system—another element that disappeared when AXON winked out. And he was the only experienced hunter in the crew. When the haelocron jerky ran out, she needed him.

There was pressure from both sides, and no obvious correct path forward.

Kroyle had to march without a shirt, or a backpack. The wounds on his skin flared like giant welts that wept a yellow puss, and any touch at all grated on him. Sijani gave him a regular dose of the analgesics in the first aid kit and that kept the pain under control, but medicating pain was a tricky task. It was a dynamic and exponentially increasing problem. Kroyle's condition was getting worse, and his body was adapting to the medication, meaning that if they wanted to maintain the comforting affect, each dose had to be increased. And what would they do when they ran out?

Both of those problems—Quinton and Kroyle—were time dependent. Shorten the duration of their stay on Dienne and the consequences were minimized.

Lapoint proved to be more mobile than Cassi would have considered for someone with a broken ankle. Pelly's knee-crutch allowed him to keep a brisk walking pace. Once he got through his periodic bellyaching and griping about being led by a group of kids, he fell in line and did everything asked of him. Cassi's trust in him was growing, but he still wasn't one of them, and never would be.

They took six days to reach the *Bee* not just because of the physical complexity of traveling cross country on a planet without any roads, but because Cassi wanted to take the long way around. Cassi wanted to come at the *Bee* from behind.

"Tell me about them," Cassi said, walking up beside Lapoint as they got closer to the crash site. "Your flight crew."

"Not sure what you want to know, Skipper," Lapoint grumbled. The way he said 'skipper' sounded like he was mocking her. Without MURPHI, her options for protocol enforcement were limited and he seemed to take pleasure in that. But he still drilled down to the point quickly. "It's not like what they are now is what they used to be."

"Okay. But give me something. Even physical descriptions might be helpful."

Lapoint laughed.

"Hondo's the skipper. He's about this tall," Lapoint held up his hand as high as he could reach, then he held his hands out as wide as they would go, "and this broad. The guy used to be an Alliance Spacemobile Marine. He didn't talk about his service all that much, at least, not with us, the survey crew, I mean. Hondo is, or at least was, a clockwork marine. Punctual, to the point, and he didn't let little details escape him." Lapoint shook his head. "If he still has his full faculties about him, there's a good chance he will have anticipated this move of yours and he's got some trap waiting for us."

"Good to know. What about the others?"

"The other one is Beja Oswald, our flight engineer. He's ex-military too, though I'm not sure what he used to do for them. I'd call him tall and lanky, but in a used-to-run-track kind of way."

"It's only the two of them?"

"They killed everyone else." Lapoint looked away. Cassi hadn't forgotten that he'd lost the people he worked with. It was likely they were close friends. Lapoint was grieving.

"Either way, I wouldn't ignore the physical prowess of either of them. If you get into a physical match up with either of them and you don't have guns to level the playing field, it will take at least two, if not three of you to match one of them."

Lapoint exaggerated the limp with his knee-crutch, as if to suggest that he wouldn't be much help. "One-on-one, hand-to-hand scenarios won't end well."

"They rarely do," Cassi said.

Bauer called a sudden halt to the column and all of them dropped down, into knee-high grass. Lapoint performed an awkward and reluctant belly flop. With his knee bent in a perpetual ninety-degree angle, the boot on his wounded foot stuck up in the air.

Someone came over a hill—Sijani.

She had mud smeared over her face and hands, and though it looked like she'd simply been rolling in the brush, she was using what she could from the environment around her for camouflage.

She signaled them all to stay down as she walked in a semi-crouch.

"What is it?" Cassi asked.

"The *Bee*," Sijani said. "Just over the next ridge."

CHAPTER TWENTY-SIX

Lapoint told Cassi that the *Lucky Bee* still had partially functioning sensors—astronomical grade optics, RF, infrared, and navigational proximity sensors. It could all be configured quite easily to passively monitor a perimeter around the spacecraft. He didn't know that they had necessarily done that, but it was both possible and probable, which meant the cadets could be spotted on any direct approach to the downed spacecraft.

Concealed from its view by a mound of rock, the cadets worked out the details of a plan.

"So, Mission Commander," Lapoint challenged, "now that we're here, what's your plan of attack?"

Cassi had been thinking about it for days but hadn't wanted to finalize anything before she actually saw the spacecraft and had an idea what the surrounding terrain looked like.

Cassi took a centering breath. "Feign and sneak," she said.

The surveyor's brow furrowed, as if he'd expected her to balk now that she was confronted with the reality of assaulting the *Lucky Bee*.

"Bauer, you and Emica are our most mobile cadets. I'm going to have you assault the spacecraft directly."

Both of them nodded, not exactly full of enthusiasm, but willing.

"Mr. Lapoint, you told us the outer hatch on the main access airlock is compromised?"

"I did."

"So to get in, Bauer and Emica, you only need to get through the second hatch. A well-placed explosion might rip that second hatch right off its hinges."

Pelly scratched the back of his head. "That compromises the structural integrity though. If we blow a hole in it, the *Bee's* crew can get back in if we can't repair it."

"That's the feign," Cassi said. "A good feign has to have a reasonable chance at working. It's a weak point. That's what they'll be expecting, if they're expecting anything. The point is that Bauer and Emica, you look like you're trying to do just that, but retreat at any sign of trouble."

"You want us to draw them out," Bauer said.

Cassi hesitated, then swallowed and looked each in the eye. "Yes. Hopefully, we can get the flight crew to pursue you, and abandon the *Bee* to give chase. Quinton, you and Kroyle provide overwatch security." She called up a topographical map on a shared window and indicated where she wanted them positioned. It was a high rocky outcrop where they would have a direct line of sight onto about two hundred and seventy degrees of arc around the spacecraft.

"Lie in wait and shoot the bastards," Lapoint said. He formed a gun with his thumb and index finger and mimed shooting. "As soon as they're out in the open. Pop. Pop. Pop."

Cassi glared at him. Huddled under the cover of the alien forest, a mottled mix of shade and light broke up and distorted the features on his face. "They're your crew."

"They killed my friends."

"The goal here is to take them alive," she said.

"So why have an 'overwatch' at all then?" Lapoint asked.

Cassi spoke more to Quinton and Kroyle than to the geologist. "You need rules of engagement. You might need to make a decision in a very short time frame. I authorize you to use lethal force if you deem it necessary to protect any one of us. If it looks like they have firearms and are about to use them... take them out."

Quinton's fingers massaged his temples. His eyes were closed, but he nodded acknowledgment.

"Aye ma'am," Kroyle said. He spoke through clenched teeth and shifted, uncomfortable in inflamed skin.

"There's a lot of 'what ifs' in there, kid" Lapoint argued. "You can't be ideal like that. In the time it takes for someone to draw a firearm, your friends here could get killed."

"That's why I have to rely on them to use their best judgment."

"Pelly, Sijani, Mr. Lapoint, and myself, are going to be the breach team. As soon as the *Bee* is abandoned, the four of us will approach the secondary starboard airlock. We can gain access using Lapoint's code, and once inside we can secure the downed spacecraft.

"Then we get the overwatch team in." Cassi turned to Quinton and Kroyle again. "I'll signal you once we're in, assuming you're not watching us. If you see us get inside, and it looks like Emica and Bauer are okay, just come as quickly as possible. Otherwise I'll text you. At that point we can break radio silence anyway."

Kroyle and Quinton nodded. Neither of them were in great condition, but there was a look of determination in Quinton's face, like he'd found a sense of purpose on Dienne, amid all of this, and he'd fight to his death to see this through. There wasn't a doubt in her mind about his commitment.

That left Bauer and Emica. Cassi let out a tense breath. "You two will either have to run like gazelles or go to ground and hide. Once we're inside the *Bee*, we'll draw the flight crew off you. Sijani and I can take up firing positions from inside the spacecraft or maybe on top of it, anything so long as we can distract the flight crew from the two of you."

Bauer glanced at Emica. "If we have to, we can retreat all the way back to the *Triumph*. We can hold out there and then loop back once things quiet down. It will give us a secondary defensible position. It's not great, but it's something."

Cassi flashed a crooked, forced smile. "Hopefully it won't come to that."

That was the plan. Cassi wasn't proud of it. And being honest with herself she didn't have a lot of confidence in it. There were a million different things that could go wrong. What if they changed the access codes? What if Emica or Bauer got caught? Was she leading her squad into a disaster?

She gave the team a few minutes to prepare themselves, drop gear, redistribute water and ammunition.

Cassi looked up at Dienne's blue sky. She wondered if Commander Dodd and Lieutenant Singh were still safe in their stasis pods. Dodd had once told her that command wasn't about making the perfect decision. It was about making *a* decision, and then making that decision work. And sometimes there was a cost to making it work.

Quinton and Kroyle moved into position, climbing up the edge of the rocky valley the *Bee* had crashed within. There they took to concealing themselves under moss and shrubbery that grew out on the rocky outcrop.

At the same time Bauer and Emica circled down to a point where they could close the gap to the primary airlock as quickly as possible.

About five hundred meters from the *Bee*, in a small bog, Pelly had gathered up a heap of deadfall. He lit the fuse on one of the makeshift bombs they'd built and ran back toward Cassi. The fuse burned for ten seconds.

WHAM!

Black smoke began billowing into the air, generating their first distraction.

The *Bee* remained quiet.

Bauer and Emica made the decision to go. With Pelly's fire roaring, Bauer and Emica raced and dove for the main access hatch.

They made it, unchallenged.

Inside the airlock, the two of them raced to rig up their explosives. Cassi estimated that would take about sixty seconds. She felt every tick on her tracker's display.

It hit sixty... then seventy.

"Come on," Cassi whispered.

Eighty... ninety...

Emica texted: *Go.* That was the signal. They'd got it.

Just as Emica turned to dash away from the explosives, the hydraulics on the massive *outer* airlock hatch whined. The torronite pressure door rolled into its locked position.

"What?"

Emica: *Trapped.*

Quiet pangs hit the torronite from inside.

Lapoint shook his head, his lips pressed tight together. "I was afraid of this."

Pelly dropped down behind Cassi, out of breath. "What'd I miss?"

"Bauer and Emica are trapped," Sijani explained.

"Oh." He sucked in a few more deep breaths.

Pelly thought for a moment as he reached for and downed some water. Then took a few more breaths to get his heart rate under control. "Tell them to disconnect the hydraulics to the inner door if they can."

"How will that get them out?" Lapoint asked.

"It won't. But it will keep the flight crew from getting in."

Cassi relayed the message.

They all waited until a soft thud thrummed through the torronite.

Emica: *Really trapped now.*

Bauer and Cassi's best friend now had the outer door locking them in and the inner door disabled, trapping them inside the airlock like a bank vault.

Quinton: *Secondary airlock compromised.*

Cassi bit her tongue. She didn't know exactly what that meant, other than she couldn't use that as a point of entry. Her plan was falling apart so quickly, crumbling through her fingers.

She'd gambled with Emica and Bauer and the dice hadn't come up good.

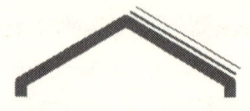

CHAPTER TWENTY-SEVEN

Cassi turned to Lapoint. "Can we get in through another access hatch?"

"I don't think so, kid."

"What about the stasis pod ejection ports?" Pelly asked.

"What about them?"

"If I can get into a maintenance panel, I should be able to login to the system and trigger a safety circuit to launch a stasis pod. That's essentially another airlock. We might be able to get in that way.

Emica sent another text: *Cassi?*

Cassi: *Hold on. Coming.*

She pointed to the nearest port that hung underneath the main body of the spacecraft. Unlike the *Triumph*, the *Bee* had managed to land right side up, with a downward pitch, her needle nose buried in the dirt.

Pelly and Sijani nodded.

Lapoint squinted, shielding his eyes from the sun. Bauer and Emica were trapped inside that thing. Cassi would shake the planet to its core to get them out. Pelly and Sijani were onside. But Lapoint was still a question mark.

The man shook his head and swore. "You kids are crazy."

Cassi grabbed his collar, balling the fabric into her fist. "I need you in too. We need you on this."

Lapoint stared at her, uncertainty in his wide eyes.

"You're under my command. When I say move, you will move. Understood, Lapoint?"

He swallowed, then nodded.

Cassi released her grip, took a deep breath, and then whispered. "Go."

She armed her K205 and led the charge across the open gap between their observation position and the *Bee's* hull. She got far out front, and then slowed down. Lapoint couldn't keep up with her at a full sprint.

FLASH!

The zing of ionized air cracked like lightning. The thick scent of ozone overwhelmed her olfactory nerves.

Lapoint fell.

"Go! Go! Go!" Sijani waved Pelly and Cassi on. She was the closest to Lapoint.

Cassi stumble-stepped and hesitated. But the increasing pitch of the capacitors charging on the *Bee's* ion ray forced her to make a quick decision. She and Pelly tore forward and dropped under the cover of the escape pod ejection port projecting from the hull. There the cantilevered ion ray couldn't reach them.

The capacitors hummed.

Geometry offered them protection. The ion ray was mounted near the top of the ship. At about two thirds of the distance they had to cover, the protruding outer hull provided cover from the ray. It couldn't hit them without cutting through the spacecraft itself.

Sijani and Lapoint didn't need to make the full distance, only about twenty meters.

"Move! Move! Move!"

Quinton and Kroyle provided cover fire, their shots pinging off the torronite hull. Hand weapons were ineffective against a spacecraft, but the shots let the *Bee's* AI know there was another threat on the field, forcing it to split or prioritize its actions.

Sijani grabbed Lapoint by the shoulders of his jacket and dragged him kicking across the ground.

The ion ray fired again.

Lapoint screamed.

Sijani got him inside the safety perimeter, as the ray charged again.

Cassi sent a text to the overwatch team. *Get out of there.*

The ion ray hit their position about seven seconds later, cracking bedrock with a hit that rumbled through the ground. The weapon was designed to cut through asteroids.

Lapoint rolled on the ground in agony, cursing. His left foot, what had up until a few seconds ago been the good one, now ended in a bloody stump. The ray had seared the flesh, leaving it blackened, but the wound was cauterized, the ends of the blood vessels stitched together by the heat, at least enough to keep him from bleeding out.

The first shot had struck Lapoint's shoulder, leaving a similar burn. He rolled on the ground, the dirt and grit contaminating the wound.

Cassi's heart raced as she cowered under the *Bee's* hull. The sprint stole the wind from her lungs and her body desperately needed oxygen. She took deep, heavy breaths.

Lapoint's leg was gone and it was because of her. She'd ordered him up, ordered him to run and now he was fighting for his life. Doubt clamped onto her like a ratcheting leg shackle, complete with chain and steel weight. He was hurt and it was her fault. Had there been a better choice? A better move? Cassi stomped on the doubt, pushing it down the way they'd trained her to at the academy. She could ruminate on poor choices later. For now, she had to push forward, make the plan work.

"We have to get pressure on those," Pelly said, pointing to Lapoint's wounds.

"Eject the stasis pod," Cassi told him. "Sijani and I can treat him."

Taura already had her medical kit open. She pulled out a pressure dressing and a sterilizer spray. Lapoint screamed when she sprayed him with the cold jet of foaming mist. The chemicals inside reacted with his wound, generating thousands of little pink bubbles, stirring the blood into a pink froth. She pasted the bandage in place and tied it down, tighter than it needed to be.

Lapoint cried.

Pelly opened the maintenance panel and skimmed over a readout, babbling to himself. "This isn't like the *Triumph*. This a Phoenix Mark Three, which means the pods run off an independent bus... and the power line is..." He pulled out a little multitool from his belt and quickly undid a couple screws, popped open another plate and flung it on the ground. "The launch sequence is interlocked to the main board and monitored by the... hey, that's amazing..."

"Pelly, focus."

His tongue worked into his cheek as he cut a couple wires. A little alarm started ringing. "Now you want to shut this down, but if I cut here," he pulled the knife and cut again. "You've got nothing, Machine. Nothing. And then... here."

He turned back to Cassi and waved his arm. "Get out of the way. This thing has explosive charges."

Cassi helped Taura drag Lapoint right up to the hull, away from the ejection port. The three of them curled up into tight little balls, pressing their bodies up against the torronite.

Pelly shouted. "FIRE IN THE HOLE!"

He short circuited a pair of terminals.

The blast sounded and felt as if he'd just lobbed a grenade into a window.

The stasis pod shot free of its launch cradle and slammed into the ground. The metal pod tumbled end over end and cartwheeled up a hundred feet in the air. Strobe lights flashed. It crashed over the far side of a hill, knocking over trees and marking the vegetation with a broad scar.

Cassi's ears rang with a shrill, high pitch.

Pelly curled up on the ground, face buried in his arms.

"Pelly!" Cassi scrambled over to the kid and shook him.

She pulled back his arms. The exhaust singed his face. It left dark jet streaks of soot and pink abrasions across his skin. Both of his eyes were closed and when the first tear wept out... it was red.

"I can't see," he said.

Cassi bit her lip. Pelly was down. She couldn't do this without him.

Sijani crawled over him. "It's Taura," she said. "I've got you."

"I can't see!"

"Go Cassi!" Taura shouted.

Cassi had to go in.

Alone.

CHAPTER TWENTY-EIGHT

Crawling into the *Lucky Bee*, Cassi felt more at home than she would have thought. There was something comforting about being surrounded by engineered walls. Every panel, wire, pipe scaffold, and bolt had a specific purpose to its presence.

Her first obstacle was getting through the stasis pod's inner airlock door, the door that kept the spacecraft's internal atmosphere from getting blown out into space if the pod launched. Once inside, she had to find the release to let Bauer and Emica out of the main airlock, all without being hunted down herself.

The pod chute had an emergency release on the inside, and that opened into the darkness of the *Bee's* water recycling and nuclear power plant. The familiar scents of metal, human sweat and musk permeated the air.

Cassi fumbled around in the darkness, her eyes still used to the bright outside, her ears still ringing. But over the ring, she heard something else, the soft purr of servo motors.

She turned just as a KONG maintenance robot pounced on her.

Two arms reached out and claw-like hands clamped down on her wrists. She struggled and fought to break free, but as strong as Cassi was, as hard as she'd pushed her body in all her cadet training, she wasn't a machine, and she might just as well have been trying to push a mountain.

It lifted her by the wrists until her feet dangled, like a strung up wild animal. She screamed, if nothing else to call out to Sijani. The machine's mechanical fingers constricted around the K205 mounted on her forearm, warping the metal, tightening around her arm like a massive handcuff.

Text flashed across her targeting goggles. *WEAPON SYSTEM FAILURE*

"Threat, neutralized," the KONG reported.

She wanted to believe that the KONG's programming wouldn't allow it to kill or hurt her. But that hadn't been the case with the robots that attacked them at the survey site. Still, for the moment, it seemed content to hold her for the crew.

All Sijani had to do was crawl up through the air lock door. She could shoot the KONG... if she could get a clear shot... but she was busy keeping Lapoint and Pelly alive.

The robot carried Cassi awkwardly through the spacecraft's hallways. Her mind raced, searching for a way to escape.

Like the *Triumph*, the *Lucky Bee* was constructed as a series of cells, each of which could be completely self-contained in the event of an emergency. Each cell had at least two pressure hatches that could be closed quickly in the event of an emergency decompression. On the *Bee*, they operated like large irises. Red and white reflective paint marked a safety zone around each—because if the system detected a decompression, the iris would slam shut. For that reason, each iris also had an emergency release that would allow the astronauts to slam it closed in the event the governing AI did not detect a decompression.

As the KONG carried Cassi through the threshold between the water recycling cell and the primary power plant, she swung her legs around and kicked open the transparent cover over the emergency release lever.

She ran her feet up the opposite wall on the backswing in an attempt to topple the machine, but it compensated and stepped over the threshold.

Cassi swung back, stretching her leg, foot and toes and she caught the release.

The KONG's optic shutters opened, a mechanical emulation of surprise.

A strobe light flashed and a klaxon sounded. But the KONG was right on the threshold.

The iris slammed shut, heavy torronite doors constricted around the KONG, crushing its steel chassis.

The robot lost its iron grip around Cassi's wrists. She broke free and fell to the floor. With a shot of adrenaline and instinct, she rolled away and came up, ready to fight.

The KONG twisted and flailed, struggling to free itself from the mechanical door iris. Electronic whines and chirps bellowed from it like some kind of robotic profanity. Green hydraulic fluid and yellow oil oozed from cracked panels. It reached for the emergency lever, but its arm was about a foot too short.

Scrambling, Cassi found a maintenance toolbox. She popped it open and pulled out a twenty-pound torque wrench.

"Here, let me help you with that."

The KONG's optical sensors turned toward the lever and that gave her an opening.

As hard as she could Cassi swung the massive wrench like a baseball bat. The robot's head crunched, broke from its articulating neck, and slammed into a bulkhead. It bounced off the floor and rolled to the far side of the cell.

The body fell limp in the doorway.

Cassi shook out her right wrist. Her K205 was out of commission. Fortunately the KONG hadn't crusher her forearm. It was already starting to bruise, but she still could still move her fingers and flex her wrist, still carry the heavy torque wrench.

Where are the crew?

Cassi crept through the spacecraft, hyper-aware of the fact the *Bee's* AI could be monitoring her every move.

The AI!

Cassi had been so fixed on thinking of the *Bee* and her crew as pirates, as antagonists, she hadn't thought of the artificial intelligence that ran the ship. If the AI identified her as hostile, it could have closed the pressure doors, trapping her in a cell... a safety confinement protocol.

But it didn't.

She slid into the craft's mess deck. For cadets, such places were a lot more like a confined study hall, but on a civilian ship, the mess was part dining room, part entertainment complex. It had twin haptic immersion pods for virtual reality gaming and physical conditioning, a full holographic projection wall, and soft lounge couches. One wall featured an automated kitchen with an old cuisine printer.

Cassi's stomach gurgled.

She opened the haptic pod, checked over her shoulder to make sure no one from the flight crew were sneaking up on her, and logged into its terminal.

Biometrics unrecognized. Unauthorized attempt at entry into system logged.

Cassi took a breath. The *Triumph's* AI had promoted her to the rank of ensign. When the *Bee* established contact with the *Triumph*, her new rank would have been transmitted as part of a standard protocol manifest packet.

She checked over her shoulder again, half expecting Hondo to be creeping up on her with a knife in his hand. But the mess was still quiet.

"Cassiopeia Requin... Ensign, Alliance Expeditionary Fleet, safety override," she said. As an Alliance-registered vessel, the *Lucky Bee's* AI system would have been subject to safety and inspection overrides.

The AI paused. Had Hondo thought to hack-proof it?

Bee AI: *Justification for override?*

"Emergency landing occurred. Full access required to assess condition of personnel and all support systems."

Bee AI: *Access granted. Welcome aboard, Ensign Requin.*

Cassi: *Identify coordinates of all personnel.*

Bee AI:

searching...

searching...

searching...

Timeout on request. Ensign Cassiopeia Requin is the only person on board. Location: Haptic Pod 03.

What? Cassi ran a quick diagnostic scan. It was possible the crash had damaged the AI enough that there were sections of the spacecraft it couldn't see.

But one-by-one, the diagnostics came back clear. The AI was working. It flashed real time views of from each of its video systems. She saw the KONG, still limp in the pressure door iris, both from the back and the front.

Well, if Hondo and Oswald weren't on the *Lucky Bee* then...

Her fingers flying on the keyboard, Cassi brought up the external cameras and turned them toward the ridge were Kroyle and Quinton were watching over the assault operation.

Both cadets were on their feet, hands in the air, K205s absent from their forearm vambraces. Rale Hondo stood behind them with a military grade tri-barreled plasma rifle trained on Quinton.

Oswald had come down the hill and had a pistol of his own on Sijani, Pelly and Lapoint. He was walking them back up the hill. Sijani pulled Pelly with her, his head down, eyes closed, his arms reaching out in front of him. Oswald dragged the semi-conscious Lapoint by the neck of his jacket.

Cassi's mind raced. Why hadn't they killed the cadets? Either they'd had the fortune of sneaking up on the *Bee* when the crew were out, or its sensors had detected their approach much further away. Hondo had quickly maneuvered to capture the cadets.

But Cassi now controlled the *Lucky Bee*. She held some big cards. She locked all other users out of the *Bee's* mainframe AI system and overrode Hondo's administrative privileges. She searched for the weapon system governor, hoping that maybe she could lock out that plasma rifle and pistol, but no luck. Those weapons weren't linked to the *Bee's* AI. What she did have, however, was full control over its ion ray.

And there was her answer. Hondo was keeping her cadets alive for leverage.

CHAPTER TWENTY-NINE

Outside, Oswald marched Sijani and Pelly up to Hondo. The leader grabbed them and tossed them on the ground. He made them lie prone, faces in the dirt, fingers interlaced on the backs of their heads, ankles crossed. They couldn't look back at either him, or Oswald.

Lapoint lay on the ground, his severed leg still bleeding profusely. Sijani had managed to stave off the worst of the bleeding, buying him some time, but Cassi guessed he would need some kind of surgical intervention soon if he was going to survive.

Cassi called up the ion cannon's maintenance screen and scrolled through a wall of readouts.

ION CANNON 3 STATUS: OPERATIONAL

At least she had some offense.

The ray produced by the ion cannon was an incredibly precise weapon. It was meant for asteroid mining operations—pumping energy into rocks to break them apart. If she had the time to line up, it could cut with near surgical precision. It was meant to be used in space, on objects dozens or even hundreds of kilometers away, where micron-changes in position mattered.

She considered using the ray to make a precise shot at the weapons Hondo and Oswald were carrying, but if she tried that, she would have to hit both of them simultaneously or risk at least one of them firing a retaliatory shot and killing one or several of the cadets. Blasting the weapons out of their hands wasn't much of an option.

Hondo glared at the spacecraft, as if he knew that she could see him. His eyes were bloodshot, his skin wet with sweat.

"Come. Out."

Cassi didn't have time to formulate a detailed strategic response. She connected to the audio on the cadet trackers to broadcast her reply.

"We're injured," she lied. "We can't come out."

Would Hondo or the others even understand? There were too many variables with too much at stake. She had to assume the worst, that the infection had turned Hondo and Oswald into homicidal maniacs.

But how do you deal with that? It was another problem that didn't have a canned solution. She didn't even know if there was a 'right' move. Wrong moves would get her friends killed. Even if she made the right moves, Hondo could still pull his trigger.

She ran her fingers through her hair. Sweat coalesced under her hairline and ran down her back.

He hadn't killed any of the cadets yet, and that was something. If he was truly possessed with some animal instinct to kill everything, he likely would have done so. He only needed one or two cadets alive to negotiate.

Maybe something more was going on.

Was there a person inside, fighting the infection? Was his immune system beating it back?

Cassi zoomed the camera in on Hondo's face. As quickly as she could, she called up biometric assessment software. The stereo vision from multiple cameras created a three-dimensional model of Hondo, right in front of her. Because the optics were designed for deep space, it picked up and mapped out every little hair, every little crevasse in his skin, every mole. The software tracked his pupils, assigning vectors to their focus, measuring, and updating their diameter. It even had the resolution to pick up blood vessels in the whites of his eyes.

What are you thinking?

It tracked his pulse. Cassi cross-referenced Hondo's biometrics with baseline measurements. It was standard medical protocol, the AI medical applications could use that data to provide flash diagnoses, sometimes catching issues before astronauts even knew there was a problem. She applied the screening apps for psychological stress. Most spacecraft had at least basic AI psychological assessment tools to monitor confinement stress, mission stress, signs of the spectrum of post-traumatic responses.

Medical warnings flashed like little textual firecrackers... suggesting Hondo was suffering anything from a transient ischemic attack to Avalonian bat flu.

His gaze darted about, suggesting he was having trouble concentrating. His pulse was elevated, and his pupils were dilated. They were all stress indicators. And the thermal imaging showed he had a fever. He was as hot as Quinton.

Is he fighting it?

Her working hypothesis was that Hondo and Oswald were infected with some kind of germ. If it were an infection, maybe it could be medicated out of him. Or if his immune system was fighting it, the homicidal tendencies might wear down with time.

In that case, Cassi might be able to get her crew through this by stalling. But for how long?

She had to get him talking.

"Tell me what you want," she said, her voice broadcasting from each cadet's tracker.

"Surrender spacecraft. Come. Out."

"I can't come out. I'm injured."

He lifted the butt of his rifle to his shoulder.

"The ion ray is armed. I have control of it. If you shoot any one of my squad members, I will fire on you."

He hesitated. His finger still wasn't on the trigger, but it was close, outstretched and resting on the trigger guard. Too close.

Get him talking.

"Who am I dealing with? What is your name?" she asked.

Hondo licked his lips. His gaze shifted, like he didn't know where she was.

His gaze kept lining up with the spacecraft's bridge, like he wanted to shoot her through the torronite.

"Tell me your name," she repeated, following her instincts. Lapoint had said he was a retired Alliance Marine. "I'm an ensign with the Alliance Expeditionary Fleet, Ensign Requin. This is a direct order marine, name rank and service number."

As if Cassi struck a nerve with a little rubber mallet, his answer came out by reflex. "Hondo, Rale Washington, Sergeant—retired, Oscar Seven Two Three Four Three..." in the midst of rattling off his number, he shook his head.

"Come out!" he screamed.

Oswald shouted at the other cadets. "Face in dirt! Face in dirt!"

Kroyle could not hold still. The inflammation within his skin had only grown worse over the past few days, and the medication in his body was only getting used up with time. He wormed around, scratching himself against the rough ground, trying to get into a tolerable position.

"No," Oswald said. To emphasize the order, he pressed the pistol against Kroyle's back. "No move."

The camera Cassi was using had enough of an angle that she could see the agony in Kroyle's face. However tough this was on all the cadets; it was worse on him. He closed his eyes and squeezed little tears out.

Hondo pulled Quinton up, his fist balled in the fabric of the cadet's shirt. He forced Quinton between himself and the ion cannon, using him as a human shield. Though smaller than the ex-marine, she would have bet on Quinton to take a swing at him anyway. But he was dehydrated, hungry, and ravaged by a fever that would have rendered most humans unable to stand up. Quinton was in no position to turn the tables, make a grab for the gun, or try to spin and take out Hondo with a right cross.

Hondo was no longer talking.

Cassi licked her lips. "Two members of my squad are trapped in your main airlock. You have the rest. I..." she couldn't bring herself to use the word *surrender*. At the academy they often joked about how it wasn't in a cadet's vocabulary. *Never surrender. Never quit.* Now that it seemed as though that was her only option, Cassi couldn't bring herself to say it.

"I'm injured," she repeated. "If you give me your word you won't kill anyone, I will stand down."

Hondo glanced at Oswald. His pulse slowed and his pupils constricted, as if her words relaxed him, if only a little. Or, if perhaps, her words confused him.

A plan slowly came together in Cassi's mind. It wasn't much of one, just a few vague ideas. But that was the way most plans started out.

Hondo nodded but lifted the rifle. "You lie."

Quinton swallowed. It took him a moment and some prodding at the open end of a plasma rifle to figure out Hondo wanted him back on his face. He slowly climbed down beside the others, his wounded leg outstretched.

"Watch," Hondo ordered Oswald. He pointed at the cadets. "Kill if trick."

"I'm standing down," Cassi reported. As a show of faith, Cassi retracted the ion ray on its cantilever arm, pulling it into a protective storage bay. A torronite capsule shield closed over it.

Hondo had two weapons at his disposal, a Tek rifle like the one Lapoint had stolen and the pistol Oswald carried. The *Lucky Bee's* skipper descended the hill toward the spacecraft, opting to bring the rifle. While the Tek rifle had more inherent power, inside the closely confined bulkheads of the commercial spacecraft, a long weapon would be tricky to manipulate. Maybe she could use that.

Though the ion ray was retracted, the targeting system was still operational. She used the AI to target and track Oswald's pistol and then over-rode the safety interlock that kept the system from firing close to a living creature. The shot, if the computer could do it, would melt the pistol right out of Oswald's hand. It might take a few fingers with it too, and there was a possibility that it could even kill him. That wasn't the kind of risk instructors at the academy would normally approve of, and Cassi wasn't sure she wanted to roll that particular die, but it was better to be ready in case that was her only option.

The ion ray's retraction took about five seconds. If Oswald didn't move, it might take the system another few seconds to pinpoint the pistol's position and perform any fine adjustment, provided he stayed where he was.

"Cadet squad," Cassi said. She tried to emphasize the next part, without emphasizing it. "Stay where you are. Comply with the *Bee*'s crew."

She set the program macro. Ten seconds, approximately, from her code word of command to a disarming shot... if it worked.

It was a long shot gamble.

And even if it worked, she still had Hondo to worry about.

CHAPTER THIRTY

Cassi raced through the *Bee*, slipping back through the mess hall and into the sleeping pod cell.

Hondo arrived faster than she'd hoped. He crawled through the access corridor she created when Pelly blew the survival pod. Now he was in the hatchway, plasma rifle in front of him.

She skidded to a stop at the mouth of the cell. Her feet slipped on the corrugated metal floor and she fell, hitting the ground hard.

He fired.

The plasma rifle thundered inside the spacecraft. The sudden pop of ionized air hurt her ears. The super-heated round punched through a bulkhead, just over her shoulder.

In the quiet that followed, the high pitch escalating sound of the weapon's capacitors recharging rang through the confined corridor.

Cassi scrambled back to her feet.

Blood.

The shot frightened her so much, Cassi hadn't realized it grazed her shoulder. Pain seared across her left arm. Blood oozed out over her sleeve and dribbled on the floor.

The plasma rifle cracked again, and she felt the air split just over her head. She dropped, after the fact, sprawling on the floor.

There was another pressure door on the other side of the sleeping cell and instinct told her to go for it. But that would give Hondo an unobstructed shot at her.

Cassi ducked behind one of the industrial sleeping pods. They were built tight into the cell's frame, right into the bulkheads. The next shot hit the steel just in front of her. Little red-hot globules of molten metal bounced off the impact site. A few struck her, burned through the fabric of her uniform, and stung her skin.

Behind the pod, she called up the far door through the link to the *Bee*'s AI on her tracker, and with a flutter of fingers, she over-rode the inner release and closed the iris.

The sudden slamming together of metal on metal gave her the slightest distraction as Hondo glanced back over his shoulder at the sound. Cassi dove through the other door, the one in front of her, just as a third shot sang through the hold.

It grazed her calf.

Hondo's boots clanged on the steel floor as he charged like a bull for the door.

Cassi grabbed the emergency release handle and pulled.

Torronite slammed against torronite.

Cassi tore off the panel and with trembling fingers, she used the maintenance wrench to unscrew the manual bolt.

Behind the door, she heard Hondo punch the touchscreen, trying to get the door to open.

Cassi cranked and cranked as fast as she could with the giant wrench and finally the nut came loose. Little warning LEDs flickered indicating the cell hatch was no longer operational.

She pulled the bolt out and flung it across the room, disabling the manual crank. Inside, Hondo swore at her.

Now for the other side.

Cassi tore off a vent screen and pulled herself into a narrow, rectangular tube. The tunnel was dusty, every surface covered with a grimy film that smelled like gymnasium floor. Most people couldn't fit through the air shafts, but for a rake of a cadet who'd barely eaten over the past week, it was possible.

And once she got going, she slipped through, like riding down a slide in a park as a kid.

She clambered over one vent and then to the next.

The plasma rifle rang out again, this time a round cut through the ventilation shaft, right behind her, close, but now she had a couple breaths before the rifle could recharge.

She punched out another screen and dropped back into the water-reprocessing and power generation cell, hitting the floor with a hard thud. She'd made it back to the other side of the sleeping quarters.

Cassi tore off the maintenance panel on that door. One more bolt and she'd have Hondo completely trapped inside.

But just as she fixed the torque wrench on it, it started to turn. The iris started opening.

With her tracker, Cassi ordered the *Bee's* AI to keep the door shut. Hydraulics pumped, trying to force the torronite panels closed.

But the manual system was designed with a massive mechanical advantage over the computerized one. If there was a fire inside, the crew had to be able to get out, regardless of what protocol the AI was running.

Cassi got the wrench onto the bolt and stopped Hondo from opening the iris any more than a couple inches. It was enough of a gap to reach through and shoot at her, though.

"Stop," Hondo barked. "You. Weak. I... marine!"

He growled and grunted, pulling on the emergency lever. His strength pulled the torque wrench up, prying the smooth neck free from her fingers.

"You're forgetting something," Cassi barked back. "Physics."

Torque was the cross product of force and the length from the point of rotation. Because the torque wrench was three times as long as the emergency crank, she only needed to apply a third the force he did to match his torque. Cassi braced herself against the wall so she could use her legs. She wrapped her fingers around the black rubber grip at the base of the wrench and pulled.

Even with the mechanical advantage, it felt like he was on the verge of crushing her against the bulkhead.

Cassi's knuckles turned white. Her face flushed red. Her legs and arms shook. Blood dribbled from the wounds on the back of her leg and her arm.

The bolt connecting the emergency lever to its inner lift hydraulic snapped. CRACK!

Cassi fell on the floor, along with a piece of the bolt.

Hondo swore.

She did it. He was trapped!

Cassi lay back on the ground, her heart beating so hard it felt like it might push all the blood out of her open wounds.

She couldn't stop now though. She crawled to her hands and knees and then sat back on her legs, kneeling. Opening the tracker, she issued one more command.

On the roof, the torronite shield rotated open and the cantilever arm quietly unfolded. The ion ray swung around, and a window popped up on her display. The AI made fine adjustments as it re-acquired the target.

Oswald's finger was still outside the trigger guard.

The border of the screen on her tracker turned red.

LOCKED

"Fire."

The thrum from the ion cannon rumbled through the *Lucky Bee's* floor.

Oswald screamed.

Quinton must have been feigning delirium. As soon as the ion beam blew the weapon out of Oswald's hand, he jumped up and attacked.

Oswald's hand was bloody, but he fought back. As Quinton tried to wrestle him over, Oswald grabbed a fist full of Quinton's short hair and used it to drag the cadet to the ground.

But before he could follow Quinton down, Sijani scrambled up and joined in the fight.

On her feet, Sijani wound up and threw a powerful roundhouse kick, slamming her shin into Oswald's thigh with a hard slap of bone on flesh. The kick buckled his leg, and the man went down.

Sijani jumped on him, pinning him to the ground.

Pelly scrambled into the fray, groping blindly, but he snagged the man's legs and wrapped his arms and legs aground them.

Together, the cadets twisted the struggling man onto his chest and bent his legs back, heels to his buttocks, immobilizing him as Sijani pulled his hands around to his back and bent his good hand into a wristlock.

"You're under arrest," she grumbled.

Cassi lay back on the metal deck and closed her eyes.

Safe.

CHAPTER THIRTY-ONE

There was no escape from the pressure of command. With Hondo trapped and Oswald overpowered, the immediate threat was pacified, at least for the moment. But it wasn't dead.

The cadets forced Oswald into one of the *Lucky Bee's* remaining stasis pods. Locked inside, he kicked and punched at the walls until his knuckles were bloody until the process flash-froze him, locking him in stasis.

Hondo paced about inside the bunk cell. He tore open the ventilation shaft and cut himself up trying to squeeze through it. He tried to login to the *Lucky Bee's* network, but Cassi locked him out, relieving him of all command authority. He tried setting a fire and nearly killed himself with smoke.

Cassi decided that entering the cell and moving him would be too dangerous. So they kept him inside and she posted a rotating watch.

Pelly still couldn't see. The skin on his face had blistered with burns and the tissue around his eyes swelled them shut. Sijani scrounged some medical supplies and injected him with the anti-pathogen agent and used some bio-glue to seal his wounds. She went over him meticulously, to minimize any scarring.

Quinton's fever got worse. He'd managed to hold himself together outside, but once inside the ship he vomited all over himself. Still being Quinton, he looked up at Cassi and said, "There. You're not the only cadet on this mission who lost their lunch." Shortly afterward, he collapsed on the metal deck.

Sijani gave him some medication to control the fever. Bauer found a hand cloth and a bucket of water to keep him cool. They injected him with as much anti-pathogen agent as the medical AI would allow, but they still had no idea what it was they were fighting.

Kroyle was the worst of them. His skin festered with blisters, red, angry. He could barely talk and even though they had more pain medication now, in the end Sijani decided to isolate him in the trauma tank where he could be sedated and monitored by the medical AI. At first, he tried to fight it. Kroyle argued that Quinton was worse off. It took a direct order from Cassi to get him to slip into it.

They used the last of the bio-glue on Lapoint, sealing up his ion ray amputation. The old geologist cracked open a bottle of Verilion rum as Sijani worked on him. Bauer and Emica took shots with him and Emica looked about ready to puke her own guts out after she swallowed.

Lapoint laughed. "Ha! Not a cadet anymore, kid!"

Sijani took her shot after she'd finished her gluing. She looked exhausted, and not at all that much interested in the drink, but when Bauer handed her the little shot glass, she knocked it back.

"Ensign Requin! It's a right of passage," Lapoint prompted.

She stared at him. "No thanks."

"Come on, Cassi," Bauer urged.

"Really, I'm fine." She wanted to ease up and relax with them. But she was still on mission. They still had a homicidal maniac confined in the spacecraft wreckage. And though she appreciated the intention behind the invitation, it seemed like drinking would be letting her guard down. It didn't feel right.

"Another round for us then," Lapoint said.

As the sun went down that night Cassi looked up at the stars. One of them was Avalon's star, so distant the light she saw now had left it before humans had even colonized the system's fourth planet. She thought about home, and about her mother isolating herself from the universe. Raena Requin had served for years in the Alliance Expeditionary Fleet, most of that time on a corvette, and as long as Cassi had known her, she'd said very little about her experiences. They couldn't all have been this awful, could they? Cassi did not at all agree with the hard-line Isolationist stance on exploration. But being out here now, she could at least understand why someone might choose to lock herself up in a cocoon of solitude.

Cassi didn't sleep that night. She kept watch, listening to Hondo roam back and forth in his confinement cell, tearing into paneling, flinging around anything loose he could get his hands on, cursing, shouting at her with inhuman abandon.

At first light, she gathered a few emergency rations in her backpack and some extra ammunition for her weapon. She left Bauer in charge, awake, but massaging his temples and sipping water as he dealt with a particular type of hangover that Lapoint referred to as "Verilion Dawn."

Emica caught her as she slid out the main airlock. "Where are you going?"

"Back to the *Triumph*. I have to check on Dodd and Singh. Bauer's in charge until I get back."

"Hold on, I'm coming with you."

"Don't worry. I've got a K205." It was only when she said that out loud that Cassi realized how stupid of a move traveling alone would have been.

"Yeah. And you've got me. I'm coming with, Cassi."

Cassi had been wanting some alone time, some time not to worry about command, where she'd only have to be responsible for herself, but that responsibility wasn't something she could just shrug off. She was glad Emica wanted to join her and that it wasn't just out of some sense of duty.

As Dienne's sun rose, the two set out together.

They made their way to a beach and then just had to follow that around to the *Triumph*. It wasn't the most direct route, but it was much easier terrain. Cassi thought about returning to the *Endurance* crash site again, but it was at least two days away and she didn't want to leave the other cadets alone for that long. And there wasn't much they could do there anyway beyond body recovery and salvage.

"I think I found something," Emica said, after they were a kilometer away from the others. She had that excited tone in her voice Cassi had come to know, the way you speak when you're trying to hold in a smile.

Emica explained as she walked, looping her hair behind her ear. "You know how we have all this radio-frequency interference here on the ground?"

"Sure."

"Well, with the *Bee's* facilities I went back to assessing some water samples. And optically I couldn't see anything more than I could with MURPHI's optics. I tried calling Pelly and the radio was still nothing but white noise. I kept thinking it was the bedrock or something, but I remembered asking Mr. Lapoint about that and he said the ferromagnetic rock in this area is minimal. So then on a hunch, I rigged up an antenna to isolate the signal from the water."

"You did that just now?"

"Last night. I couldn't sleep. Anyway, there's radio noise coming from the water."

"The water's electromagnetic?"

"No. It's regular water, I think. But there's a bacterium in it that emits a signal."

"Huh?"

Emica stopped and grabbed Cassi's shoulder. They were on a beach now. Small waves lapped at the gravel behind her. Overhead a bird screeched and looked down on them. Its shadow swept over Cassi, chilling her skin.

"Cassi, there's a bacterium in the samples that I've been looking at and I've identified an odd organelle, something we haven't seen before. I think it works like a little transmitter receiver."

Emica gave her a moment to digest that—cells with little radios.

"How do you know it's a bacterium organelle?" Cassi asked.

"The signal dies when you boil the water. And of the unidentifiable cells in the water... there's a subset that all have this common structure that's not like anything else I've ever seen. It's got a high metal content; I suspect little nano-scale wires. Granted the *Bee* doesn't have an exhaustive xenobioloigcal archive, so maybe there's something like it out there somewhere else, but I really don't think so. It's unique to this planet."

Emica started biting her lower lip. It was her way of holding in a smile, even though she really didn't have any need to hold anything in, not now. Her hand gestures grew more expressive, fingers flaring out as she spoke.

"Any bacterium can send a signal to any other bacterium within range. I don't think the range is all that far, but if they can transmit and receive signals from each other, in principle, they could do all sorts of things."

Cassi keyed in on the gravity of the implication. "They could form a network."

"Exactly. Each bacterium is potentially a relay in a giant network."

Cassi's brow furrowed.

Emica stared at her. "Cassi, it's not inconceivable that there's a single giant intelligence on this planet."

A wave crashed over the rocky shore. A couple of birds called back and forth. Cassi's mind raced with the magnitude of the implications. Would something like that be intelligent?

"We talked before about the induced psychosis being some kind of biological defense mechanism," Emica said. "What if all of this was just because it wants to be left alone?"

Cassi let out a deep breath. "Yeah." She started walking again.

Emica kept up. "Well?"

"There's a lot of maybes there, Em. Come on. Let's focus on the task at hand."

"This could be a major scientific discovery, though."

"Yeah. When we get off Dienne, we'll have to relay this, quarantine the planet, and send in research teams."

Emica's face was glowing. "We could get a paper published in Scientific Galactica."

Cassi swallowed, and then forced a smile that seemed to make Emica happy. That was one possible outcome. She wished she was as optimistic as her best friend.

WHEN THEY ARRIVED AT the *Triumph*, they found its outer hull split open as if someone had crushed it with a giant nutcracker. Black soot marred the main airlock, though the fires had long since burned out.

"We made the right decision abandoning it, I suppose," Cassi said.

"*You* made the right decision."

Together the friends climbed through the wreckage. It felt like returning to a much smaller world. Cassi knew every inch of the spacecraft. She'd spent so much time studying it, preparing for their qualification mission—and now it all seemed so small, so confined.

They made their way though the upside-down passageways onto the bridge. It was shot up from a Tek rifle, little thumb-sized holes dug into the control panels and the main view screen. One of the fire extinguishers had erupted from a puncture and looked like someone had cracked open a soft drink and shook it until yellow foam exploded from within.

There were other bullet holes through the stasis pod doors. Cassi opened them to see that the rounds had gone right through. If she'd chosen to leave Dodd and Singh where they were, they'd both be dead right now.

Outside, the cadets removed the debris they'd piled up and dug down to the stasis pods.

"Well?" Emica asked.

Cassi checked each one, reading the little LED displays and let out a deep breath. "Both are okay."

"They're alive?"

Cassi nodded.

Emica gave her a hug. "You did it, Cassi."

"Did what?"

"We all survived."

Cassi climbed back up and sat on the alien ground. She opened her canteen and realized she hadn't had anything to drink since Emica had told her about the RF-networked bacteria. The water was as safe as it was going to get, but maybe what made her hesitate was a sense that it was borrowed water, maybe even taken without permission, stolen. But she had to drink.

The glug glug glug of the water made her suddenly conscious of how quiet it was out there. A soft wind rustled the forest leaves and stirred the water. Waves lapped at the pebble shore. Insects flew about. Dandelion fluff spiders floated by.

"We're not out of the woods yet, Em. It could be weeks until someone launches another rescue mission."

"Or minutes."

"Huh?"

Emica shared a virtual window that showed a shot of a blue sky. A white vapor trail cut across it. "Bauer just patched this through."

"What is it?"

Emica's smile couldn't have been broader. She zoomed in to the end of the white streak showing the flat black spacecraft that looked like a dust buster with a tail. "It looks like a DX-32."

"A dropship?"

"Our ride home."

CHAPTER THIRTY-TWO

When Cassi and Emica arrived at the *Lucky Bee*, a squad of spacemobile marines had deployed in a defensive formation around the crashed ship. Tactical drones zipped through the air, flying in a surveillance pattern. Twelve-foot-tall mechanized armored units with shoulder-mounted cannons faced out into the alien wilderness, each carrying enough firepower to destroy a city.

In front of the *Bee* the DX-32 Rhino dropship stood on five legs. The Alliance Expeditionary Fleet logo was embossed in the dropship's armor along with an etching of the Orthe Colony four-star flag underneath, indicating its home port. Orthe was where Emica's parents were from, though Emica herself had grown up on Avalon. Its rear hatch had opened down into a ramp that rested in the dirt. The dropship reminded Cassi of a loyal dog, a Great Dane maybe, sitting back on its haunches, waiting for a command from its master.

"Halt!" a voice boomed from one of the armored mechs.

Both Cassi and Emica stopped and raised their hands.

A pair of marines in combat armor hopped out of the *Bee's* airlock. One carried a pistol on his hip, a heavy one that made their K205s look like toys. The insignia on his shoulders had a single thin bar suggesting he was a second lieutenant. The other, a corporal, with a heavy combat quad-barreled rail gun, loped along beside him. Their faces lay hidden behind sealed masks.

"I'm Ensign Cassiopeia Requin. This is Cadet Emica Junko. We're glad to see you. We were—"

"We know who you are," the second lieutenant said. His voice came out mechanical, sub-human. "Just stop right there."

"Are we under arrest, or something?" Emica asked, half joking.

"I need you to remove your K205s, ensign, cadet." The second lieutenant's armored chest plate had green gun tape on it. Someone had scrawled "Garabedian" over the tape in thick permanent marker.

"But we're—"

Cassi stopped Emica from saying anything else with a look. From the marines' point of view, the last two Alliance spacecraft that entered Dienne's atmosphere had been attacked.

"They don't know we're not infected," Cassi said. And the reality was that she didn't know that either. Not for certain.

As Garabedian called for the squad's medic, a psychological cold front crept over Cassi. She thought about Emica's hypothesis. The bacterial network could very well have already planted whatever it was that was inside Hondo, inside her. It could have infected all of them, and now it was just lying dormant and waiting for a trigger to activate it.

THE ORTHE MARINES CRAMMED the cadets together inside the dropship. The Rhino had come down with a detachable cargo hold, a boxcar, crudely outfitted for carrying passengers with rows of seating like roller coaster cars up front. The marines stowed their gear, weapons and folded up mechanized armored units in the back. The marines themselves flew in a separate passenger compartment, the one built into the drop ship, all grumbling about how tight it was, but happy to be in a different cell than the cadets and whatever pathogens they might have picked up.

They posted a single marine in the boxcar, someone to keep an eye on Hondo. The corpsman sedated the *Bee's* captain and they strapped him into one of the seats up front, his arms tied across his chest as if about to be mummified.

Kroyle was still inside the *Bee's* trauma tank. The marines carried the entire tank into the cargo carrier and strapped it down with the rest of their gear. Inside, heavily medicated, Kroyle still twitched in subconscious discomfort. They told Cassi that there was a medical officer on board the *Armistice* who could do more for him, but they had to analyze his blood first to know specifically what they were dealing with. And that had to wait until they got him up to the facilities on the spacecraft.

She wondered what they would find.

More than that, Cassi wondered about the psychological trauma of it all. Having that anemone wrapped around her leg, even for just a minute, had been terrifying. She couldn't imagine the horror of something like that slowly suffocating her. She touched the tank as the marines carried it by, as if Kroyle might feel that though the metal and the fluid keeping him alive. If he couldn't feel it, at least she could. And that counted for something.

The marines retrieved Dodd and Singh in their stasis pods, the mechanized armored units making short work of the two-day hike, returning to the dropship with the pods over their shoulders. The medic checked them and loaded them into the cargo bay along with Oswald—humans stacked one on top of another and locked into place with thick black webbing that clamped to eyelets in the deck, like crates of supplies.

Quinton pulled on his pressure suit and took his place in between Cassi and Bauer, his body drenched in sweat. It steamed the inside of his helmet, fogging the polymer face shield. He'd probably lost a good ten pounds over the last week. He struggled to lock himself in, his hands shaking as he fastened the restraint clip.

Quinton looked older now. That kid who'd followed Bauer around had come out of the fire, forged stronger, and maybe even a little wiser. Cassi pounded his fist, the way he and Bauer did it. That made him smile, but she couldn't tell whether Quinton was taking away an 'attaboy' from her or issuing her one. Maybe it was a little bit of both.

Sijani allowed a pair of tears to run down her cheeks as the Rhino engines wound up and the dropship broke contact with Dienne. They had no windows to stare out of, only a connection to the Rhino's video feed, but she watched that, and Cassi wondered if there wasn't a part of Sijani that was staying behind on the hostile world.

Pelly sat patiently beside Sijani, as if in meditation, nestled in a pressure suit that looked too big on him. The swelling around his eyes had gone down. He reported that he could see now, a little anyway, but the kid still looked like a boxer who'd gone one round too many.

Lapoint had scrounged up a pressure suit from the *Bee*. The corpsman had stabilized his wounds, but he'd lost his foot for good. When he finally got back to his home world, he'd have to be fitted for a robotic prosthetic. Surprisingly, the geologist hadn't complained about it, no whining or grumbling. He seemed, at least for the moment, happy to have survived.

And as the sky faded from the clear blue of breathable atmosphere to the black void of space, Cassi closed her eyes. She was done. The mission was complete. Someone else was in charge. The pressure of command relieved at last, she allowed herself a moment to relax. When sleep came, she didn't fight it.

She slept. They all slept.

CASSI WOKE WEIGHTLESS, her stomach unsteady. The nausea wasn't as bad as coming out of the transit, but it still felt like someone was playing soccer with her stomach. The cadets around her were asleep... Sijani, Bauer, Quinton...

Where was Hondo?

The marine guard floated in the zero-gravity environment about a foot over the floor of the cargo hold, arms outstretched. A syringe protruded from the flexible rubber seal between his helmet and his neck, one small weak point in his combat armor. Tiny blood corpuscles floated around him like spherical insects.

Cassi opened a communication channel with her tracker. "Lieutenant Garabedian?"

"What is it, Ensign?"

"It's Captain Hondo. He's... not here."

"What do you mean he's not there?"

She broadcast video, showing Garabedian the sedated marine, and the empty chair where Hondo should have been.

The second lieutenant swore. He patched through to the pilot. "Barbaduk?"

No answer.

"Hold on, Ensign, I'm going up front."

Bauer woke up. "Cassi? What's..." his words trailed off as he recognized the problem. Hondo was loose on the drop ship and they'd lost radio contact with the pilot.

"The cockpit is sealed off," Garabedian reported.

"Can you cut into it?"

Bauer shook his head. "Not unless he has a blowtorch handy."

Garabedian took that as a challenge. He called back over the channel, his voice full of marine bravado. "Oh, we can get through."

"Wait," Cassi said. "You can't blast your way in. The cockpit and the crew cab could rupture and vent into space, you could lose navigational control, guidance, communications." There were a million things that could go wrong if they started shooting.

"Hold on, we're getting a message from Control," Garbedian reported. With a brief squelch of static, he merged the channels.

"... Flight Romeo Delta X-ray One, you need to reduce your velocity."

If Hondo heard that, he didn't respond. The DX-32 kept on its course, still accelerating, even through a second and then a third warning.

"He's going to ram the *Armistice*," Pelly said.

"He wouldn't be that stu..." Bauer trailed off again. A normal person wouldn't be that stupid, but that alien pathogen inside him might want to do exactly that.

"That doesn't make any sense. We're in a marine dropship," Garabedian said. "If he wanted to attack the *Armistice*, why would he try to ram it? He could just use the ion cannon."

"He's locked out," Cassi, Emica and Bauer all answered in unison.

"Oh."

The *Armistice* loomed ahead of them on the video feed. It was an Alliance Expeditionary Fleet heavy cruiser. Cassi checked the flight control data. The DX-32 was indeed in a burn pattern, accelerating when it should have been decelerating to match orbital velocity with the *Armistice*.

"Flight One, cease burn immediately," the *Armistice's* flight control officer ordered. Her words came through crisp and sharp.

"Armistice Flight Control," Garabedian called. "This is Mace One Six, our pilot has been..." he hesitated, as if unsure how to describe the situation. "We've got a civilian of unknown mental condition who has taken over control of the Rhino."

"Acknowledged Mace One Six. Hold one. We have to figure this out."

"That's not good," Pelly whispered.

"Flight Control, can't you perform a remote override or something?" Garabedian asked.

After waiting a few seconds for an answer that didn't appear to be forthcoming, Sijani spoke up. "They can't. Any spacecraft is hard wired so that pilot control is primary. It keeps anyone from being able to remotely hack the dropships."

Garabedian asked, "Is there another way to get into the cockpit? A hidden maintenance panel or something?"

Pelly shook his head, but then hesitated. His helmet tilted forward slightly. "Well, there is one, but it's outside. You'd have to spacewalk to get to it."

Bauer looked at Cassi.

"How much time do we have?" Garabedian asked.

Emica looked up from her tracker. "About five minutes until impact."

"The *Armistice* can steer out of the way, can't she?"

Pelly shook his head. "The Rhino has a much higher thrust to mass ratio. At this distance, there's no way a heavy cruiser can dodge us. And it's probably less than five minutes."

He turned off his tracker audio so that only Cassi and the other cadets could hear him. "Right now, the *Armistice* commanding officers are weighing their options. They're establishing a minimum distance at which they have to shoot us down, and that's probably... well, it will give us about three minutes."

Bauer nodded to Cassi. "I'm coming with you."

They both unbuckled themselves.

Bauer flew to the cargo door and opened the access panel. As he did, Cassi gathered a coil of cargo strapping to form a tether. Fears of losing contact with the Rhino ran through her mind, forcing her to think through the details of the plan as meticulously as she could, under the circumstances. She didn't want to get stuck out in the vacuum space, waiting for either their oxygen to run out, or to freeze to death. Fortunately, strapping was something the cargo container had a lot of.

The panel that controlled the cargo door locked Bauer out. The cockpit had absolute control over the drop ship, including the locking mechanism on the cargo door.

Bauer tore the panel open and cut the wires. "Ready for breech?"

Cassi glanced around at the other cadets as she cinched up the strapping around her and Bauer's waists. Emica and Sijani managed to strap the sedated marine into a chair, buckled themselves in and everyone gave her a thumbs up.

"Go."

When Bauer crossed the wires, the cargo container ruptured and blew anything not strapped in out into the cold void of space, including Bauer and Cassi.

Their lifelines snapped tight.

The strapping around her waist nearly folded Cassi in two. She doubled over. Her guts somersaulted and she choked back a wave of bile. Beneath them Dienne passed by in all its blue-green glory. Clouds, oceans, land mass, it all sped underneath her, so far below.

"Climb, Cassi!" Bauer called.

The *Armistice's* flight control officer came over the radio, wanting to know what was going on. Garabedian told them to wait and not to fire. He told flight control the marines had a plan to regain control of the drop ship. They were trying to blow it off course, feigning a reason for the breach, in case Hondo was listening. He told them the marines were going to force the cockpit door open.

As he argued with flight control over whether that was possible, Cassi and Bauer pulled themselves up their tethers.

Hondo piloted the ship into a roll, attempting to break them off with the pull of centripetal acceleration. Cassi pulled herself up the strapping, her relative weight decreasing as she moved closer to the axis of rotation.

They got to the drop ship hull and inched their way up the torronite armor, their fingers finding hold in the tiny crevasses between the plates.

"You've got about a minute," Emica reported.

Cassi moved as fast as she could, fighting to keep up to Bauer.

They reached the access panel.

"I need two hands to open it," Bauer said, hanging on to the drop ship, unable to let go.

"Hold me," Cassi said. "With your legs."

Bauer didn't have time to object. He wrapped his thighs around her waist and scissored his legs tight.

"Bauer, I have to breathe."

"Yeah, but I can't let you go."

Cassi let go, putting all her trust in him. Her arms had been burning and she hadn't been sure how much more she could have held on, but now, Bauer had both his and her weight to support. The roll was getting faster. Their relative weight was increasing.

She worked as fast as she could.

Cassi authorized maintenance, and unscrewed the access panel bolts, each one breaking off and spiraling out into space.

Bauer started to slip.

If they dropped, they wouldn't have time for a second run.

"Thirty seconds," Emica called.

The panel opened inward against a full atmosphere. She had to push against the full vacuum of space, she had to push against Bauer.

"Do it," he said.

She punched upward.

A jet of white air blew out, like a whale spouting. The Rhino bled cockpit atmosphere into space.

Bauer let go.

Cassi caught a handhold.

Bauer cartwheeled away from the drop ship, only to be snapped to safety at the end of his tether.

The *Armistice* came up, its lights glowing in behind them, as it spun in a relative sense. Cassi had to keep her eyes forward just to keep oriented.

A boot heel slammed down on her fingers. Hondo desperately tried to kick her away. Once. Twice.

Her middle finger snapped.

Cassi held. She reached up with the screwdriver and struck, driving the blade through his pressure suit and into the flesh of his calf.

The man screamed.

Another jet of air blew free from the pressure suit hole in his leg.

He kicked again, but with only a quarter of the force. He'd decompressed and lost air. His eyes rolled back in his skull as his face turned purple.

Cassi pulled herself through the maintenance hatch.

"Flight One, alter your trajectory now or we will destroy you!"

Cassi climbed into the pilot's seat and logged into the control system.

"Change of command protocol… commanding officer: Ensign Cassiopeia Requin AVLN T72 715 524. Updating user security rights."

"This is Ensign Requin," she called over the radio. "I have control of the Rhino. Breaking collision course now."

She took the controls and fired the retro-thrusters, braking hard. She veered the dropship into open space.

CHAPTER THIRTY-THREE

Still in orbit around Dienne, Cassi completed a brief but cramped quarantine while confined within a medical suite aboard the *Armistice*. Clean now of the grime of Dienne, and dressed in a fresh service uniform, she looked more the part of a junior astronaut officer than something the dog coughed up.

As she prepared to go check on Kroyle and the other cadets, a solid barrier wall on one side of the suite transitioned from an opaque frost to a glass-like transparent surface. Captain Daiki Higashi, commanding officer of the *Armistice* stepped into view, flanked by Commander Jett Bentley, an Orthe political commissar.

She saluted as they entered the suite.

Higashi walked in with his hands clasped behind his back, head forward. The man had thick creases radiating from the corners of his eyes, and shocks of silver hair streaking back from his temples amid his short black hair. His shoulders seemed wider than most, like his uniform sported shoulder pads with no other purpose than to make the commanding officer appear intimidating.

Cassi forced herself to maintain eye contact.

Bentley tapped in some commands on his tracker and then glanced at the camera in the corner of the room. Cassi couldn't be positive, but she was relatively certain he'd just turned it off.

The political commissar appointment was not a standard appointment on a spacecraft in the Alliance. It certainly wasn't a position on any Avalon vessel. But each member colony of the Alliance had its own set of rules and customs. The function of a political commissar as far as Cassi understood it, was officially to ensure civil control over the spacecraft, however, in practice, Bentley was the *Armistice's* executive officer, the captain's right hand.

"We need to discuss some details of your report, Ensign," Higashi said.

Once she had showered and dressed, Cassi dictated a mission summary, an official account of the events on Dienne. She had Bauer review, revise, and co-sign it. Then she'd entered it into the *Armistice* local archive server, which would be automatically uploaded to the Alliance galactic archive when it next made contact with a node—presumably when they got back to Avalon space. It was standard procedure, and it would have been her final task as mission commander before completing the Dienne mission.

Perhaps now that the chaos of their arrival had settled down, the captain wanted to examine the situation they were in more closely, find out what really happened. Cassi smiled. "Yes, sir. Of course. Do you mind if I ask about the condition of my crew first? Cadet Kroyle was in a serious condition when we came aboard. Cadet Quinton had a fever."

The captain looked at his political officer.

Bentley checked a virtual window and huffed through his nose. He looked up at Cassi. "Your lad Quinton's got a fever, but the medical officer has him on a round of antixenos that could sterilize a planet. Looks like he'll be fine. The Kroyle kid though…"

Higashi eyed the window and rubbed his chin. "They're working on it. We've got some of the best fleet medical officers in the Alliance on this vessel, Miss Requin. He's having a reaction to whatever toxin entered his system."

"Will he be okay?" she asked.

The captain and commissar glanced at each other. Higashi lowered his head. "I'm not a medical officer. It doesn't look great, at this point. I think they're trying to stabilize him until we get you back to Avalon. They might have better luck when they get him to a research hospital there."

"How soon will we be heading back?"

"Ensign," Bentley interrupted. "It's not customary for junior officers to ask so many questions."

"It's alright, Jett. They're her crew."

"Yes, sir."

"We have some business to square away here first. Now, Ensign, did you have any contact with the *Endurance* before it was shot down?"

"Yes, sir. Not a lot. As I stated in my report, there was a lot of radio interference. And it's possible they were jammed."

Higashi nodded. He turned away for a moment and pinched the bridge of his nose between his fingers.

"Captain Higashi knew Captain Bolton," Bently offered in a whisper.

"I'm sorry, sir." Cassi said.

When the captain turned back, he was composed, but colder, focused, with the kind of intensity that comes over a fighter's face when he steps into a ring. "The xenobacterium pathogen. Your cadets made quite the discovery down there. It can signal other bacteria of the same species via radio-frequencies?"

"Yes, sir," she replied. "At least, we think so. We didn't exactly have an accredited xenobiological wet lab at our disposal. But the basic science behind it holds."

"And you think this is some kind of collective... intelligence?"

Cassi looked back and forth between the captain and the commissar. They'd turned off the cameras. This conversation was off the record, intentionally, though she couldn't quite figure out why. "That's just a hypothesis, sir—a possibility Cadet Junko suggested."

Perhaps it was because the captain was making her nervous, but she broke into a technical explanation. Since they'd been on the *Armistice*, Pelly had analyzed the noise and found patterns in it, Marsaglia planes in high dimensional plots of the radio signals suggesting that it wasn't completely random but contained repeating patterns. The noise contained buried signals, order within the chaos. Junko had speculated that the xenobacteria developed a pathogen that attacked the frontal lobes of the human brain, interrupting executive function, inducing a specific psychosis that would turn a potential threat to the network against members of its own species. But it wasn't efficient at delivering the pathogen. It had to get the pathogen into the blood, which was why anyone who was wounded and exposed to the water would develop the psychosis.

When she stopped to take a breath, she looked up and realized she'd been speaking fast, like when Pelly really got going.

Higashi rubbed his chin.

"It's just a theory," Cassi reiterated.

"And a very good one," the captain said.

"What are you thinking, sir?" Bentley asked.

Higashi paced in front of Cassi's medical suite. He took his time answering the question. "Show me the surface radio-survey again," he said.

Bentley called up a projection of the Dienne surface. "The drones weren't able to make it higher resolution than this, in the time we had, but here it is sir."

Cassi recognized the crash sites, the survey outpost. They'd been so far apart when she'd been on the surface, but now, zoomed out, it seemed like such a small area of land. More to the point, the map showed hot spots of radio-interference, and they projected perfectly with three bodies of water... where the cadets encountered the land striders... where Lapoint's flight crew went swimming. It looked like an invisible nest of some sort.

"That," Higashi said, "is a hostile alien intelligence."

"Sir, that might be jumping the gun a little," Cassi said. "For all we know it could be, more like an allergic reaction."

Higashi turned on her. "Commander Zignew Bolton and his entire crew are *dead*. You could never have met a more compassionate officer, nor a sophisticated gentleman." There were tears forming in his eyes. "That man..."

The captain inhaled sharply and composed himself, straightening his back. He flicked the virtual map of Dienne's surface turning it off. "Commissar, assemble the senior staff in the CIC."

"Aye, sir."

Higashi stormed away. Cassi brought herself to attention and saluted as he left.

She turned to Bentley. "May I ask about the captain's intentions, sir?" She wasn't entirely sure she wanted an answer.

Bentley nodded slowly. "Whatever that is down there, it has shot down multiple Alliance spacecraft. It even got close to taking out the *Armistice*. I believe Captain Higashi's intentions are to target the intelligence and destroy it."

"Destroy it?"

"Orbital nuclear bombardment, Ensign."

Cassi swallowed a dry lump in her throat.

CHAPTER THIRTY-FOUR

Cassi's heart pounded as she made her way through the heavy cruiser. Sijani texted her, beaconing Cassi to Kroyle's medical suite.

The ensign dashed through the maze of corridors in the *Armistice* and found her way to a second medical bay where they were holding Kroyle. The place was deserted and eerily quiet. Centered in the suite, inside a dedicated trauma pod, Kroyle floated in amniotic-like fluid, a scaffolding of tubes down his throat, eyes open, but his stare vacant, unseeing. His body seemed so still, his breath slow and shallow, despite the fact that on a cellular level, Kroyle was fighting for his life. And losing.

"Cassi, where is everyone? I can't contact the medical officer."

"The senior staff are in the combat intelligence center," she said, the words coming out matter of fact.

"Doing what?"

"I think they're trying to decide on whether to nuke the crash site."

Sijani nodded. "Probably the most prudent course of action."

"I don't think it is."

"Now isn't a good time to go all bleeding heart, Cassi. Whatever it is that's down there... it's killed a lot of people. If anyone else goes down there—"

"They could quarantine the planet."

"How?" Sijani crossed her arms. "There's a good chance that the *Lucky Bee* was already there illegally. There's too much money to be made. If they have a chance to wipe out whatever is down there, I say do it. All they have to do is map out the radio noise signature on the surface and..." She made a fist and popped her fingers out in a burst. Boom.

Cassi stopped herself from saying anything else on the issue. Arguing the point with Sijani was irrelevant. Neither of them had the power to stop the *Armistice*.

Cassi studied the readouts on Kroyle. The fluid in the tank was filled with artificial cells and microscopic stents and shunts that acted like an external immune system, tracking the storm of cytokines stirred up in Kroyle's body by the alien toxins and counter-acting them, down-shifting the storm of inflammation inside.

"The medical officer said he was stable, when she was here," Sijani told her, pacing back and forth. She'd changed into a new undersuit and washed, but her eyes were still sunken, her movements slow. She clearly hadn't slept since coming on board. "The data is all over the place and changing by the minute. Those toxins are eating him alive. I feel so helpless."

She was right, as far as Cassi could tell. His skin was breaking down—red and inflamed in patches, and even torn open in spots with soft tissue directly exposed. He was skeleton-thin. They'd all lost weight on Dienne, but for Kroyle it had come off in layers of lean muscle, leaving him emaciated.

An alarm beeped. Inside the tank Kroyle shivered. His hand drew up over his chest, wrists flexed downward.

That alarm should have patched straight through to the medical officer, or... someone. But it wasn't just the MO in the CIC. The whole the medical team was on deck. Higashi had wanted input. There wasn't much a fleet medical technician or a marine corpsman could do directly for the cadet anyway. The trauma tank AI knew more about keeping people alive than most doctors even. Still, if there was a chance an MO might be able to stabilize Kroyle, they had to try.

Cassi texted Pelly, hoping that he might be able to hack the system, override and get a message to the MO. It was breaking the rules, the kind of thing that under normal circumstances could get a cadet kicked out of the program, but they were both willing risk that if it meant saving Kroyle.

Pelly: *Can't reach her.*

Sijani placed a hand on the tank and glanced back and forth between the fluid bath and the readouts. "I don't know what to do, Cassi. I think his brain is hemorrhaging."

Cassi had a look at the readouts herself. "The trauma tank is supposed to stop the hemorrhage, isn't it?"

"It can't."

Sijani tried to work through the problem by talking it out. "There's no existing protocol to counter the anemone toxins, so it has to develop a tailored biochemical response in real time."

She pointed to a window with stacks of lit up LEDs. "Look, the neural processor is working as hard as it can."

The machine was running simulations in real time to predict the best counter measure it could deliver, but it didn't seem to be coming up with anything.

Pelly: *I'm in. MO on the way. But Cassi, you have to see this.*

Requin:?

Pelly patched a video feed through to her tracker. It was the passive, system-wide report on the *Armistice* weapon systems. Even the ventilation fans seemed to go quiet. A soft klaxon rang, and a mechanical voice echoed through the ship. "Preparing for nuclear strike."

"No," Cassi said out loud, as if the system might hear the objection of a rescued Ensign.

The entire spacecraft shuddered as a series of missiles launched.

Finally, the medical officer stormed into the suite. She was a stocky woman with thick forearms, a woman who looked as ready to wrestle a bear as she was to respond to a medical emergency. "What's wrong?"

"I've been trying to page you for like the last fifteen minutes, ma'am," Sijani snapped.

Gritting her teeth, the medical officer ignored the cadet and read through the reports coming off the trauma tank. She glanced at Kroyle and tapped a screen.

A robotic arm inside the tube, picked up a syringe, located a vein in his arm, and injected a drug that forced Kroyle's muscles to relax. It stopped the seizure, or at least the outward symptoms of it.

"Is he okay?" Taura asked.

The medical officer tapped another screen. "This is his brain activity. He's in trouble. Let me work."

"Kroyle?" Sijani said. "Will? If you can hear me, we made it. We're going home. Just hold on a little longer."

He squirmed and shivered in the tank, the relaxant not quite pacifying him.

Outside, the missile engine flared, accelerating it with forces beyond anything a human could hope to withstand without pancaking. The system showed a countdown to intercept. The decision was made. The missile was on its way.

"Pelly?" Cassi called him over the radio. "Can you abort the missile?"

"Um... no, ma'am."

"There's got to be something." She felt raw and cold, and sure that this was the wrong decision. The xenobacteria was life, possibly intelligent life. They were just having trouble communicating.

Sijani knocked on the side of the tank with an open palm. "Willister, hold on. Just a little longer. One breath at a time."

Cassi took Sijani's hand and pulled her away. "We have to let the medical officer work."

Sijani turned like a feral animal and yanked her hand away, defiant. Fierce.

The medical officer swore and punched a panel. "The bleeding is too profuse…"

"Kroyle?" Sijani wouldn't be pulled away. Cassi was pretty sure she wouldn't leave even if the marines came in with a twelve-foot mech and tried to bulldoze her out of there.

The seizure returned, he thrashed violently, slamming against the inside of the tank, millions of tiny air bubbles obscuring his face inside the dark fluid.

And then it stopped.

Alarms chirped and beeped.

The machine jolted him with electric current forcing him into a massive convulsion, followed by a complete relaxing of his musculature.

"No!" Sijani shouted.

The countdown to the missile detonation reached the last seconds. The optical feed showed the ground approaching fast, like a camera zooming in, expanding details by the millisecond. Then it went black.

The feed cut to the *Armistice*. Light flashed on Dienne's surface. A blemish of dust and dirt swirled around the light, like a hurricane.

The trauma tank shocked Kroyle again, repeating the process three times, until it flashed red text on the main panel. Slivers of red light reflected off the medical officer's face.

She closed her eyes, shook her head.

Taura placed her forehead against the tank. Tears fell from her eyes onto the transparent surface.

Willister Kroyle was dead.

Text flashed Cassi's virtual widow, across the system feed. TARGET DESTROYED.

Cassi didn't even want to breathe. She felt sick. Sijani hugged her tightly, in desperate need of her own support.

Her tracker buzzed.

Quinton: *Cassi, you need to see this.*

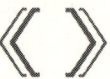

QUINTON WAS IN THE xenobiology lab. When they'd taken the cadets on board, the *Armistice* only had so many medical suites available where they could be quarantined, and since Quinton had an active fever, he got the 'presidential' quarantine suite—tucked into a corner of the lab in a cage normally reserved for larger biological specimens. However, his location gave him a small window that offered a view of the dropship hangar.

He patched video of what he saw through to Cassi.

"That's Hondo," he said, his voice a whisper. "They had him in here. I mean, not right here with me, but they were keeping him in the lab, trying to treat him for the decompression, but when he became conscious, he started fighting. Hard. It took a squad of marines to bulldoze him into a corner. I think they might have broken one of his legs. But that guy's freakishly strong."

"I know," Cassi said.

On the deck a pair of marines dragged the infected captain out toward an airlock. They had his hands zip-tied behind his back. He was still inside a pressure suit, quarantined from the marines who also wore their own pressure suits, even though the entire hangar would have been pressurized. Hondo fought against them. He kicked his feet and struggled to root himself to the deck, but for all the effort he might just as well have been a drunk bar patron getting hauled out by a team of bouncers at the end of the night.

The marines wheeled a stasis pod along beside him too, with *Lucky Bee* stamped on its side.

"Cassi, I think the marines are planning to blow them out through the air lock," Quinton said. "That's the only thing over there. That's illegal, isn't it?"

Sijani still hadn't let go of Cassi, but she was looking on too. She sniffled and squinted at the screen, and then let go and looked at Cassi, her bloodshot eyes asking the same question.

There was a good chance that Higashi, Bentley and the senior officers of the *Armistice* debated exactly that question in the CIC. It wasn't clear how they could have justified an execution. Maybe they thought they could justify it as a direct threat to the vessel, and act of war against weaponized bodies... or something. However, any way Cassi looked at it, tossing humans out into space was wrong.

"It is illegal," Cassi said quietly. She wondered if perhaps Higashi was turning a blind eye to the law for his own vengeance, or if he and his officers were just scared. Either way, Hondo and Oswald were heading for the airlock. Higashi was wiping out every last trace of that xenobacterium.

"We have to do something," Sijani said.

Hondo managed to trip one of the marines and sent him sliding across the floor. Even with his arms shackled behind his back, he jumped on and began hammering the grounded marine with knees to his helmet.

Cassi bit her lip, her mind racing. She wasn't sure there was anything she could do to help Hondo and Oswald. But an idea popped into her head.

"Quinton?"

"Yes?"

She took a deep breath. "I need you to do something for me."

CHAPTER THIRTY-FIVE

Cassi charged through the battle cruiser calling the other cadets and explaining as she went. She slid into Emica's suite. Pelly had already joined her, and the two brought up an array of semi-transparent virtual windows. Pelly's eyes were wide as he worked his magic and hacked into the *Armistice* network. Bauer and Sijani came in behind Cassi.

"This might buy us some time," Pelly said. "I disabled the automated airlock system. The problem is that they can still open it manually."

In the hangar, Quinton sprinted between Rhinos and caught up with the marines. One team was stuck at the inner door of the interlock, two marines staring at the display screen, tapping at it, trying to figure out what was wrong with it. Three more marines struggled with Hondo, one on each arm and third fighting to catch his kicking legs.

"Stop!" Quinton barked.

The marines with Hondo all looked up. Quinton bowled all four men over as he slammed into them high, arms outstretched.

The marines shouted and swore.

"You can't do this!" Quinton shouted. He climbed back to his feet. "It's illegal."

"Stand down, cadet!"

A sergeant let go of Hondo to grab Quinton. But the cadet wheeled the marine over his shoulder and sent him crashing to the deck.

In the medical suite, Pelly tapped a final screen and sat back with a deep breath. "Got it. But we don't have much time—maybe a couple minutes."

Emica nodded, lost behind her own virtual window. "I've got the sequencer online. I just... where are the samples?"

Bauer sat down and pointed. "They're over here."

Emica rolled her eyes. "That's halfway across the lab."

"Two minutes..." Pelly said. "Then they'll figure out the network's been hacked."

It wasn't enough time to run through the heavy cruiser to get down there. They were going to lose all evidence of the Dienne xenobacterial intelligence for the sake of about eight feet.

Bauer cracked his knuckles. "I got it. Em, can you open the sample window?"

"Sure, but how are you..." she trailed off as she watched Bauer operate one of the robotic arms used for handling radioactive samples.

"That's not long enough," Pelly said.

Bauer pinched his tongue between his teeth as he rolled up his sleeve and pushed a hand through the virtual window. A network of green laser dots reflected off his skin as he assumed haptic control of the arm. Flexing his fingers, the robot mimicked the action in real time.

"Bauer what are you doing?" Cassi asked. "There's no way you can make that."

"They're going to destroy the samples anyway," he said. He picked up a test tube and stared at the camera, judging the distance.

The cadets held their breath.

He tossed.

The robotic arm flung the test tube across the room where it landed directly inside the sample port.

Bauer closed his eyes, only showing the shock on his face now that he'd made the throw.

"Ninety seconds..." Pelly said.

Emica ran the samples through the genetic sequencer. The machine stripped the individual cells down into their constituent components and ran the alien DNA through a high precision counter. The machine carefully and meticulously ran through the billions of basepairs, recording the entire bacterial genome.

In the hangar bay, the marines backed away from Quinton and Hondo. Heavy footsteps thudded on the deck as one of the marine armored mechs stepped into the fray.

Quinton rolled his eyes.

The machine pounced on Hondo. It lifted him up into a kind of wrestling hold fireman's carry. Hondo struggled like a child in a tantrum, but the massive metal machine held him fast, with so much pressure around his diaphragm that his face turned purple. The mech's head turned toward Quinton and for a brief moment the cadet, mouth full of blood, shoulders heaving, actually looked like he might try to face off with it.

"Stand down, Quinton," Cassi whispered.

He took a few deep breaths and then raised his hands.

An alarm blared. The other marines cracked open the airlock's inner door with the manual crank. They grabbed the stasis pod that held Oswald and pushed it into the bay. The mech followed, its feet clanking on the deck with every step. It threw Hondo against the back wall of the airlock, hard, the kind of toss that could have broken bones.

The mech backstepped out, just as the marines wheeled the doors closed.

Another alarm chimed. Strobe lights flashed. A disembodied voice echoed through the window. "Airlock One Four clear to open in three... two... one..."

Quinton whimpered as the *Bee's* stasis pod blew out of the airlock into space.

Hondo clawed at the window, a wild animal, scratching, with nothing really to hold on to. Cassi turned away, seeing only in her mind the man's desperate final moments. He wore a pressure suit, but no air tank. He would slip away into the cold vacuum of space, breathing only the air he carried with him, a bubble that would slowly build up with carbon dioxide and put him to sleep, if the cold didn't freeze him first.

The outer airlock door closed.

"Sequence complete," Emica said.

Pelly fed the complete sequence into his tracker, and as soon as it was finished, he scrubbed all evidence that the sequencer had been run. The only thing that anyone might notice was the little acrylic test tube, now empty, in the sample port, easily written off as a sloppy mistake.

"Got it," he said. He sat back and tapped a virtual kill switch.

The virtual windows all winked out and suddenly they were just cadets and an ensign, sitting in Emica's medical suite. Except for Quinton.

"Numpty?" Cassi called.

He fell to his knees as the marines scrambled around him, yelling, barking like a pack of dogs.

"Sorry, Cassi," he whispered. "I lost them."

"Don't be sorry, Quinton. You did good. We got what we needed."

On the other view feed, only seconds later, lab technicians stormed into the lab, led by Bentley, the commissar. His temples were wet with sweat, and his commands uncertain, but he directed his staff to gather the samples.

"Is that all of them?"

"I think so, sir."

"We can't just think so."

Cassi tensed. Would they count the vials? Discover one missing?

"We had six, sir," the lab technician said. "They're all here. And it looks like the cadets had... ten."

Bentley strode over, crossing his arms. He looked over her shoulder but didn't seem to focus on any one thing.

"You think he even knows what a sample looks like?" Pelly asked, picking up on the authority posturing of the officer.

"Very well," Bentley said. "Can you incinerate them, or do we need to chuck those out the airlock too?"

The chief tech smiled. "We have a sample incinerator right here," she said, pointing to something that looked like a small oven. Another technician handed her the samples and then placed them inside and closed the door.

"You sure you want to do this, sir? I mean... it is an alien life form. Shouldn't we—"

"The captain was very explicit," Bentley said. "I'm giving you a direct and legal order. Incinerate them. All of them."

"Aye, sir."

Pelly encrypted the data and transferred it to each of the cadets, multiplying their chances of successfully getting it off the *Armistice* and back to Avalon. When her tracker indicated it received the data, Cassi let out a breath.

They hadn't completely saved the bacterium, but they'd accomplished the next best thing. With a few hours in a properly equipped lab, even one on the academy campus, they could use the sequence to print out a copy of the xenobacterium. It wouldn't have the same characteristics or memories, but it was at least something.

The last image Cassi saw of Quinton was him on his knees, marines closing zip ties around his wrists.

CHAPTER THIRTY-SIX

Two weeks after returning to Avalon, Cassi stepped into the commandant's office wearing her dress whites. The high collar, damp with sweat, scratched against her neck with every little movement. Her shoulder epaulets were black with academy lettering embroidered at the bottom, the single thin gold bar indicating the rank of ensign. Wearing the bars made her feel like an impostor, like she was impersonating one of the academy instructors. But they were still hers. No one had taken them away, or at least not yet.

A second-year cadet acting as the commandant's aide presented her. "Ensign Cassiopeia Requin, sir."

Cassi saluted.

Commandant Beryl West stood at a large bay window that overlooked the parade square and training grounds of the academy. A light rain smacked the window glass. Outside, first year astronaut cadets ran through the fields, slowly getting soaked in their physical training gear, as others worked to set up the last of the temporary bleachers. Tomorrow, her crew and about three hundred other cadets would be out there getting their stars.

Another officer Cassi didn't recognize rose from a chair aside the commandant's massive cherry wood desk. She was tall and wore her dress uniform with a professional casual manner that suggested she was in the whites more often than not. Pins at the base of her epaulets indicated she was with the fleet's legal corps—a lawyer.

West waved the aid off and she slipped from the room, closing the door behind her. That left the three of them in a quiet stillness. The room was soundproofed and though Cassi suspected that it was meant to help cadets relax in the presence of the school's commanding officer, the silence seemed to amplify the sound of her heartbeat and her breathing.

The lawyer stared at Cassi but said nothing.

West studied Cassi through a faint reflection in the glass. She'd grown used to the commandant's inspecting eyes. He left it to his staff to find flaws in the cadets. The Beryl West Cassi knew usually looked for common ground, asked how cadets were getting on, what they thought of the coursework or the exercises and cadets always replied with enthusiasm. Of course, that commandant was the parade version, not the commanding officer version she was there to see now. "Stand easy, Ensign."

She relaxed, a little, as much as she could. She didn't like the way the lawyer was staring at her, like a wolf stalking prey.

With a wave of his hand, West brought up her file on a virtual window. The first item—her forged admission form. He read it over. "This was signed by your father when you were just a child."

Cassi swallowed. She'd almost forgotten about that. She kept her chin up. The commandant turned to face her directly, patiently waiting for her response.

"Sir, is that what we're here to talk about?"

"Among other things." He clasped his hands behind his back and that puffed out his chest. A former spacecraft skipper, the commandant projected a natural aura of command.

"That form is a forgery, sir."

He stared straight at her. Based on his reaction, or more accurately, his lack of a reaction thereof, Cassi suspected that he and the lawyer had figured that out well before she set foot in the office.

Her pulse quickened and her gut tightened. All this way and she was in the program based on a lie, a lie she could be criminally charged with.

"Why?" the commandant asked.

"I wanted to get into the academy, desperately. I wanted to be an astronaut officer more than anything, sir. But my mother's an isolationist and refused to support my application."

Cassi looked at the lawyer, but she didn't say anything, didn't react, as if she'd had some training in that kind of thing.

"I realize the predicament that put the academy in sir," Cassi went on. "Technically they accepted a minor without parental consent. And if anything would have happened to me then, well, there could have been serious repercussions for the entire program... audits, investigations... Even though that was three years ago I accept full responsibility—"

He waved a hand, cutting her off. "That's fine, Ensign. You're not the first cadet to forge a form. It's history. You've earned your position as an astronaut officer. As far as I'm concerned, it doesn't have to leave this office."

"Sir?"

But she figured it out as soon as she questioned him. West brought up the form as a litmus test to see how truthful she was. Apparently, she passed.

The lawyer made a note on a virtual screen Cassi couldn't see.

"I read your full report, Ensign," West said. "I spent some time considering the details. I also spent some time reviewing Daiki Higashi's report."

"Did he mention the xenobacteria, sir?"

West nodded. "He did. I'm fascinated. I'm something of a xenobiology enthusiast myself. A bacterium that's able to transmit radiofrequency signals... remarkable. But it emits something that induces psychosis?"

"It's just a theory, sir. We didn't have the opportunity to study it in detail. We only had rudimentary instrumentation that Cadet Junko and Cadet Pelly were able to cobble together out of the wreckage. And Captain Higashi destroyed all traces of the life form."

The lawyer made another note.

Cassi didn't say anything about the copy of the genetic sequence they'd copied. She was about to, but something made her hesitate.

"He deployed a tactical nuclear strike on the surface of the planet," Cassi said.

"And you disagreed with his decision?"

"As noted in my report, sir." She understood the objections of a cadet-turned-Ensign weren't going to carry much weight, but she wasn't going to lie, or falsely stand behind Higashi's decision.

"Well, that's what I'd like to talk to you about."

"Sir?"

"First off, you need to consider Alliance Standing Orders."

The lawyer spoke up. "Article Eighty-Three, Section Five."

West went on. "We have yet to encounter any fully sentient alien life, not our equal, present circumstances excluded. But we have standing orders detailing appropriate action should one be encountered."

"Sir," Cassi hesitated. She wanted to be delicate, yet precise with her words, but sometimes you just had to swing the sledgehammer. "Where in the standing orders is xenocide explicitly mandated?"

The lawyer spoke. "The commanding officer of an expeditionary vessel is, by definition, venturing into unknown circumstances and has a responsibility to defend the interests of the Alliance and human life. Captain Higashi detailed evidence of clear and present danger to humanity. The alien intelligence brought down the *Triumph*. It destroyed the *Endurance*. It made unrelenting attempts to destroy the *Armistice*."

Cassi voiced her objection directly to the commandant. "With all due respect, sir, we don't know that. We don't know what the xenobacteria's intentions were. In fact, we don't even know it had *intentions* at all. Its sentience was hypothetical."

"Be that as it may, the standing orders are very clear that the commanding officer of an Alliance spacecraft has the authority to identify hostile threats and respond accordingly."

"With a measured response, sir... with a responsibility to tread lightly. The act of walking is supposed to leave footprints, not craters."

"Be that as it may, Ensign, Captain Higashi identified a threat and destroyed it, and that's the end of it."

Cassi felt sick.

"I need you to revise your report. I'll provide you with a copy of Higashi's. Yours will reflect his version of events."

"But sir..." Cassi's mind raced. "I can go to the media if I have to. He blatantly executed two civilians. All he had to do was lock Captain Hondo in a stasis pod. Back here, we would have had a chance to extract the pathogen, the bacteria, or whatever it was that induced the psychosis."

"And risk bringing that alien intelligence to a populated colony."

The lawyer took a step forward, passing through her virtual window. "Ensign, it may not seem like it, right now, but we're on your side."

"How? How are you on my side, ma'am?"

West lowered his head. "Cadet Quinton assaulted a team of marines on that vessel. He's in a Fleet Consolidated Brig for the moment. Captain Higashi has agreed not to press formal charges. I'll still have to strike Quinton from the astronaut officer program, but he won't have a criminal record."

There it was. That lawyer stared at her for a while and then quietly suggested it was an offer she should accept. There was nothing anyone could do about the bacterium, and it was entirely plausible it was just that... a unicellular life form, and Higashi's actions carried no more moral consequence than swatting a fly.

And Quinton was stuck in a fleet prison... for following Cassi's orders.

West placed a hand on her shoulder. "There isn't always an optimal outcome, Cassiopeia. This business is messy at the best of times."

Cassi looked into his eyes. He was right. And she couldn't leave Quinton in prison.

CHAPTER THIRTY-SEVEN

The next day, Cassi stood in her dress whites with her crew on the Alliance Cadet Corps Academy parade square, along with about three hundred other graduates. A light rain continued to fall from a gray sky, beading on their fabric of their dress uniforms, on the mirror shine of their black shoes. Behind them, other cadets, family, romantic partners, guests, other service members and even a few members of the general public looked on, seated in bleachers, many with heads covered by umbrellas.

Word got out about what happened on Dienne, or at least a polished version of the events.

The *Triumph* crashed. The *Endurance* was lost in an attempted rescue. Cassi led her cadets to safety until they were rescued by Captain Higashi and the *Armistice*. Dienne was placed under quarantine while an investigation was conducted—a political inquiry that could be tied up in the courts and successive colony governments for years until people forgot what it was they were even investigating.

The Dienne Crew, as people were now calling them, were the last in order of precedence through the star ceremony.

The cadets were not graduating from the academy. They still had a full year to complete the astronaut officer program where they would be posted to an Alliance spacecraft or elsewhere in the expeditionary fleet operations. But the single gold star over the left breast pocket on their uniform would signify that they were qualified astronauts, members of an elite caste of space explorers.

The master of ceremonies called the cadets up by their crew teams and when it was their turn, Cassi led the Dienne crew onto an elevated stage on the center of the parade grounds. Or at least she led the surviving members. They all wore black arm bands with Kroyle's name embroidered in yellow letters on them. They couldn't wear anything for Quinton though. The audience had been applauding throughout the ceremony, but now the applause grew in both volume and intensity.

"Cadet Anson Bauer," the master of ceremonies bellowed. "Cadet Bauer will be presented with his star by his uncle, Lieutenant Commander Thray Bauer, a senior engineering officer serving on the *Solstice*." Bauer walked out onto the stage with long proud strides. Cassi expected he might ham it up, stick out his tongue or bring his hand to his ear to encourage applause, but he kept to the drill—straight back and dignified. His uncle shook Bauer's hand, flashed that characteristic bright white smile, and took time for a polite political wave to the audience. He pointed out at Bauer's younger cousin, a kid still a few years away from academy admission. The emcee went on to tell everyone that Bauer had been the captain of the varsity avalanche team and received a piloting distinction.

"Cadet Taura Sijani." The whistles and cheers erupted from Taura's admirers, particularly as the camera drones zoomed in on her photogenic smile and plastered it on the thirty-foot projection screen over the stage. Taura's mother, a colony socialite, was there to pin her star on. She smiled for the camera too, anti-aging treatments making her look more like a sister than mother. She had been ecstatic about her daughter joining the academy but had no real desire for Taura to actually serve. Rather the impetus for service in the fleet derived from the weight it carried in colony politics. She pinned on the star and gave her daughter an exaggerated, prolonged hug, which though mostly for the cameras, was full and genuine.

Pelly was the second youngest cadet ever to earn a star. His was presented to him by a hereditary chief from the Dakum colony. Along with the star, the chief made a small speech and presented Pelly with a ceremonial Dakum eagle feather.

Sweat collected under Cassi's collar. Cool rain landed on her face, as she watched Emica's father present her with her star. Isan Junko had served with distinction on several Orthean space galleons, and he was now retired. The man beamed with pride as he pinned Emica's star on her jacket.

Looking out, Cassi saw Mason Lapoint in the bleachers, looking uncomfortable in a dress shirt and tie, but happy to be there, a goofy smile on his face. She wondered what kind of deal he'd cut with Higashi to keep quiet about what happened on Dienne. He had a cane with him. Evidently someone had paid for his foot to be regrown rather than fitting him with a robotic prosthetic.

She found Quinton too, sitting toward the back, the collar on his leather bomber jacked turned up against the rain. He should have been up there with the rest of them. And even though he was several hundred feet away, a speck in the crowd, Cassi could barely bring herself to look in his direction.

The master of ceremonies asked for a moment of silence to remember Ensign Willister Kroyle. They promoted him to the rank of ensign posthumously and at the request of his parents, the fleet had given him a space burial. Cassi and the cadets had still been on the space station and attended the funeral when his body had been shot toward the Avalon sun. And though it was raining out, Cassi wanted to believe that there was a part of Kroyle shining down on them now.

When it was Cassi's turn for her star, before the master of ceremonies said anything, one of the cadets still on the parade square shouted something out, his specific words lost in the rain. All through the ceremony there had been little inside jokes, nicknames hurled out, calls of "we're in trouble now," and the like. And at first, she thought it was a reference to her space sickness. Sure enough people were starting to call her "Retro Requin."

But then, the third-year cadets-now astronauts, came to attention. In drilled unison, they all snapped a formal salute. To her.

The audience erupted into thunderous applause.

A video of her father flashed on the big screen, a still shot zoomed in on his face along with the words: *Master Sergeant Koen Lawson, Alliance Spacemobile Marine Corps, (Cassiopeia Requin's father), deceased.*

The video transitioned to a shot of her admission form, the form she'd forged to get into the Cadet Corps in the first place.

Master Sergeant Lawson had a vision for his daughter to one day become an officer of the Alliance Expeditionary Fleet—so much that he signed her into the service when she was only three years old. All she needed to do was qualify.

That generated a few murmurs as people commented. Someone shouted out, "no pressure" and that caused a few laughs.

Cassi swallowed and glanced sidelong at Commandant West and the other officers. That was all a lie. But they all kept it up.

"Congratulations, Cassiopeia."

Her mother stepped in front of her. Where had she come from?

Lieutenant Commander Raena Requin, retired, wore an older fleet dress uniform, but she looked just as sharp in it as she had in the old videos Cassi used to watch. But that didn't make any sense at all. Raena was an isolationist and wouldn't have anything to do with the AEF.

"Mom?"

Raena's mouth was pinched tight, her glare intense. The muscle atop the woman's jaw flexed tight. She tugged on Cassi's uniform, stretching the fabric out, jarring her. She pinned the star over Cassi's heart, quick, efficient. She leaned in and whispered. "You know how I feel about this."

"Why are you here?"

Her mother gave her a brief squeeze on the shoulders, perhaps what she may have considered a hug. "We'll speak later."

Bauer stepped forward as her mother stepped back. "Three cheers for Ensign Requin!"

Cassi looked over at him, mouth open. He wasn't actually doing that.

"Hip hip."

The bleachers boomed with the expeditionary fleet *Huzzah!*

"Hip hip."

"HUZZAH!"

On the third HUZZAH the cadets tossed their berets skyward.

CASSI MET HER MOTHER after the ceremony off base, at a high-end restaurant where the servers wore red jackets and white gloves. Raena was there with her gentleman friend, Assistant Professor Shuben Cakaul. Cakaul still had the same wiry beard Cassi remembered, but it was lined with premature grays and he had little bits of bright orange chicken wing skin caught around his mouth, from having started eating without her. His hair was tied back in a braid, not unlike her mother's, that stretched down between his shoulder blades. He wore a suit jacket, that stretched with a single button done up around his rotund belly.

Emica had offered to come with her, but Cassi needed to face her mother alone.

The hostess pulled out a chair for Cassi and quietly whispered, "congratulations, ma'am." She offered a timid smile and backed away. Highlights from the graduation had been broadcast on the major networks all over Avalon, but that single interaction was about the only moment of fame Cassi would enjoy from it.

Cakaul and Raena sat opposite her, the two of them intimately close. Though it was only early afternoon, the lighting in the room was soft. Tea light candles flickered between them. Shadows danced in curious patterns over her mother's face.

Cakaul leaned forward, folding his hands in front of him, thick knuckles out toward her.

Cassi stole the conversational initiative from them. "I really appreciate you coming, Mother. I know you didn't approve of my joining the Fleet, but it's nice that you're here now. It means a lot to me."

Raena remained completely stoic in her response. She sat with her back straight, hands folded in her lap.

"Cassiopeia," Cakaul said. "We're here to offer you a chance to do something good with this."

Perhaps she should have kept her mouth shut. Of course, there had to be a catch.

Cakaul was a loud breather. Each breath sounded labored as it huffed through his nostrils.

Raena placed a hand over Cakaul's knuckles. "I read all about your ordeal on Dienne."

Read? She'd read the polished version. That was the only version there was. Unless someone else had said something.

"I'm so sorry you had to go through that. I suppose sometimes a woman must make some mistakes herself to genuinely appreciate the magnitude of the consequences. It's a part of being young, I suppose. But now that you've seen it firsthand, I'm sure you're coming to realize that the universe is not ours to expand into at will. Humans don't leave footprints. We leave craters."

"Do you see now, Cassiopeia?" The professor leaned even further forward. "Your crew mate died because he stepped where he wasn't meant to step."

Cassi's skin grew cold. She'd tried to relax, a part of her hoping that just maybe this might be an opportunity to turn things around with her mother, that they might at least start talking again. But clearly, that wasn't happening. She—they were here with an agenda.

"Leave Willister out of this."

Cakaul's brow furrowed. "You can't just leave a person out. That's just the kind of brainwashing the academy instills."

"You have no idea what you're talking about, Professor. Just tell me what you want," Cassi said.

Her mother handed her a pin. It was about the same size as her astronaut qualification star, but it was embossed with a capital I inside of a circle. The Isolationist logo.

"We want you to join the movement," Cakaul spoke. "You have some influence now. If you publicly call the Alliance for what it is, all the major networks will interview you. You can get others to see the expansionists for what they are..."

"I am an expansionist," Cassi said. And not only that, but if she said anything Quinton's charges would re-appear, and he'd go to prison because of her.

They both looked at her as if she'd just committed blasphemy right in front of a deity.

Cassi leaned forward, staring directly at her mother. "I'm sorry Mother, but I can't be what you want me to be. For better or worse, I'm an explorer."

"If you go down that path, you won't ever be more than a vile monster," Cakaul said.

Cassi stared at her mother, hoping that Raena might respond, might summon some deeply buried love for her and reject the professor, but she didn't even flinch.

Cassi left the pin on the table. "Goodbye, Mother."

Cakaul swore. Whether at her or because of her, Cassi didn't know, and she didn't care. She just stood up and walked out of the restaurant, heading back to her real family.

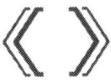

CASSI MET HER CREW at the Sky Guy Pub n' Grill, a couple blocks away from the academy campus. She'd never been one for bars. The music was loud. The floor was coated in a layer of sticky grime. The scent of human sweat mixed with spilled beer and the perfumes and colognes of locals, officer cadets with liberty and the human servers. The Sky Guy was one of those bars that catered specifically to cadets, run by a retired Rhino pilot who kept old photographs on the walls of graduated classes going back through the two-hundred-year history of the colony.

Still, the Sky Guy was home, or at least a version of home. It was evening, and the third-year cadets were all waiting for their first assignments to roll in.

Emica had had time to change into her civilian clothes. She wore her hair down in a large braid that hung forward over her right shoulder. It had been a long time since Cassi had seen any of her friends in civilian attire. The black wool sweater, and denim jeans gave her a country girl kind of look, something different for Emica, but as usual she looked awesome. Cassi still wore her dress whites.

Emica greeted Cassi with a great bear hug, that lifted her off the ground, and hurried to buy her a drink.

When Sijani joined them, in a light dress with spaghetti strap shoulders and heels that made her taller than Bauer, nearly everyone in the pub was staring at her. Guys engaged in conversation stopped mid-sentence as she walked by. Some were sheepish about staring, casually scanning the room and allowing their gaze to linger on her just a little longer than on anything else. Others outright gawked. Sijani had a date with her, someone from off colony that Cassi felt like she should have recognized but couldn't quite place. He was a few years older than her and too well dressed for the Sky Guy, in a designer suit.

"Where's Bauer?" Sijani asked, joining Emica and Cassi. She looked like she wanted to show off her date. But Bauer was off in the washroom.

Emica blushed as she shook his hand. "Avery Balthazar?" she said. "It's an honor to meet you." She bit her lip as she glared at Taura with wide eyes afterward.

That was where Cassi knew him from. The heir to the Balthazar shipping company dynasty. The guy probably had enough money to start his own private colony somewhere. He shook Cassi's hand and she found herself trying not to blush.

He smiled. White teeth, wide jaw.

It was just like Sijani to bring a minor celebrity to the Sky Guy.

Bauer's friend and avalanche teammate Saul Duschene had asked Cassi out for the night. But in the end, she and Emica had decided to go stag. Being an ensign, it didn't feel right to date a cadet, even if they were from the same class. Or at least that was what she told herself. When she really thought about it though, she supposed she just wanted to be with her crew one last night.

Pelly was still underage for the bar.

She wished Quinton would have come, though. No one was even sure what his plans were. She thought he'd show up. Instead, there were just a couple of empty bar stools. One for Quinton, and one for Kroyle that sat with a full drink on the table in front of it.

The news came in all at once.

About eighty percent of the patrons in the Sky Guy were cadets, most third years with new star pins. Their trackers vibrated in tandem.

The background drone of conversation behind the music stopped.

The collective attention of hundreds of astronaut officer cadets turned downward toward virtual windows, and they read their orders.

The live band stopped playing, the lead singer coming on the microphone only to tell everyone they were going to take a break. And that she hoped the orders were good.

Cassi barely noticed that though. She skimmed through the words, racing through the official orders, and then glanced up, breath caught in her throat. She slid off the bar stool, too excited to remain sitting.

Emica smiled at her, beaming.

Bauer got back from the washroom, his dress jacket over his shoulder, walking with casual confidence, checking out the ladies in the band coming down from the stage.

When Avery offered his hand, Bauer just nodded. "What's up?"

He slid in next to Cassi and took a big swig of beer.

"Like you don't know," she said, checking him with an elbow.

"Was there a disaster or something?" Bauer's act wasn't fooling anyone, but he still went through the motions, like goofing his way through it diffused the tension.

Emica wiped her eyes, gently so as not to smear her mascara, then took a sip from a drink with a little paper umbrella. "You first, Cassi."

Cassi blew out a deep breath. They were all looking at her—Emica, Bauer, Sijani and her date. She read from the virtual window projected in front of her chest. "Assignment: *Avalon Fleet... deep space cruiser... Steadfast.*"

Bauer spit out a mouthful of beer, spraying it all over her.

She swore, wiping his beer-spit off her face. "Bauer!"

The big jock almost fell off the bench. "Requin, you got posted to Avalon's flagship?"

"Well, it's not the flagship yet. They're embarking on space trials in two weeks. But yeah, there's orders attached." Cassi twisted her window to share the projection with Bauer.

Emica hugged her, wrapping her arms around Cassi, and squeezing tight. "I can't believe you got the *Steadfast*."

Cassi wanted to be happier about that. She was happy. In so many ways, she'd earned that. But the victory came with a bitter aftertaste, a lingering question. Had she really earned it? Or was this some kind of kickback, a payoff, for keeping quiet? At least it wasn't on the *Armistice*.

In an effort to deflect attention, Cassi turned to her bunkmate. "Well, Em?"

Emica smiled. It was genuine and deep. She straightened her back. "Looks like I'm assigned to the *Intrepid*... flight control officer."

Bauer held up a fist. "Way to go, Em!"

She punched his knuckles.

Cassi grabbed another napkin and wiped the droplets running down her neckline. "Bauer, you're such a turd."

"Yeah, but a turd who got a Rhino."

Cassi slapped her hand on the table. "You did NOT."

He flicked on his projector and spun the hologram around, showing the girls his orders.

Emica took another sip of her drink. "I didn't think it was possible, but if they put this guy in a Rhino cockpit, it's going to make him even more arrogant."

As if on cue, Bauer unfolded a pair of sunglasses from inside his breast pocket and slid them on. Then he held up a hand. "One at a time, ladies. One at a time."

They all laughed.

That was when Quinton walked in. His jacket and hair were wet, like he'd been outside walking around in the rain. His hands were tucked inside his pockets. His head hung forward, though he managed to smile. Cassi couldn't tell if it was genuine or something he'd forced on, but she suspected the latter.

He knocked fists with Bauer and the girls, took the time to fully shake Avery's hand, whom he clearly didn't recognize, and they filled him in on their postings.

He turned to Cassi, as if to square off with her. He looked bigger now somehow. Maybe it was just that she hadn't really seen him since Dienne and he'd put on weight rehabilitating, or perhaps for some other reason in his time in the brig. She wanted to apologize to him, but given all the commotion in the bar this wasn't really the place.

He held out a fist, a kind of minimal peace offering, but it was something and she knocked her knuckles against his. And before the ensuing silence got too awkward, Cassi's tracker buzzed with a message.

Pelly.

Cassi projected a hologram of the fourteen-year-old's head. He looked around, a broad, dimpled smile on his face.

"What spacecraft are you on, Pelly?" Emica asked.

He glanced down and blushed. "I... I didn't get a spacecraft."

"You didn't what?" Bauer said.

"Oh, Pelly," Emica said. "As soon as you're old enough, you'll have your pick of—"

"They placed me on Base Grix."

Bauer slammed a hand down on the table. "My man! Alliance Intelligence, right?"

"I... I'm not sure what I'm allowed to say." His blush was all the evidence anyone needed. The kid was going to become a computer hacker with top secret clearance, stopping wars before then even started. They all raised their glasses to Pelly. An intelligence posting was rare, right out of the academy. Usually they selected officers who proved themselves in the field.

"Taura?" Emica asked.

"I didn't get a spacecraft either," she said. "But maybe I'll see Pelly on Grix."

Bauer kept his beer in his mouth this time, looking at Cassi and then forcing himself to swallow it. "Intelligence?"

"Medical officer training." She glanced sidelong at Avery briefly, and then smiled. "They let me change my request when I got back."

"You can do that?" Emica asked.

Sijani shrugged as if to imply that perhaps not everyone could, but she'd managed to finagle her name into the pool.

"I never figured you for a doc," Quinton said. "I mean, not that you wouldn't be great at it, just... I don't know..."

Sijani leaned forward, towards Quinton, chin down, eyebrows raised. "Sometimes you don't really figure out where your strengths are until fate steps in and drops a challenge on you."

Bauer held up his glass, toasting to that.

CHAPTER THIRTY-EIGHT

The last time Cassi saw Thad Quinton, they were on the academy tarmac together.

A light rain was coming down. She wore her gray garrison uniform, complete with the astronaut wedge cap and the brass insignia of the *Steadfast*. She carried one duffel bag, one backpack and a stainless-steel barracks box footlocker, with a sticker on the side that read: venture into the void.

He was in that old bomber jacket and jeans that were threadbare at the knees. It was like the guy didn't own any other clothes. The rain gummed up the gel in his short hair, making it matte against his skull.

She was with two others assigned to the *Steadfast* as well, Saul Duschene and Yelena Sankova. She'd been trying to get to know them, since they were going to be working together moving forward. It was her own dumb luck that the guy she'd turned down for a date a few days ago was now serving on the same spacecraft as her.

Quinton had his own gear with him, stuffed into a pair of old civilian duffel bags. They didn't even let him keep the basic travel kit.

When Cassi saw him, she dropped her gear on the wet concrete and dashed over.

He smiled at her.

A boom rumbled across the grey sky, a DX-32 Rhino dropship. It had glossy black numerals, 03, painted against the flat black armored paneling on its side. Underneath, AEFS *Steadfast* and underneath its home port: *Avalon*.

It slowed to a hover over the tarmac, lights flashing, as ground control robot marshals guided it to a touch down position. Despite the crosswind, the pilot made the landing look easy. A sheen of ice coated the dropship's underbelly.

She'd said her goodbyes to the others already. Lots of hugs and tears, especially with Emica. In a way it felt like her family was breaking up. But she'd turned the page and was ready for a new beginning. None of them had heard much from Quinton. After grad night, they'd taken away his tracker. That too belonged to the Alliance Expeditionary Fleet, and he didn't have a civilian version of the device, at least not yet.

She was glad to see him, one last time, even if it was only for a moment.

"Hey, Numpty," she said, punching his shoulder softly.

Quinton cocked a smile. "Cassi."

"So? You figure out what you're going to do yet?"

Quinton leaned closer so he wouldn't have to shout over the whine of the Rhino's engines. "I'm joining the Spacemobile Marines."

"What?"

He shrugged. "I get to skip Alliance officer indoctrination, and the educational components. They'll accept the astronaut officer training on par. They're starting me on a platoon leader's course and depending on my performance, figure out where to go from there."

Cassi wiped the rain from her face. "Well, you have experience trekking through unknown terrain. I don't know why you'd want to do more of that though."

"Hey, next time I won't have to do it with an infected leg wound. And it turns out I'm pretty good at shooting things and blowing stuff up... when my commanding officer lets me have a gun."

FIRST COMMAND

Behind her the Rhino's rear hatch dropped open, creating both a personnel gangway and cargo ramp underneath the dropship's tail. The other junior officers started loading their gear onto the back with the help of a dropship crew chief and a general-purpose robot.

The rain picked up. Cold water ran down the back of her neck.

Cassi snapped her tracker off the mount on her chest, held it up and put her arm around him. She looked up at the little iris and smiled, snapping a picture. Quinton plastered on a dorky half-smile.

"Where can I send this?"

"I'm still on the Alliance social net."

She tagged his account and sent the picture.

"Ensign Requin!" the crew chief called. He stood on the ramp, holding a tablet, leaning out from under the tail, using the device to keep the rain off his head. "I need you to get a burn on, ma'am!"

"Guess that's me," she said. She still had her arm around him, not sure that she really wanted to let him go. He felt larger now, the musculature in his shoulders was broad, powerful. He wasn't that kid who'd landed on Dienne anymore. She felt the power that allowed him to manhandle those marines on the *Armistice*.

"Good luck, Cassi. I mean, you don't need it. You'll be captain of the *Steadfast* in no time."

"You too." She couldn't think of much else to say.

He turned and looked straight into her eyes; his face close enough she felt his breath on her lips. Faint traces of his cologne hung in the warm air that came off his skin, a sweet citrus with a sandalwood base.

"Take care of yourself, Numpty. They don't send marines into the nicest places in the galaxy. And they don't give them the easy jobs. Don't let them harden you, okay?"

"Yeah."

She turned and hugged him, deeply and without really thinking it through, she kissed his cheek.

As if she had crossed some kind of line, Cassi pushed away from him, but he was so solidly planted to the ground he didn't budge and she took a couple steps backward stumbling, the skin on her face a little warmer than it should have been.

The Rhino was waiting, and she didn't want to make a bad first impression. Cassi hiked up her barracks box and duffel bag, then bounded up the ramp.

"Requin," Quinton called. "Try not to puke on the way up."

The crew chief scanned her biometrics, confirmed her identity, and drew up the ramp— sealing her inside. The engines spun up, their high-pitched whine dominating the splatter and smack of the rain against the dropship's hull and the tarmac.

Cassi climbed up to the crew compartment and locked her helmet on, bubbling herself up. The suit pressurized when she plugged the hose into the outlet. She fastened her restraints and the safety interlocks all flickered green. The crew chief came by, double checked each passenger and tugged on their restraints, running through his check list before locking himself in and using the dropship AI to double check himself. "Cabin secure," he reported.

The Rhino's engines thundered when the pilot got clearance, and Cassi broke from the surface of Avalon with a thud.

Don't miss out!

Visit the website below and you can sign up to receive emails whenever Charles K James publishes a new book. There's no charge and no obligation.

https://books2read.com/r/B-A-RRWO-INGNB

BOOKS 2 READ

Connecting independent readers to independent writers.

About the Author

Charles K James lives in Southern Alberta with his amazing wife, two awesome children and a couple of Guinea pigs. When not writing, he works as a medical physicist. He also enjoys reading, hiking in the mountains, and judo.

Read more at https://charlesjamessfauthor.com/.

Made in the USA
Coppell, TX
24 September 2024

37631384R00166